The King and the Fire Chanter

Map of Medarya

To the
Sphinx's Pass

Lotus Lagoo

Enchante

Gwar's Ca

Great Plain

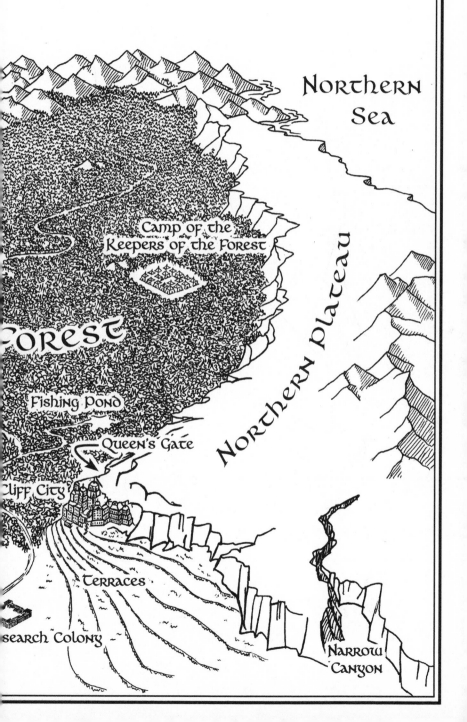

NORTHERN
Sea

Camp of the
Keepers of the Forest

NORTHERN Plateau

FOREST

Fishing Pond

Queen's Gate

Cliff City

Terraces

Research Colony

Narrow
Canyon

Arron Wend

The King and the Fire Chanter

by

Arran Wend

BOOK ONE

of

The Runes of Medarya

Copyright © 2006 Arran Wend

Cover Art by Stephanie Pui-Mun Law

Interior Art by Louis Ebalo

Map by Arran Wend

Library of Congress Cataloging-in-Publication Data
Wend, Arran
The King and the Fire Chanter / Arran Wend – 1ˢᵗ ed.
p. cm. – (The first book of The Runes of Medarya)
2 0 0 7 9 2 3 7 7 5
ISBN-13: 978-0-9793284-0-4
Manufactured in the United States of America

This book was typeset in Cochin by Linotype
and Rùn Teine by Arran Wend

Antiquity Publishing

visit us at www.antiquitypublishing.com

This book is dedicated
to our readers.

The King and the Fire Chanter

CONTENTS

Prologue 1

Part 1: The Estate 9

Part 2: The Flight 77

Part 3: Medarya

    1. The Dwarf Caves 111

    2. The Enchanted Forest 171

    3. The Riddle 213

    4. The Chanter 267

    5. The King 319

Epilogue 355

Appendix 357

pROloGue

*(Note to the reader: You are welcome to skip this part. It
was written for boring sorts of people who like deep
concepts and mysterious foreshadowings and such.
The action begins with Chapter One.)*

"**M**other, tell us another story of Medarya!" This
was a nightly ritual for Shane and Mia. Their mother had
an endless supply of stories from that mysterious place,
and the children never tired of hearing them.

"All right," Serena agreed with a smile. "Let me
see…" Her steel-grey eyes got the far-away dreamy look
of a bard reciting a saga, and she began:

"Thousands of years ago, in the land behind the sun,
in a place called Medarya, there lived a powerful mage
who had a dragon for a pet—"

"Yeah," Mia chimed in, "a cute baby dragon!"

"Mia," Shane objected, rolling his eyes, "it wasn't *cute*.
Dragons are mean!"

"Okay – the sorcerer who had the cute, fuzzy little
mean baby dragon!" retorted Mia.

Serena went on patiently: "This mage was a cunning and desperate man, well-learned in his art and feared by all — "

"He was a wicked sorcerer!" Mia piped up again.

"He wasn't a *real* sorcerer," Shane corrected. "There's no such thing as magic. It was science – he was a *scientific* mage. They only thought he was a sorcerer because he knew more about science then anybody else."

"He was, too, a sorcerer, Shane! He was! And there *is* such a thing as magic – isn't there, Mother?"

"No, Mia," said Mother soothingly, "Shane is right. There is no such thing as magic – at least, not the kind you are thinking about. But there is a kind of magic in words. Just think of it – the people who made *this* story lived thousands of years ago. They captured their thoughts in words and etched them into stone. And those words lay there silent for five thousand years, until we came along and found their stones. Now their ancient thoughts have once again come to life in our own minds. That's a sort of magic, don't you think?"

Serena settled herself more comfortably on the bed

and continued: "The mage and his dragon lived in a magnificent city cut into a cliff. Its white granite stone glistened with veins of gold. They lived among a noble people who had silver-white hair and wings — "

"Wings like *me*!" interrupted Mia again.

"Mia, will you please stop interrupting," Shane said impatiently.

"You're just jealous," returned Mia, "because you don't have... because you're *deform*... I mean, the mage didn't have wings either."

"Now, Mia," said Mother a little severely, "be nice!"

"Yes, Mommy."

"May I continue now?"

"Yes, Mommy."

Serena resumed her story. "...The mage set a cruel trap for the Medaryan king in the depths of the wild land. But the king was wise, and he spoke to the forest and enchanted the trees..."

"How did the king enchant the forest?" This time it was Shane's turn to interrupt.

"With words," answered Mother. "Ancient words. The inscription reads this way:

> The king was wise in the language of the forest, and spoke to the trees in their own speech; and they heard his voice, and obeyed his words."

Mia mumbled sleepily, "Mommy, could the trees really hear him talk?"

"No, of course not," answered Mother. "Trees don't have ears. And even the forest animals which did have ears would not have been able to understand what he said. It's just a legend..." But Mia didn't hear the rest of her explanation. She was asleep.

"What was the forest language like?" asked Shane, who was still very much awake. "Was it like Medaryan?"

"No, it was an entirely different language, and very mysterious. You know the Rune Rock out in our peppermint garden. The top half of it is written in the forest language, I think."

"What does it say?"

Mother sighed wearily and shook her head. "I don't know. I simply have been unable to figure it out. That rock does not give up its secrets easily."

Suddenly she laughed. "The Rune Rock really is well named, isn't it? After all, that is what the word *rune* originally meant – 'secret' or 'mystery', and then 'secret writing'. The top half of the stone is a mystery, and the bottom half is, quite literally, a riddle – in Sumerian. Why *Sumerian*, the oldest recorded language on Earth? And how did these two languages come to be together on the same rock? It is all very baffling.

"Anyway... I have to get back to my work now," she said, gazing at her daughter fast asleep in her bed, "and it's time for you to be in bed, too."

Shane trudged off to his room while Serena went back to her office near the children's rooms to continue her research translating this Medaryan saga. She had been at it for several months and was almost done.

Shane lay in bed for a long time after that, puzzling over

the Sumerian riddle carved onto the Rune Rock in their garden. He knew it by heart:

> Thee, neophyte king, awaits my rancor.
> Drink with me my bane of canker.
> Plague, spring forth! For fools can't hold
> The molten rock to burn the gold –
> Though song from yonder ledge be told.
> Lead, firegrasses! Path behold!

Shane loved riddles. This one held him like a spell, with its five-thousand-year-old words taunting from the past. Could words hold magic? Equally puzzling was how this rune stone in Sumerian – a language spoken by people who had once lived in ancient Mesopotamia – had been found at the archeological site in Medarya, so far from its home. Then there was the indecipherable inscription underneath the riddle – that, too, was a puzzle. With these questions circling about in his head, Shane fell asleep.

While Shane slept with the ancient rhythms forming his dreams, in the faraway land where the runes had been found an ancient creature stirred in fury – for man had returned. That ancient creature was the reptile Gwar.

The Riddle in Sumerian Cuneiform

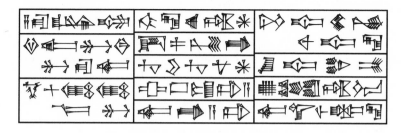

Transcription of the Sumerian

Zara, lugal gibil, sag šur-ĝu ša murabðug.
Namuš sim-sima-ĝu ḫala-zu ḫeam.
Asag, ziga! Ḫuru ḫunu-am;
šir ᵍᵉˢkug-bia ðugabi
na izi kugsig babila šu nubibðu.
ᵈŠumunða ḫeeð! Kaĝiriš igi ilaš!

English Translation

Thee, neophyte king, awaits my rancor.
Drink with me my bane of canker.
Plague, spring forth! For fools can't hold
The molten rock to burn the gold –
Though song from yonder ledge be told.
Lead, firegrasses! Path behold!

PART 1

The Estate

chapter one

The first time Shane and Mia met Damien was the morning they thought they had caught a thief in the peppermint garden. He was eating the chocolate berries. He was so covered with dirt and brown-red berry ooze that they couldn't really see what he looked like except for the dark hair and black eyes and the cloth wrapped around his head, dirt-stained and only half on. He was so intent on picking the berries and stuffing them in his mouth that he didn't notice the two children approaching.

Mia was barely ten, yet she was the bossy one. "You're a pirate!" she challenged stoutly.

Shane stepped protectively in front of his little sister before the startled pirate could get a good look at his accuser. "Or a thief," Shane observed, sizing up the intruder. The boy looked pretty tough, though he could hardly be more than two years older than Mia – a year younger than himself.

The strange boy stood scowling for a minute. Then he

lunged to the ground and grabbed a stick that looked something like a pirate's sword. Brandishing the weapon, he cried, "I am Pirate Damien Black, Terror of the Seven Seas! Fight for your life, you lily-livered land-lubber!"

Shane hesitated for an instant. He hadn't meant to start a fight. But now that it was facing him, he did what he had to do. Seizing another stick from the ground – not as stout as the pirate's, but serviceable enough as a sword – he met the attack head-on.

The pirate fought well. Shane did his best, but he clearly was not in his element. He wished he could handle his sword as well as the pirate handled his. He evidently had had a lot of practice, for his sword seemed only an extension of himself.

They fought, sword to sword, over hillocks and under arches, around and among the exotic trees and plants of the garden. Then without warning Shane disappeared into a tall clump of ferns. The pirate made a few random jabs at the ferns, then crouched like a cat, glancing left and right for a sign of his foe. "Show yourself, scurvy bilge-rat!"

Shane suddenly emerged from the ferns about twenty feet away, near some tall fruit trees. "Here's your rat!" he cried.

"Aaargh!" The pirate let out a throaty growl and lunged after him, swinging his stick furiously in every direction. Shane blocked the vicious slices and jabs and slowly retreated, luring the attacker back into the clump of trees.

Mia quickly realized what Shane was up to and let

out a squeal of anticipation. The pirate shot a quick glance in her direction, then did a double-take, very confused. What he saw was not a girl – it was an angel! He had never had an angel mistake him for a pirate before. He was so surprised he even forgot to fight – but only for a moment. A well-aimed thwack on the head brought him rudely back, and he rejoined the battle.

By now Shane was getting the hang of sword fighting and began to use his superior size to his advantage. The pirate soon found himself backed up against one of the trees. In a flash, he darted behind it and scampered up into the lowest branches, where he continued raining down blows from his new vantage point.

Unfortunately for the pirate, he didn't know about the gnarl vines. An instant later he felt something twine itself around his two ankles and jerk him from his perch. There was a brief scramble as he tried to keep his balance and free himself, but the next thing he knew his head was swinging three feet from the ground, his feet bound securely in the branches above, his sword lying harmlessly in the grass just out of reach. Shane stood over him, panting but smiling triumphantly.

The pirate saw the angel step up for a closer look and turn her head upside down so she could look at him right-side up. "If you eat too many of those chocolate berries you'll get sick," the angel said.

"No, I won't," contradicted the pirate. "Berries don't make you sick… unless they are poison berries. But I saw a bird eat one and it didn't die." The pirate was managing to be very stubborn even while hanging upside-down

from a tree talking to an angel.

"I didn't say you would die, I said you would get sick. They're like candy. Daddy made them that way. He's a genetic scientist," Mia informed.

The pirate got an even more stubborn look. "You don't *make* berries. They *grow*. Where did you get them? I want to grow some." Without waiting for an answer he turned to the question that had ended him up in his predicament. "Are you an angel? My dad says they're real, but my step-mom says they aren't."

"No," said Mia, looking upset. "I'm a girl. See? I have wings. And you're a boy, like Shane, because you haven't got any wings." Mia turned away with a people-should-mind-their-own-business look.

"He's not a boy," said Shane. "He's a pirate. He said so himself."

"Let me down!" demanded the pirate – then added after a pause, "Please." This was a drastic measure, he knew, and very un-pirate-like, but with his face growing uncomfortably red and his dignity at low ebb, he thought a little politeness might not be such a bad thing after all.

"Okay," Shane consented, "but only if you agree to be our prisoner."

The pirate saw he had very little choice. Reluctantly, and a little awkwardly, he nodded his head. Shane and Mia unwound the gnarl vines and carefully let him down.

"Are you really a pirate?" demanded Mia. "What is your real name? And how did you get in here?"

"I told you, I'm Pirate Damien Black. My real name is Damien Knight – Damien for short." Still eyeing Mia's silver white wings and hair, he said, "I'll tell you how I got in here if you promise not to tell on me. My step-mom'll kill me if she finds out I got out of our yard."

Shane and Mia both raised their right hand, trying to nod solemnly rather than eagerly. "We promise," they said.

"Pirate's honor?" he insisted.

"Pirate's honor," they affirmed.

"I dug a hole under the wall behind my fort. It came out over there," he said, pointing to the rock garden wall that enclosed the peppermint plants. There were clefts and crags and ledges planted with all different kinds of mint. Water trickled down the rocks, making the ground muddy in spots. Broken away from the wall, a large stone jutted out with Sumerian cuneiform writing chiseled onto it, and underneath the cuneiform were some strange, decorative rune-like figures – the Sumerian Rune Rock.

Mia went to investigate. Behind this stone and hidden by the leafy plants was indeed a hole. She disappeared and came back a minute or two later almost as dirty as Damien. "Your step-mother is calling for you," she said, looking earnestly at him, "and she doesn't sound very happy. You better go or you'll be in trouble."

Damien was embarrassed. He was sure Blackbeard had never had to go home because *his* step-mother was calling him. He turned to leave.

"Wait!" exclaimed Shane. "You agreed to be our prisoner. Tell you what. I'll let you go if you promise to come back tomorrow and finish being our prisoner."

Damien didn't think he had much choice. He was an honorable pirate. With a quick nod he dashed off toward the hole.

"Tomorrow you will have to pass a test to see if you are a worthy pirate!" Shane called after him. But Damien didn't hear. His head was already inside the hole and soon his feet also disappeared.

chapter two

That evening, Shane and Mia could hardly keep their mouths shut. They had thought they had only caught a thief but they had actually caught a pirate. At dinner they acted very much like kids who were up to something – not that it was so unusual for them to be up to something. But this time it was clearly something really special.

"Pirates" was one of their favorite games. They even had a sunken pirate ship for a fort. Shane and Mia agreed to hold a secret meeting with each other that night to discuss how to test Damien to find out if he was brave and worthy.

Mother and Father knew something was up but they generally let their kids get into a little mischief as long as nobody got hurt, and Shane and Mia didn't argue with each other. The children were not able to leave the Rockwell estate except on rare occasions, and, extensive as the grounds were, the 30 acres were not always big enough to easily contain the children's active imaginations. Father tucked them in bed with an indulgent twinkle in his eyes.

Shane lay in bed looking at the opposite wall. It had two large tree trunks set vertically against the wall. Notches were cut into the tree trunks to provide foot and hand holds for Shane to be able to climb up to the loft above. Once you were sitting in the loft you could see a small door, large enough for a child to crawl through. If you unlatched that door you would see another door latched on the other side which led from Mia's room. Mia also had a ledge in front of her door which she had decorated with pretty plants and flowers – that were most difficult for the maid to water, since Mia had no steps up to her ledge.

It was in Shane's loft that they had agreed to hold their secret meeting. Once their father's footsteps had receded down the hall, Shane silently slipped out of bed and climbed up his tree-ladder. He had barely reached the top when he heard Mia's soft tap from her side of the door.

"We have to make sure he's a brave pirate," whispered Mia once she had settled next to Shane.

"And true," added Shane. "Lying is a bad habit. We could hang him upside down again, and tickle him."

"No! No tickling. I hate it when you tickle me!" Mia complained. "We could use truth serum."

"Or give him a riddle."

"We could make him eat a slug-fruit pie."

"Or a sandwich."

"And not tell him how they wiggle like real slugs all

the way down."

"We can make him walk the plank."

"Blindfolded."

"And feed him to the sharks."

"Or the wild beasts."

"Like Cyril?"

"Yes – or Lyric. She's meaner. We can take him to the fire pit."

"What would we do at the fire pit?"

"I don't know."

"We could keelhaul him."

"What's that?"

"It's… well, I'm not quite sure, but pirates always do it to their prisoners."

They both fell silent as they ran out of ideas.

At last, Shane spoke again. "I think the pirate should walk the plank. We will blindfold him and lead him around until he is completely lost. We will take off his blindfold when he gets to the feeding rock at Sharks Lagoon and make him stand with his hands tied behind his back. Then we will call Lyric to cut off any escape. I want to see if he will panic and jump to the sharks or bravely face a wild beast. Finally, we'll agree to set him free if he promises to climb a gnarl vine tree and get us the fruit from the top. If he really does it then we will know he's also true and clever."

Mia looked at her brother with admiration. He didn't always talk much, but when he did what he said was always worth hearing. "Agreed," she said.

After Mia had returned to her bed and started to fall asleep, Mother came looking for her. Quiet as a shadow she sat at the edge of Mia's bed. "I have something for you," she said softly, showing Mia a beautifully sculpted white stone that glistened in the pale beam of moonlight streaming in from the window, with elegant golden veins lacing the granite-like sheen. It had a sharp middle prong pointing forward and two outside ones curving gracefully back to the handle. It was about the size of a large man's hand and had intricate carvings on its blade and handle.

"It's shaped like a mysterious flower," said Mia, eyes wide and all sleep gone.

"It does look like a fleur-de-lis, doesn't it?" agreed Mother. "I think it is a knife of some kind – maybe a ceremonial knife? I found it in a compartment that nobody else noticed, under the throne of the king in the ruins of the Cliff City at the archeological dig. I only discovered the compartment because I was translating the runes carved on the throne. I don't know what the intricate carving on the blade means, but on the handle it has an inscription that says it should be given to the princess daughter of Mia-Ryall. She was the queen whom you were named after. The sagas say this stone was always given to the princess who was to become the next queen. When the last queen died, the king hid it under his throne with the instruction that if it was ever found it must be given to the next princess. So it really belongs to you rather than to a stuffy old museum. But that is our secret. Okay?" And then she added with unexplained urgency, "If you ever have to leave here, I want you to take this with you."

"Okay," agreed Mia, who loved secrets. "But, I'll never have to leave here, will I?"

"Oh, you don't need to worry about that. I just mean that this stone knife is important, and belongs with you wherever you go." Mother kissed her on the forehead.

Mia fell asleep gazing at the beautiful object bequeathed to her. Did it make her a princess too?

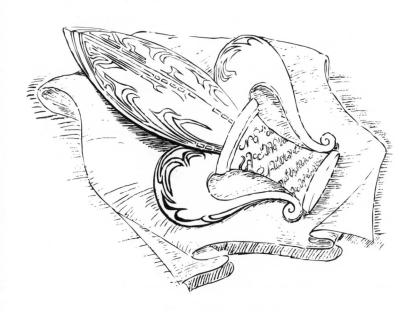

chapter three

It was reminiscent of the Middle Ages, when people believed the world was flat. Many thought Columbus would fall off the end of the earth trying to reach India by sailing west. Or when people believed the sun revolved around the earth. Galileo was arrested for insisting that the earth circled around the sun. Even with scientific proof, some people angrily refused to believe that the sun was at the center of our solar system.

So it was, centuries later, when another planet was discovered in our solar system. Many rejected the idea, calling the photographs and artifacts brought back a hoax. Perhaps they would have found it easier to believe if the new planet had been discovered in the Kuiper belt, out beyond Pluto. But this was not the case. They also might have found it easier to accept if the planet had been a barren wasteland pocked with craters. But this, too, was not the case. The planet was found on precisely the opposite side of the sun from Earth. It was about the same size as Earth, shared Earth's orbit, possessed an atmosphere very similar to that of Earth, and abounded with plant and animal life — much of which, however, was unlike that of Earth. It was called Meta and was declared a United States territory.

The Government was most concerned about introducing new viruses and bacteria to Earth, which could cause an epidemic. Another major concern was that some of Earth's diseases would be exported to Meta, against which the biological systems on that planet had no defenses.

The Government established a tightly-run research colony on Meta. Every precaution was put in place to avoid contamination. Most of the personnel invited to establish the colony were scientists of biology, physics and genetics. But there was also an archeological division which included one linguist to assist in the analysis of the writings found in the ruins of an ancient civilization. Her name was Serena Whitman, and she had a doctorate in linguistics from Harvard with a specialty in ancient languages.

Serena immersed herself in the rich artifacts and ruins of the newfound culture, working eighteen-hour days and often forgetting to eat or sleep. She soon found her obsession was shared by a young genetic scientist named Garrit Rockwell, who was studying the petrified wing structure of the humanoid skeletons in the ancient tombs. These skeletons were consistent with the elaborate carvings and statues of the stone city. The only creatures depicted by the carvings that were still alive were the large silver-white winged cats that prowled the plains. They were carnivores, larger than a Siberian tiger.

Serena was fascinated by the cats and the role they seemed to play in the ancient culture.

chapter four

It was about mid-afternoon and Damien sat on a large stone in the garden with his elbows on his knees and his chin in his hands, awaiting his doom. Presently he saw Shane and Mia making their way across the estate grounds. They were both wearing pirate hats. Shane had a large purple feather in his hat and he wore a red captain's jacket with a shiny plastic sword at his hilt. Mia wore a patch over one eye and tall black boots. She had a toy dagger tucked into her left boot and her silver-white wings and hair gleamed in the sun.

"A pirate's word is his honor, so you scallywags may take me prisoner," growled Pirate Damien Black. He surveyed his captors through narrowed eyes as if trying to anticipate their next move.

"Aye, matey, we be here to test yer courage." Shane put on his best pirate sneer. "If ye survive." He bound Damien's hands behind his back securely, but not tightly enough to actually hurt.

Mia was skipping about, darting here and there with little yips of excitement.

Damien looked at her critically. "You're supposed to be a pirate. How come you're still wearing those costume wings?" he asked, abandoning his pirate manner momentarily. He had evidently decided overnight that she wasn't an angel. Mia didn't answer. She just turned her head with a sniff and an offended look.

"Mind yer eyes, swab," said Shane before Damien could continue his line of inquiry. "First I'll be blindfoldin' you so ye won't know yer way back to our lagoon – if ye survive to try an' come back! Har! Thar ye'll walk the plank to the sharks. Mayhaps after that, an ye show yerself brave, we'll set you free – but only providin' ye gives yer word – yer pirate's word – that ye'll climb atop yon gnarl vine tree – they's alive, ye know – and fetch us the fruit that's up thar. Be ye agreeable to it now? Eh? Speak up, scurvy cur."

Damien paused deliberately as if to consider his options. "Arr," he agreed. "If I survives the plank, pirate's word I'll climb that gnarl vine tree and fetch ye that fruit – or die tryin'." He tried hard to sound appropriately scared, brave and sullen all at the same time.

With the prisoner blindfolded, the trio set off towards Sharks Lagoon, their circuitous path twisting all over the estate grounds until Damien was thoroughly lost. In the distance he could hear what sounded like claps of thunder or explosions which drew nearer as he was led on. Soon he felt damp air stinging his cheek, smelled the rotting wood of a lagoon and heard the sloshing of water against it. Nothing, however, prepared him for the sight before him when the blindfold was finally removed, for Damien was used to the world behaving according to calculated reason.

Fog clung to the lagoon, shrouding everything in a mysterious twilight so that all that could be seen was the lagoon and what touched it. Half hidden, as if emerging from the gloom, was a pirate ship, its guns blazing. Water sploshed here and there with flashes of red light. It was just like the Pirates of the Caribbean ride at Disneyland. It looked astonishingly real and spooky.

The rock on which Damien was standing jutted way out into the lagoon. "This is the Sharks Lagoon feeding rock," explained Shane. "You will walk the plank out to the end of the rock. I suggest you don't jump in."

Damien didn't need to be told not to jump in. Just below his feet the fish were swarming all around, roiling the water as they jostled each other for a chance at the first bite of food. Some of them did look like sharks – not very big ones, so Damien wasn't sure how dangerous they really were; but still, they seemed pretty hungry. He considered the circumstances of this strange dilemma, and figured things probably wouldn't get any worse. But just then Mia appeared at the edge of the lagoon leading a huge beast, and Damien's heart leapt inside him. This time his fear was no act. The creature was like a giant Siberian tiger, but with wings like a great silver-white eagle.

As soon as it saw Damien, the animal crouched down, its ears flattened against its head. "How did that young one get in here?" it growled to Shane – at least, this is what Shane and Mia heard. All Damien heard was a ferocious snarl.

"He—" began Shane. But before he could think of how to answer, the great cat sniffed the air and her expression changed. "Poor thing," she rowled, a softer tone in her voice. "He's scared half out of his wits." Rising up on her haunches and flapping her muscular wings, she bounded toward the boy. Damien shut his eyes tight and steeled himself for the pounce. Terrified as he was, he held his ground and didn't cry out... at least, not until the massive cat started to lick him.

"It's tasting me!" he yowled.

Suddenly the cat whipped around and in one flying leap, graceful and terrible at the same time, she pounced on Shane, pinning him to the ground. "Your father and mother are going to be very angry that you brought another child in here," she snarled furiously. "You know the rules!"

"Please, Lyric," whimpered Shane. "We didn't bring him in here. He showed up and we just... we just made friends with him, that's all. He's the only friend we have! Please don't tell." The cat stepped back off of him without replying. Shane picked himself up off the ground, brushed the dirt and twigs off his captain's coat, and hurried over to untie Damien's hands.

"You two have been cruel brats, terrifying that poor kitten the way you did," spat the giant cat.

"It was my idea," said Mia defiantly, looking every bit the brat that she had just been accused of being. "So tell on me if you want to. I don't care!"

Lyric regarded Mia very seriously. "I think your mother and father will have to hear about this," she said. Then she looked back toward Damien, who still stood, wide-eyed at the end of the feeding rock. She appeared to be about to say something to him, but then, seeing the expression on his face, she seemed to think better of it, and without another sound she turned and disappeared into the fog.

"What was that?" asked Damien once she was gone, his voice hardly more than a hoarse whisper.

"It's OK," Shane tried to reassure him. "That was Lyric. She's our cat."

"Yeah," added Mia, coming to join them on the rock. "Lyric is our pet. And we have another one too. His name is Cyril."

By now astonishment had replaced the fear in Damien's expression. "And you were talking with her?" he asked incredulously.

"Sure," Mia replied. "Didn't you hear what she was saying?"

"It just sounded to me like she was snarling," he said.

"She *was* snarling," Shane agreed. "You kind of have to get used to the way she speaks. She sounds less cat-like when she isn't so angry."

"But... but..." Damien stammered, still trying to make sense of it all, "but... she has wings! And she can *talk*! How in the world—?"

"Oh," said Mia by way of explanation, "she's a Medaryan Cat – you know, from Meta."

"Yeah," agreed Shane, "so she isn't from our world."

Damien was unconvinced. "Meta?" he said. "What do you mean? There's no such thing as Meta. My dad says it's a hoax, and he works for the Government, so he should know. And Step-mom agrees with him too, which almost *never* happens."

"But Meta does exist," Shane insisted. "Father and Mother were both researchers there. That's where they met. And they brought back Lyric and Cyril as kittens. They both still work for the CMR, too – that's their job."

"What's the CMR?" demanded Damien.

"That stands for the Center for Metan Research," said Mia in a knowing tone, remembering the exact words her father had used when she had asked the same question. "Its purpose is to learn everything there is to know about Meta. It's run by the Government, and a lot of what they do is *top secret*."

"Cool!" Damien exclaimed. An idea suddenly dawned on him. "So you must be from Meta too. That's where you got your wings!"

"No, don't be silly," said Mia impatiently. "*I'm* not from Meta. I already told you, I've got wings because—"

"Come on, you guys," Shane cut in before she could finish. He seemed uncomfortable with the direction the conversation was going. "We need to figure out what to do if Lyric tells on us."

"Are you going to get in trouble because of me?" Damien sounded genuinely concerned.

"Probably," said Shane glumly. "We're not supposed to have other kids here. If our parents find out they might forbid us to play with you any more." In reality he was more concerned about losing a new friend than about being punished.

"Same here," Damien concurred. "I don't think Dad would mind, but my step-mom is a control freak. She doesn't like me to do *anything* without her permission. There's no way I would breathe a word about you! Do you think we could convince Lyric not to tell your parents?"

"I don't know." Shane looked doubtful.

"It's worth a try at least," urged Mia. "Come on, let's go find her."

This proved to be easier than expected. They practically stumbled into her just a few paces from the lagoon. She was sitting at the edge of the fog bank, facing them, a distracted twitch in her tail. Shane suspected that she had overheard their conversation back at the rock.

"Um, Lyric," said Shane hesitantly, "I'd like to introduce our new friend. This is Damien Knight. He's from next door. Damien, this is Lyric."

Damien wasn't quite sure of the proper etiquette for addressing a talking cat. "It's a pleasure to meet you," he said stiffly.

"The pleasure is mine," she replied formally, but there was a gentle purr in her voice that put him at ease. Damien realized that it did not take too much concentration to understand her feline accent now that he was prepared for it. "I hope I did not give you too much of a fright back there. Mia did not explain why she wanted me to come with her, and she obviously did not tell you, either. The unexpected sight of a Medaryan winged cat must have been quite a shock."

"It's all right," Damien replied. "I've recovered now, thanks." Then with a quick breath he continued rapidly, "But please don't blame Shane and Mia. It's not their fault. I snuck in here yesterday all on my own. I didn't mean to get them in trouble."

Mia began to cry. "Please, Lyric," she pleaded, "it's not fair. Shane and I are always cooped up here on the estate, and we never get to have any friends. And then when we finally find one, we get in trouble for it, and he'll get in trouble for it, too, and then he'll never be able to come back and play any more and – and you don't even care!"

This last vehement outburst was met with total silence, and Mia was suddenly afraid that she had gotten herself into even worse trouble. But when she looked at Lyric through her tears, it was sadness that she saw rather than anger.

"Shane, may I talk to you alone?" Lyric asked quietly. He nodded and followed her a short distance away, just out of earshot. After a few minutes of hushed conversation, he returned to the others alone, his face sober.

"She promised she wouldn't tell Mother and Father," he reported, but refused to say any more, even when they pressed him to tell them how he got her to agree to that.

"Guess I have to go home now, don't I?" said Damien regretfully.

Shane's face brightened a bit. "No, you don't. Lyric

did say you could stay for now, so let's go back to playing." He slipped back into his pirate brogue. "Ye were brilliant, me hearty – steadfast and fearless! From now on ye must be called Savage Pirate Damien Black the Stalwart. 'Twould be an honor to us if ye'd join our ship."

"Nay, mateys, but the honor 'ud be mine. This calls for a solemn blood pact."

They made their way around the lagoon to the gangway that led aboard the ship, and Damien commented, "I like the fog effect. How do you do it?"

"Fog ferns," explained Shane. "If you look at the ferns carefully you can see mist seeping out of their fronds. From our house you can't even see the ship. All you can see is a big cloud. It also muffles sound. And those plants are called firegrasses –because they look like flames when they flicker in the wind." Damien had to admit that they did resemble fire, with their flame-shaped blades in myriad shades of orange and red and yellow, green and purple. They were the only vivid colors he could see in the murky fog.

"Sometimes I have heard the cannons from my yard. I always wondered what the noise was."

Once inside the ship-fort they made it through the nasty business of poking their fingers with a pin to mingle their blood while taking the oath to be true until death:

> If I'm false, if I lie,
> Poke a needle through my eye,
> Break my sword, slit my throat,

Keelhaul me on a pirate's boat.
Pirate's skull, cross of bone,
Honor pledged endures like stone.

They held their right fingers together and chanted under the flickering light of the mock lanterns which hung from hooks on the wall, swaying with the boat. The flame-like effect cast ghostly shadows of the ship's wheel at the helm and the old wooden table that was set in the center of the small room. On the table was a treasure map.

"Mia wants to add something to our pirate's treasure chest," said Shane as he studied the map. "It's located right here," he told Damien, pointing to a spot marked with an ✖. "Let's go."

The three pirates trudged out of the ship following the pirate's map, Shane in the lead. Stumbling through the thick fog they headed south from the ship's stern. When they reached a forked rock they turned due west until they got to a hollow tree. Shane retrieved two shovels from the hollow of the trunk. Then the three of them proceeded ten paces north until they came to a small mound of earth.

"Here it is," announced Shane.

Damien had been studying Mia's wings as they went along.

"Can you really fly?" he asked her, a bit skeptically, "or are you like one of those flightless birds whose wings don't actually work?"

Mia stretched her wings and then folded them

smugly. "Of course I can fly," she said.

Damien was about to ask her to show him when Shane thrust a shovel in his hand. "Help me dig," he interrupted.

"Don't mind him," Mia whispered to Damien, just loud enough for Shane to hear. "He's just sensitive because he has always wanted wings."

The two boys worked hard and within a few minutes they had dug up an old wooden box encased in leather. It had brass clasps over its curved lid. Inside were various interesting treasures, including a hand-drawn map of Meta and some scattered gold coins. Mia handed Shane the object that they were to bury with the rest of their treasures – the white stone her mother had given her, its marbled gold veins glistening in the sunlight.

"Wow," said Damien with fascination. "What is it? A knife?"

"Mom thinks its may be a ceremonial knife, but she's not sure," said Mia.

"She gave it to you?" asked Shane incredulously.

"Yes, she did," said Mia, pursing her lips together stubbornly, "but I can't tell you any more because it's supposed to be a secret. That's why I want to bury it."

"Well, okay. Let's get it buried, then," said Shane.

As Shane started to close the chest, Damien stopped him. "Wait," he said, taking off a silver chain hanging around his neck, "I would like to add this too." He placed it in the box with the stone and shut the lid. Then they lowered the chest back into its hole and covered it with earth once again.

On their way home Damien reminded them, "By the way... I still have to climb a gnarl vine tree. I gave my pirate's word."

"Oh, that's easy," said Mia. "All you need to know is that you can't touch the vines from underneath. It tickles them and they grab you."

Damien eyed her guardedly and decided she was telling the truth. When they reached the gnarl vine trees he lithely climbed one of them, careful to avoid the vines, and threw down some of the fruit from the top.

chapter five

The genome is the human genetic code. There are a hundred and sixty-four genes in the genome, each with thousands of proteins. When science first cracked the human genetic code, the possibilities for medical advancement and improvement of the human condition seemed wide open. But a series of genetic experiments went awry while the field was still in its infancy, and the results were so horrible that many rational people realized something had to be done to regulate the practice of genetic science, or permanent damage to the human race could result. The major nations of the world held a number of summits, and after much bickering, wrangling, name-calling, and negotiating, the Treaty for International Genetic Engineering and Research Standards was eventually hammered out. After TIGERS, it had been forbidden to cross the human genome with that of any other species, and breaking the code was punishable by the severest of penalties, commensurate with the potential dangers.

One remarkable and unexpecte, result of the research into human DNA also sparked a good deal of controversy. A prominent study of the genes of people from around the world found that all of modern man could be shown to be of a single family stock — in other words, that the entire human race alive today could be traced back to a single man and woman. A number of scientists were uncomfortable with this conclusion at first — less for its scientific implications than because of the satisfaction they knew it would give creationists. Nevertheless, the evidence was compelling, and most eventually accepted the idea (though some drew the line at using the nickname coined by the popular press: the "Adam & Eve Theory").

Garrit and Jerrod Rockwell, identical twins, were two of the most promising scientists of the new generation. They were far too fascinated by the way genetics worked to care much about the philosophical arguments. This theory was the axiom upon which they based their research, and the axiom always held true — that is, until one day when just for fun they decided to run some basic genetic tests on their friend Serena Whitman. To their surprise, her DNA contained a sequence that they had never come across before. Nor could they find a record of anything like it in the databases. It was as if a part of Serena was not exactly human.

Soon afterwards, to their even greater astonishment, Garrit and Jerrod discovered precisely the same genetic sequence in the winged humanoid mummies from the royal tombs of the Cliff City of Meta. They could think of only one explanation: The two civilizations of Meta and Earth, separated by half a solar system, must have been in contact millennia ago, and one of the ancient kings from this faraway land must have left a child in ancient Mesopotamia at the beginning of our civilizations. The recessive gene had been carried through the generations and now surfaced in Serena. Her silver-white hair and steel-grey eyes were the outward signs of this genetic link.

chapter six

Shane and Mia played with Damien every day after their lessons. Lessons during the morning and early afternoon consisted of language and literature with Mother, science and math with Father, archeology and history with Mother, engineering and problem-solving with Father, music with Mother, and finally writing with whichever parent could more easily spare the time.

Today's science lesson was to be in Father's basement lab. This was an exciting event that didn't happen all that often because of the many secret projects Father had going. The lab was a vast complex of rooms extending not only the length and width of the large house, but dug for some distance out under the yard as well. It was crammed full of experiments and scientific instruments their dad used in his research, odd contraptions he had invented to help him in his work – or sometimes just for his own amusement – and all sorts of plants and small animals brought back from Meta to be studied. Shane and Mia with an excited hush wound their way down to the forbidden laboratory.

When Mia was ushered into the lab she immediately caught the attention of some large orange flowers that were in a cage against the wall. They were snapping in her direction with loud clacks and stretching their roots earnestly through the wire mesh. One smaller flower managed to slip through the wire and drop to the floor. It was running along a crack in the floor towards Mia who yelped and jumped away.

"Don't worry," said Father, the usual twinkle in his eye. "They just want to play. They don't get to see kids very often. I guess they don't find me enough fun for them."

Up in another corner jellyfish-looking creatures were riding the air currents from the heat and cooling vents, feasting on dust motes. In the sink some greenish slime pulsated.

A portion of the room was taken up by a small pond of lily-pads, surrounded by numerous flowers in pots and planters. The pond area was separated from the main space by caging covered in mosquito netting, and inside brightly colored light-bugs flitted about and equally bright frogs hopped in and out of the water. The light-bugs were a kind of Metan bee – "except they don't have stingers," said Father. Every so often a frog would shoot out its long tongue to catch and swallow one of the bees. Then it would start to glow the color of the bug it had eaten. Each color of bee seemed to have its own hive – cyan bees hovered around a cyan hive, purple bees hovered around a purple hive, and so on. The hives had tubes attached to collect the bright honey which also glowed the color of the bee that made it.

"There is a type of phosphorus in the honey that very quickly gets into the blood stream," explained Father as he took a bottle of plain soda water and held it under the pink tube until he had added several squirts of pink honey to the water. "It's very sweet-tasting and perfectly innocuous." He gave the pink bottle to Mia and made a cyan one for Shane. Mia drank about half the bottle in one gulp and immediately began to glow pink. Shane glowed neon blue.

There were also neat machines. One that rolled up to you and offered you tea, another that carried around a bag of jellybeans. There was a self-automated vacuum machine which was having a battle with the escaped flower – the flower was scuttling up and down the crack in the floor, the vacuum machine trying unsuccessfully to catch it.

Shane was drawn to a glass terrarium at the edge of the room. In the generous terrarium was a baby cobra. Shane had been practicing the recorder since the last time he had been in the lab, preparing so he could play for this cobra and see if it would dance the way they did in the stories – snake charming. He pulled out the wood pipe he had carved just for this event. After only a few notes the small snake, obviously bored, slithered off to the far corner and curled up. Noticing this with disappointment, Shane began to blow harder on the pipe in a vain attempt to get the snake's attention.

Meanwhile Mia was kneeling on the floor, holding out her hand to the little orange flower. She wiggled her fingers and clicked at it encouragingly. The flower answered with a loud snapping noise, reaching playfully for her fingers – *tsk-tsk-tsk CLACK, tsk-tsk-tsk CLACK*, almost in time with Shane's piping.

Suddenly a series of tiny explosions occurred among several trays of potted herbs on the floor. Shane spun around just in time to see flames leaping from pot to pot. There was a moment of pandemonium – startled frogs dove under their lily-pads, the escaped flower found a way back into its cage, and Father hurried to the sink to get some water – but the fires went out as quickly as they had started, leaving a few smoldering plant pots among a tray of potted herbs. The only plants that had caught fire were a few firegrasses that had not been planted among the others by the Sharks Lagoon.

"Very curious," mused Father. "I knew those grasses contained chemicals that could burn if mixed together, but they are always confined to separate chambers within the plant, and have never ignited before. Why did they choose now to spontaneously combust? These are long-lived plants – I believe I planted this batch from seed about the time Mia was born. Maybe they have some sort of internal clock that causes this to happen every ten years or so? That *would* serve as a natural means to keep the Metan forests cleared of excess underbrush. Hmmm," he added with a frown as another thought came to him. "I just hope the ones we planted out by the Sharks Lagoon don't do the same thing."

All the commotion had caught the attention of the baby cobra. The little snake was finally peering out of the glass, its neck skin flattened into the characteristic hood, bobbing its head at Shane. Shane grinned.

Then Mia saw something on the counter that was trying to hop up onto the sink faucet. "Sucker anemone," said Father. It looked like two rubbery antennae connected near the bottom, with bulgy eyes on top and suction cups for feet. The two antennae would bend this way and that, and every once in a while a spark of static electricity would sizzle between them. Mia leaned over for a closer look and the sucker anemone jumped on her head.

"Yikes!" she squealed.

"They always try to jump to the highest spot," Father explained. "They won't hurt you. Indeed, they seem quite happy on your head, Mia."

The antennae gave a spark of approval.

Meanwhile Shane was intently studying a huge spider that was busily spinning a web at the far side of the room. The spider was about as big as a medium-sized dog, though its web was woven out of surprisingly thin strands of silk.

"I'm harvesting the spider's silk," Father informed them. "It's stronger than steel, and more lightweight than any metal. We have coated our shuttle with it sandwiched in with the titanium."

Shane was impressed. He knew that Father and Joe – mainly Joe (a scientist and colleague of Father's who was also his best friend and confidant) – had been designing a family shuttle for travel to Meta one day, but Father had been very secretive about the details. "It's a work in progress," he kept saying. "There's really nothing to say about it yet." So this must have been one of the secrets they had been working so hard on.

"How do you keep the thread from sticking to everything?" Shane asked.

"That, son, was one of the simplest, and most inexpensive, problems we had to solve. You cover it with talc. It bonds instantly and permanently to the natural adhesive in the spider's silk and you end up with a superstrong thread that is also smooth as – well, silk. I've put in an order with the tailor for some clothes made out of it. It also makes excellent lightweight armor. Weave it into a fabric the thickness of a sweater and a bullet can't go through it. Here, Shane, cover the web with talc and then see if you can put your hand through it." He handed Shane a blue plastic bottle. "Oh, but do be careful to put the talc on *first*. Once the spider's web has already stuck to something, the talc can't unstick it, and you have to use more drastic measures to get it loose."

Shane looked at the bottle in his hand with some surprise and amusement. Talc was nothing more than the scientific name for *baby powder*! He generously applied the scented white powder to a corner of the web and tried to break it. With all his strength Shane could not tear a single thread of the spider's web.

Father turned around to see what Mia was into, and as soon as he did so the spider shot some sticky silk at his and Shane's feet. Father tried to lift his leg but his feet were hopelessly stuck to the floor. The spider squirted him again and now his left hand stuck to his jeans. "Mia, bring me that spray bottle that says anti-stick acid," he said, trying to motion to the sink next to the shimmering green goo, but now both his arms were completely stuck to his sides. "Oh dear," he exclaimed, wriggling like a large eel in his vain attempts to free his arms and feet. "I think Matilda must be jealous. She's never done this to me before."

Mia squirted Father's feet with anti-adhesive but no sooner had she done so than the spider restuck them. "Oh, this is hopeless," said Father in dismay as the spider again squirted his momentarily free hands. "We're supposed to study the human genome today and the genetic code of the Medaryan cats and the winged people. Oh, dear. Oh, dear. Mia, I think you had better go get your mother."

Mia flew off to find Mother. As she flitted past the frog pond, still glowing pink, the sucker anemone antennae on her head sparking in excitement, she resembled a giant, electrified version of the busy glow-bees obliviously gathering their nectar on the other side of the netting.

Literature lessons with Serena were more normal, aside from the fact that Shane and Mia were still glowing. They were studying the literatures and cultures of the ancient Near East. Today's reading was a portion from the Sumerian epic of Gilgamesh which told of a great flood that had covered the whole world and destroyed all life.

Only one man named Ziusudra, along with his family and representatives of all the animals, survived by building a large raft.

"There are other Sumerian legends," Mother added as the children were putting their books away at the end of the lesson, "– or rather, the way some people understand their legends – which tell of a race of men who had traveled to that land from the sky. They were called *annunaki*, and were worshipped as gods. They were said to have created humans to be their servants, but when the flood came they left."

"Who were these god-men?" asked Mia.

"We don't know exactly how they fit in with history. It's Sumerian mythology. Most of it is probably no more than fable. But there is very good reason to believe that some elements of the account, at least, have a grain of truth behind them."

chapter seven

Serena had always loved languages. Ever since her childhood she had thought of them as elaborate codes just waiting to be deciphered. By age 8 she was even trying to invent languages of her own. And when she grew up, she decided to become a linguist – to the surprise of no one who knew her. So it was that when the unique opportunity came her way to study the newly discovered inscriptions on Meta, Serena tackled the challenge with her old childlike enthusiasm.

But a completely unknown language in a completely unknown writing system is a practically impossible code to crack. As a linguist, Serena knew this only too well, and being a realist too, she did not expect anything like full success in deciphering Medaryan.

Two discoveries changed her mind.

The first was the discovery that the cuneiform symbols chiseled into the rock found in the throne room were actually Sumerian. Now there could be no doubt that contact had existed between Meta and Earth in ancient times. This raised the possibility that the language of Medarya might somehow be related to a language of Earth. Serena wondered: Could it actually be related to Sumerian? But that idea soon proved to be a dead end.

The second discovery came some months later, over coffee one morning. Serena was sitting at the breakfast table sipping her coffee and, as she often did during this quiet time of the day, reviewing her notes. The jottings in front of her on this particular morning were of a few Medaryan numbers written out as words — that much she had been able to figure out, though she had no clue how they were pronounced.

As she gazed at the list, still half asleep, a familiar pattern unexpectedly jumped off the page. The word ꞓ, meaning 'two', and ꞓ, meaning 'ten', both began with the same letter in Medaryan, just as in English. Similarly, ꞓ 'six' and ꞓ 'seven' also began with the same letter (but not the same one as 'two' and 'ten'). And, finally, ꞓ 'seven' and ꞓ 'ten' both ended in the same letter. When she saw this, Serena nearly dropped her mug. She was suddenly wide awake, and a wave of realization swept over her that almost made her giddy. She knew this pattern — she had seen it again and again, in other old languages distantly related to English. The individual sounds might change, but the pattern remained the same:

English	Gothic	Gaulish	Latin	Greek	Medaryan	
t·wo	t·wai	d·o	d·uo	d·úo	ꞟ	ꞓ
t·e·n	t·aihu·n	d·eca·m	d·ece·m	d·ék·a	ꞟ	ꞓ
s·eve·n	s·ibu·n	s·exta·m	s·epte·m	h·épt·a	ꞓ	ꞓ
s·ix	s·aihs	s·uekos	s·ex	h·éx	ꞓ	ꞓ

A single agreement between languages could easily be a fluke. Two might also be coincidence. But three exact matches? And in such a small set of words? This could not be the result of chance. There was only one possible explanation – all these languages must have shared a common ancestor. Medaryan must have been related to Proto-Indo-European, the ancient ancestor of English and many of the other languages of Europe and Asia.

This was the key that unlocked the code. After that it was only a matter of time – and a lot of hard work – before Medaryan was fully deciphered and the writing could be read. It became known just how these numbers had been pronounced: duwó 'two', sékas 'six', sṓptim 'seven', and díkim 'ten'. And the scores of inscriptions in the Cliff City began to reveal their long-held secrets.

chapter eight

That evening the Rockwells had a family meeting in the linguistic library. This adjoined Serena's private office near the children's rooms. Shelves covered almost every inch of the walls, containing scores and scores of books – dictionaries and grammars of dead languages, large facsimiles of ancient manuscripts written in exotic writing, volumes with captivating titles such as *The Gāthās of Zarathustra, Studies in Hittite Historical Phonology, Indo-European Word Formation, How to Kill a Dragon: Aspects of Indo-European Poetics,* and many others, most of which were not even in English. At one end of the room stood a reading table piled with books; two volumes of Vedic hymns lay open on it. At the other end of the room sat a couch and two plush arm chairs, arranged in front of the fireplace to form a cozy lounge area.

It was here that the family gathered after dinner. Even the cats, Cyril and Lyric, were there. Lyric was sitting primly on a pillow twitching the tip of her tail.

Cyril held his regal head high as he paced back and forth. Mia and Shane had flopped themselves on the couch, fidgeting nervously. Mother, usually so mysteriously elegant, was looking rather piqued as she sat down in one of the armchairs. Father stood in front of the small gathering, his hands clasped behind his back. He cleared his throat gravely and began to speak.

"There is a matter of some importance that we need to discuss as a family. It has to do with the children's new friend." He paused to look at them. Shane sat staring silently at the floor, a very serious expression on his face. Mia scowled at Lyric whose tail gave a particularly sharp flick. "No, Mia," said her father gently, "Lyric did not tell on you. It was Shane who came forward with the news. And I would like to thank him for his maturity and wisdom in doing so. It was not easy for him."

"I had to," said Shane quietly. "Otherwise Lyric would have told you, and I knew it would be better coming from me than from her."

"You were right, Shane. But Lyric said that you volunteered to do it before she even had a chance to suggest that you should. That is commendable.

"So now you have a friend – Damien is his name, right? We are not unhappy about that. Everyone should have friends, and we wish you could have more of them. We also understand that you did not defy our rules and bring another child into the yard without our permission. He just showed up at the front door... er, so to speak... that is, it was really the back yard, of course, but you see my point – and what else could you do? I suppose I would have done the same thing.

"However, the simple fact of your having a friend brings with it some difficulties that you may not be aware of. There are some things we haven't explained to you children, and I think it is now time we did so." He sighed heavily and paused as if unsure quite how to continue. "You see, your mother and I were not able to have children... you see... and we so much wanted to have you... so we, well, we... Maybe you can explain, dear?" he appealed to his wife.

Serena gave a tired smile. "Years ago, long before either of you were born, when I was working on Meta with your father and his brother – yes," she said when Shane's head jerked up in surprise, "that is one of the things you should know. Your father had an identical twin whose name was Garrit. The three of us were good friends. Garrit was a scientist like your father. He was also a geneticist. One day he discovered quite by accident that my genes were a little different from those of most people – that I had an ancestor who was related to the winged people on Meta. For that to be possible, the Medaryans had to have had contact with Earth at some time in the past. And I believe it was antediluvian..."

"What's *anti-luvian*?" interrupted Mia.

"Oh, I'm sorry – that is a big word that means 'before the Flood'. Remember what we covered in literature class today? Our civilization continued on, but there was no more contact with Meta. In fact, the Medaryan society was completely wiped out at some point after that – by what, we are not exactly sure – so all that is left now are the empty ruins.

"In the Tombs of the Kings on Meta we found the remains of large winged cats that used to live there. There are still winged cats alive there today which are related to the ancient cats, but the modern cats are just wild animals – intelligent animals, as all cats are, but not like the ancient ones. Those cats had special intelligence and wisdom, and played an important role in the society and lore. They seemed to have been personal advisors and friends to the kings. They were frequently embalmed along with their families in the royal tombs.

"That was thousands of years ago, but the royal family and their cats were skillfully embalmed and are amazingly well preserved – the embalming chemicals developed on Meta are superior to those on Earth. Uncle Garrit found that it was possible, even after all this time, to use their genetic material to make clones. And since it was possible, well, of course he did it. He cloned three of the royal cats. That's right, Shane," she continued, seeing him glance toward the two great cats. "Lyric and Cyril were two of them. But their sister and Garrit were taken away, and… well… the penalty for breaking the code of law, like the penalty for violating the human genome, is death. We never heard from him again.

"Your father brought Cyril and Lyric to me from Meta as kittens, hidden in his luggage. They have the intelligence and wisdom of the ancient cats, and their ability to speak.

"When I was on Meta studying the race of people who, I then realized, had been my ancestors, I first came up with the idea of bringing them back. We have the technology to do it. So, later, when your father and I discovered that we couldn't have children of our own, we hit on another plan. Father's position as a genetic researcher gave him access to the mummies that had been brought back from Meta. We used their DNA to conceive you children. So both of you have the genes of the Medaryan kings. You are a prince and princess, of an ancient civilization, come back to life today. Shane, that is where you get your wisdom and Mia, where you get your wings."

Mia liked the idea of being a princess. Her antennae (which she had named Moogkey) sensed her pleasure and gave an excited spark.

Shane understood himself better now. This is why he sometimes used words that sounded too noble for a boy his age. This is why he and Mia had always been so sheltered all their lives. But he also had one burning question, one which he was afraid to ask.

As if reading his thoughts, Father added, "You should have had wings too, Shane. You got the genes for them. For some reason, they never developed – there are always factors outside of our control. That is the kind of risk we took."

Father's face darkened. "It was highly illegal, too, of course, and after what happened to Garrit, we should have known better. But... well, your mother and I were both young and wanted to have children so badly, and it seemed like the right thing to do at the time. You children have always been a delight to us, and we have never regretted bringing you into the world.

"Unfortunately, if the authorities find out about you, the consequences will be the severest for our whole family. That is why we need to meet your friend, to find out what damage has been done... I mean, can he keep a secret? We are not angry with you kids, and it's a great thing to have a friend, but I think you can understand why we are very concerned. Do you have any questions?"

Shane remained silent for a few moments longer, deep in reflection, trying to sort through the implications of this news. Finally he spoke up. "We don't belong on Earth, then, do we?" It was as much a statement as a question.

"I don't know what to say about that," Father said frankly.

"But you do belong with us," Mother added, "and this is where we are for now."

The family shuttle project that Father and Joe had been working on for years now took on a greater significance to Shane. "Are Joe and Nanny the only other people who know about us?" he asked.

"Yes," said Father, "and now Damien, too."

"I don't think Damien would cause us any problems. He is reliable."

"Let's invite Damien over to lunch so your mother and I can meet him. Why don't you ask him tomorrow morning?"

"I will," said Shane.

"But for now," said Mother lightly, "its time for you kids to go to bed. I'm tired."

Everybody went to bed early that night out of sympathy for Mother's exhaustion. But it was just as well. They all had a lot to think about.

chapter nine

Shane was in bed and about to fall asleep when he heard a *plink* on his window. Then another one. He went to see what was making the sound. Damien was getting ready to throw another pebble when he realized – just in time – that he was about to throw it at Shane's face.

Shane let down a rope ladder for Damien to climb up and motioned him to be quiet. Silently they made their way to Shane's loft.

"What's wrong?" asked Shane. "You look like your step-mother made you swallow a ghost."

"It's my dad," answered Damien. "He went away on a trip without any warning and left me with my step-mom who hates me. She's a witch – well not really, but you'd almost think. I think she's the one who swallowed a ghost. Dad didn't even say goodbye, and my step-mom says he'll be gone for a year and a half and I can't even call him."

"Damien, I'm certain your father didn't just leave

without a good reason. Maybe something bad has happened to him and you're not being told. Maybe he was taken away and not allowed to say goodbye. I'm sure he would have if he could. We need to do some detective work and find out what really happened. What is his job?"

"He's a diplomat – a negotiator for the Government."

Shane thought for a minute. "My parents might be able to help. They're really good when it comes to this kind of thing. They have connections. Oh, by the way, they know about you – I had to tell them. They wanted me to invite you to lunch tomorrow so they can meet you. Do you think you can come?"

"I don't know. I don't know anything anymore. If my step-mom ever found me sneaking over here I think she would lock me in a dungeon hanging from my knuckles." Then with a wry smirk he added, "And feed me on moldy bread and tap water and maybe a few dead bugs from the swimming pool filter."

"Well, in that case we'd just have to sneak slug fruit into her jam," said Shane mischievously. "But seriously, come over when you can. We'll wait for you."

On an impulse, Shane decided to follow Damien home to see where his room was. This knowledge might come in handy, the way matters were shaping up.

chapter ten

Damien came over early the next day, a big grin on his face. "Step-mom went to the spa for the day. She locked me in my room while she's gone, but I climbed out the window. I've got the whole day free!"

The Rockwell house was in mayhem, buzzing with preparations for their guest. Mother was fussing over lunch in the cook's kitchen. Mia was trying to explain about her new antennae to Damien and also trying to tell him how she was a princess. Cyril wanted a formal introduction to Damien who was politely listening to Mia's unending barrage. Lyric was smugly pacing about, flipping her tail here and there with an important air. Father's friend Joe was also there for the day, and was busy repotting some net root plants that were creeping into the pool. (Net roots were like a ground crawling vine with roots as thick as human fingers that grew so rapidly you could watch their shoots zipping out in all directions and sprouting feathery green leaves as they went. They were interesting because the full grown plant would grow into a dense and spidery mesh which was a large replica of its particularly shaped seed. Each seed was unique. Once the net roots claimed their space they tenaciously fought to maintain it. Not having realized this, Joe had planted them too close to the pool and now was constantly trying to chase them back. He might have been able to burn them back, but he considered them too "alive" for such barbarity.) Nanny – who had been a personal assistant to the family all the children's life – was laughing at Joe's struggle as she bustled about dusting the outdoor table and chairs, even though they were already clean. In reality she was trying to size up the children's guest. She had a good eye for a child's temperament and found that she already liked Damien. The only person missing was Father. Nobody had seen him all day.

When Mother carried out the hamburgers, they all gathered around the table, even the cats, who had their own bench. Father was still missing.

"How do you do?" said Mother to Damien with a welcoming smile. "It's very nice to meet you."

Damien stretched out his arm toward Serena to shake hands. Unfortunately, at that exact moment Mia's napkin blew off her lap and she ducked under the table to retrieve it. Moogkey, who didn't like the idea of going under the table, hopped off Mia's head onto Damien's arm. Instinctively he jerked back and Moogkey, startled, jumped onto the edge of the salad bowl. Lettuce and tomatoes flew across the table as the salad bowl flipped

up and over, landed right on top of the poor creature and trapped him underneath.

"Oh dear," said Mother, as she and Nanny rushed to clean up the mess and free the surprised prisoner. A confused and shaken Moogkey hopped back to the safety of Mia's head and sat there shivering and sparking. The sucker anemone stuck to Mia with all his might for the rest of the meal.

"Where *is* your father?" asked Serena, sounding a tiny bit irritated. "Lyric, will you hunt him down and tell him our guest is here and lunch is waiting?"

Lyric stalked off after her prey, and returned a short time later followed by Father – who was followed by the large spider, who was followed by the vacuum robot. When Mia saw him she immediately started to giggle. His usually neat, wavy blond hair was sticking out in every direction. He was still wearing his lab coat, and had on a large, crooked pair of lensless black glasses for added effect.

"Got into a tussle with the spider. She's been jealous of my attention ever since you kids were down in the lab." Turning around he noticed for the first time that he had been followed. "I'm sorry, Matilda," he told the spider, "but you can't stay here. You have to go back to the lab." Matilda wilted. Just then Cyril pounced on the robot vacuum which was darting this way and that looking for things to suck up. In a flash, Matilda pounced on Cyril, sending sticky thread in all directions and getting everybody stuck in her tangle. Then she crept back downstairs looking self-satisfied, her spirits obviously restored.

Father stepped out of his shoes which were firmly glued to the ground and, carefully avoiding the sticky strands of web on the ground, ran back down to the lab in his socks. He returned a few moments later with the unstick acid and a few glow pops. Damien was all eyes. He had never seen a father like this before. By the time everybody had been unstuck and they were all seated at the table once again, the hamburgers were cold, but luckily they were still edible and had no spider silk on them. They had been covered to keep the flies off.

Father started to serve the glow pop, and Mia began giggling again. His hands were shaking in such an exaggerated manner that he almost spilled the glow pop several times. Even Mother and Shane, who were usually more serious, were amused by his act.

"Excuse me," said Father, trying to straighten his glasses but only managing to make them more crooked. "For those who haven't tried it – glow pop," he explained to no one in particular. "My latest invention. I do hope you like it." Then he focused his gaze on Damien for the first time, and his eyes widened. "Ah, you must be the Earthling."

Now just about everybody was having a hard time keeping a straight face – especially when Father's hamburger stuck to a bit of spider silk on the sleeve of his lab coat which had been missed in the cleanup. "I'll bet you are all wondering why I called this meeting," he said with a broad gesture. The extraordinary sight of two huge, noble cats on the verge of losing their composure made him notice the stray burger on his cuff. He began to nibble at the dangling burger as he continued: "Now, you see, we have a little problem here. And the problem, you see, is the fact that *most* people don't have talking cats, or winged princesses, or affectionate (and jealous) spiders, or glow pop. And, further, the fact that most people don't know that we *do* have these things. Now that you, Damien, know it, we are beholden to you to help us in keeping other people from finding out."

"I'm pretty good at keeping a secret," Damien assured him, trying unsuccessfully to look solemn while his shoulders shook in laughter.

"I can affirm that," said Shane, unconsciously using one of his noble-sounding words. "He is trustworthy." Then he added quickly, "Damien has a problem, too, Father, and we were hoping you might be able to help. His father recently vanished without a trace, and Damien has been left with his step-mother."

"Who is very mean," interjected Damien.

"She told him that his father has gone away on a long trip and will be out of contact for a year and a half, but we think she must be hiding something. I mean, a father wouldn't just leave on such a long journey without saying goodbye, would he?"

"My step-mom is sending me to junior military academy for the next two years," added Damien, "probably just to get me out of her hair and keep me from asking questions until Dad gets back."

"I thought that if anyone could find out what happened to his father, it would be you," said Shane.

Father had suddenly become serious, taking off his glasses and actually looking fatherly for the first time. He listened intently as the mystery was unfolded before him. "Why do you think I might be able to find out what others can't? Does your dad work for the Government?" he inquired perceptively.

"Yes," said Damien, "he is an official negotiator for the State Department. He often has to travel, but he has never just up and left like this before."

"What is his name?"

"Terence Knight."

Shane's father nodded. "I can use my network of contacts to ask around. They know most of what the Government is doing – usually. However, if his sudden disappearance is legitimate, it may mean that he has been sent on a top-secret mission, and I may be unable to learn very much. Still, let me see what I can find out."

Damien thanked him, feeling more hopeful now.

Just then Nanny came out carrying a brightly colored

tray of desserts. "Slug fruit jell-o," she announced. The yellow, orange and red jell-o squares jiggled as they were set before the diners. Some pieces were even trying to jump out of the bowls. Everybody began spearing them and swallowing them in gulps – everyone except Damien, that is.

"It's not alive," Mia assured him, trying to nail a cube that had wriggled off her fork and was now hopping around the table. "It's just fruit. It starts twitching after you pick it, and keeps it up for the rest of the day. You have to be quick or it'll get away." She wasn't able to catch her little square before it dived off the edge of the table and fell to the ground with a splat. Cyril immediately jumped down and licked it up.

"Wonderful stuff," said Father. "Wiggles all the way down." This assertion did not seem to encourage Damien. "May I?" asked Cyril politely, licking his chops. Damien pushed his squirming bowl over to Cyril with a look of relief, and the cat made short work of it.

The glow pop was a different matter. Damien drank his right down and instantly began glowing a fluorescent green.

"I'm afraid this is not the best way to send you home," said Mother, looking at her own purple hands. "It will take a couple of hours to wear off. You kids can play inside until Damien is ready to go."

Inside the house, Shane, Mia and Damien had a three-way war. They stockpiled rubber bands and tinker-toy bows and arrows. They made popsicle-stick bombs and hid behind couches and sneaked up behind doors to bombard each other. At first Mia had a treaty with Shane, but then she switched to an alliance with Damien. Damien was remarkably good at strategy and with Mia's gall they finally got the better of Shane. (It was Mia's wet paper-towel wads that partly won the day.)

After that they played newspaper swords, blindfolded. It was a game Mia and Shane had made up. They rolled newspapers into swords and then the opponents were blindfolded and set at opposite corners of the room. The winner was the one who could hit the other first. There were different tactics to this game. One was to charge your opponent while wildly swinging your sword, hitting him before he could do anything. This was Mia's usual approach. Another tactic was to quietly creep around the room till you were behind your opponent, then strike. This was Shane's preferred method. Damien's tactic was the most effective, however. He lay flat on the floor while his unwitting opponent was slashing the air above, and struck at their feet.

Thus the day passed pleasantly until Damien remembered he had to get home.

chapter eleven

The next day Damien didn't come to play. Nor the next day. Nor the next. Shane grew worried and discussed the situation with Cyril.

"I think we should go looking for him tonight," advised Cyril.

"You will go with me then?" asked Shane. "Good. Your sense of smell and hearing are so much keener then mine, and so is your night vision."

"That is true," said Cyril without pride. "We are made for hunting. I will come along to protect you." In the shadows of Shane's room they made a pact to go that night in search of Damien.

After night fell, they made their way in the cloud-covered darkness to the wall that separated the two properties. Shane crawled through the hole that Damien had tunneled under the wall, but Cyril was too big to fit. Finding a spot hidden by some tall trees, he launched himself over the wall in a single flying leap and landed quietly on the other side. He and Shane now found themselves in a vast yard beyond which loomed a huge mansion. It was in the style of a French castle with an assortment of turrets and spires. Occasionally a form would pass by one of the lighted windows on the ground floor – Damien's step-mother or the maid going about her business. Keeping to the shadows and avoiding the bright windows, Cyril traced Damien's three-day-old scent from behind the play fort to the back door.

"His room is around the corner from here, in the south-east wing," directed Shane. Stealthily the two trespassers crept around to the side of the house where Damien's room was. They peered into his windows but all was dark and, Cyril could see, no one was in the bed.

Cyril sniffed the air, then turned his large head left and right as if he was expecting to see something in the yard. Then he cocked his head to the side, listening to the still air. "Up there," he purred, pointing with his nose, "I hear a cub crying."

Shane craned his neck to look up into the tallest turret. There he saw a tiny window with a dim light flickering.

"We're going up there," said Cyril. "You can ride on me." The boy climbed onto the cat and they silently flew up to the crenellations which formed a narrow ledge around the turret under the arched window. Shane crawled onto the ledge and peeked in the window at the same time Damien peeked out. They gave each other a fright and Shane nearly fell from his perch.

"Don't startle me that way!" whispered Damien

fiercely.

"Don't pop out at me that way!" retorted Shane forgetting to keep his voice low.

"Shhhh! My step-mom might hear," Damien warned, then continued hoarsely, "Look, what do you expect? There was a noise at my window, so I came to see what it was! How was I supposed to know it would be you all the way up here? I thought it was a pigeon or something. Oh – sorry, Cyril," he broke off when the cat made a low noise that might have been either a chuckle or a growl. "I don't mean I *really* thought you were a pigeon. I mean, the rustling did sound awfully big for a little bird."

By now Damien had got his wits about him again and he asked, "Did you come to get me out of here? Oh, thanks! I've been locked up here for three whole days!" In his haste to escape he plunged headfirst through the open window without taking into account how small it was, and got caught halfway out. He looked down at the drop below. "Uh-oh… Um, I'm stuck," he gasped. Shane started to pull at him. "Ever since I came home green—" he started to explain between the pulls and yanks, "well, actually, I wasn't green when first I got home…" Suddenly he came out with a pop, and the two boys scrambled to keep their balance.

"Quiet!" hissed Cyril. "You can explain once we're on the ground. But first we have to get back down without being seen – or heard. Get on, both of you, and hang on tight. We're going up first, so no one will see us from the windows below."

The boys clung to Cyril as the powerful cat surged up

into the low-lying clouds. The freezing air hit them like sheets of ice. Then unexpectedly they broke through the cloud cover into the clear air above, where the stars shimmered with a clarity that made you want to touch them – minuscule points of light in the velvet night. Immediately Cyril plunged into a dive. It was the most frightening feeling Shane had ever felt. Damien loved it. With a smooth but sudden motion Cyril pulled out of the dive and landed with four paws on the damp dirt of the Rockwell yard.

"So what did that wicked and cruel step-mother of yours do?" gasped Shane once he had caught his breath.

"As I was saying before," Damien answered excitedly, his mouth racing to keep up with his thoughts, "I wasn't actually green any more when I got home but my step-mom startled me and made my heart jump, and when it did the glow-pop green came back. Then Step-mom became furious and said I was up to something evil to look that way – all green and such – so she locked me up in the tower and has only fed me on bread and tap water for the last three days. She said I was going to stay there until it was time to leave for the academy with all the other nasty little kids (as she calls them)… and that there they were going to do much worse to me – they'd probably beat me if I tried to escape, and put me in solitary confinement (whatever that is) for the rest of my life, and starve and torture me. So boy, am I glad to see you!"

"Solitary confinement is what *she* gave you!" Cyril growled. "And starvation and torture, if you ask me –

locking you up in a cage like that." The unmistakable menace in his voice gave a hint of how truly angry he was. "You boys go inside now. I need time to think, alone. We have solved one problem – we couldn't leave Damien with that despicable woman – but in doing so we have created another. Of course, to look on the bright side," he mused ironically, more to himself than to them, "I've never known of a cat, or a child, being convicted of kidnapping. Still, there's a first time for everything. You two go to bed while I consider this. Shane, you can hide Damien in your loft for tonight. Off with you."

Long after the boys had fallen asleep, Cyril paced up and down the hall outside Jerrod's office door. So he heard the phone ring at midnight; he heard Jerrod answer it; he heard Jerrod confirm that they had been detected – a satellite photo, a brief anomaly above the clouds, a calculated projection pinpointing the Rockwell property below.

Jerrod went first to wake up Serena. "Joe just got an urgent phone call from a friend of his in the Administration. Somehow something suspicious was detected at our place, and they are going to launch an investigation first thing in the morning. The time has come to put our contingency plan into action. We have to have the children and the cats and all evidence of them out of here by seven o'clock – in seven hours. Good thing this didn't happen a couple of months ago before the shuttle was finished. Joe says it has passed all his diagnostic tests and is ready. We'll have to send the children to Meta on it. Cyril and Lyric will take care of them until we have a chance to join them."

"We can't send them to Meta by themselves," whispered Serena, turning white.

"They won't be by themselves. The cats will be with them. But we need to stay behind and face the investigation. After that we can go to Meta legally. It will be much more difficult for everyone if we don't. The cats will look after the children," he reassured her.

They went to wake up Shane and Mia. There were trunks in the children's closets already packed for this eventuality. Nanny brought in suitcases for their regular clothes, and they began filling them in utmost haste. Serena did most of the packing for Mia who could hardly keep her eyes open, but Shane assured his father he could do the job while Jerrod took care of the other preparations necessary for their hasty departure.

"After we leave the house," Jerrod instructed Nanny, "pack up everything that is left of the children's and the cats' things. Also, do a thorough vacuuming of the house so there are no cat hairs to be found. We can't leave any evidence behind. We will return in a few hours with Joe, and he will cart everything off. Even the footprints in the yard will have to be erased. Serena and I should be able to do that after Joe leaves." Nanny hurried off to start cleaning, and Jerrod went to start packing their vehicle.

Shane closed the door of his room and called Damien down from the loft. "Damien, you've got to hide in my footlocker. I made room for you to fit. You only have to be in it for a couple of hours. As soon as we are fully on our way you can come out. It will be safe then."

"How am I going to breathe in there?" Damien asked, somewhat dubious.

"I already thought of that," said Shane. "I poked a few holes in the end where your head will be so you can breathe – you know, the way you do when you want to keep bugs in a jar."

Damien grimaced at the comparison, but he was game for the adventure. Thankfully he didn't get claustrophobia. He curled up and tucked inside the footlocker and Shane got it buckled up just seconds before Father came in with the hand truck to retrieve his things. He helped Shane throw the last of his clothes into the open suitcases and began to load up the luggage. Shane winced as the trunk was jostled and bumped onto the dolly.

"Wow," said his father with a grunt, "maybe we packed this a little *too* well."

Shane followed Father down to the garage. Mia's luggage was already there waiting to be loaded into the SUV. Shane helped his father pack the luggage into the back. He tried to protect his footlocker from being banged around too much, but made an effort not to sound too anxious about it.

"Oh, wait – my stone!" cried Mia suddenly, remembering her promise to her mother. "And our map of Meta. We must get the treasure chest."

"I'll dig it up," Cyril said and bounded off into the night. Less than ten minutes later he returned dragging the kids' treasure chest by its leather strap. Just then Mother rushed into the garage with an armload of books and manuscripts. "Study the languages," she urged. "Look, this is a copy of the writing I found under the throne where Mia's knife was. See if you can understand it." They threw the papers inside the chest and Jerrod heaved it into the back of the vehicle without even taking the time to brush it off. He slammed shut the back door then jumped into the driver's seat. Nanny ran out to bid them a tearful goodbye, and they were off.

The clock on the dash board read 1:13 AM as they pulled out of the garage – a little over an hour after they had received Joe's phone call. Jerrod kept the headlights off until they were a few blocks away from their house – "just in case anyone is watching from the air," he said. "The cloud cover should help protect us from detection." Joe's laboratory and the launch pad for the shuttle were located out in the desert. At this time of night it would take only about an hour and a half to get there.

Joe met the Rockwells as they approached the gate to the laboratory compound. "I'm glad you made it!" he told them. "I think everything is set. Go ahead and pull the SUV down to the underground loading dock and we'll load the passengers and luggage from there."

While Shane and his father stowed the luggage, Lyric and Cyril looked over the ship and its stocks. Fuel and supplies were already packed and were being rechecked. "Yep, she'll get them there, no problem, and with plenty to spare," bragged Joe. He was evidently very proud of the ship which he and Jerrod had designed.

The luggage was loaded under the seats – none too

gently, Shane noted again with a wince – and strapped firmly into place. Once that was done, Mia, Shane, Lyric and Cyril were ushered to their seats and strapped in.

Mother had tears in their eyes. Father had never looked so dire. It was as if the tapestry of the children's world was unraveling before their eyes – and it was being put in their own hands now, to sew it back together, in a different way, thread by thread.

"Don't forget to study the languages," Mother urged again.

"Remember everything I have taught you," said Father as the hatch was shutting.

The flight path was already programmed into the computer. Once free of Earth's gravity, the shuttle would settle into the path of the planet's orbit around the sun and head at full-speed in the opposite direction. In a little over two months it would meet up with Meta coming around from the other side and establish an orbit around that planet. On the third turn around Meta the ship would descend into its atmosphere and make its landing on a level spot not far from the research colony.

A rumbling below the passengers' feet grew louder and louder until the vibrations filled the whole cabin and coursed through their bodies. They felt a jolt as if the earth was being torn from underneath them and they were pressed down hard in their seats as the ship left its moorings. Though they could not see it from inside the shuttle, at that moment the ceiling of the underground launch pad opened up, its nautilus-shaped panels sliding aside like the aperture of a giant camera, and the ship rose up and out into the night air. For what seemed like an eternity, though in reality it was hardly more than fifteen minutes, the vibrations continued and the irresistible force pinned them to their seats. Then, imperceptibly at first, as the ship began to pull free of the earth's gravitation and move into orbit, the heavy weight of acceleration eased and was replaced by an entirely new and alien sense of weightlessness. As if in the realm of the surreal, the radar display showed the orb that was Earth – shrinking.

"I brought something along," Shane announced once they had settled into the flight path. He released the restraints that held him in his chair and lowered himself down to where his footlocker was secured below their feet. He unstrapped it and tried to pull it out, but only succeeded in pulling himself in and bumping his head. He braced his feet against the wall and pulled harder. This time the trunk did come free, and – as the others watched, wide-eyed – he and it sailed in slow motion across the cabin until they reached the far wall. "Oof!" exclaimed Shane as he was pinned against the wall by the trunk. "This is going to take some getting used to!"

He maneuvered around to the front of the footlocker, undid the latches, and opened the lid. Out floated a few items of rumpled clothing followed by the head of a boy.

PART 2

The Flight

chapter twelve

"It's alive!" yowled Lyric.

A body followed the head. Damien saw four faces staring at him as he crawled from the stuffy footlocker.

"Hi," said Mia, her antennae twittering with pleasure.

Lyric glared at Cyril. "You don't look one bit surprised!" And indeed, Cyril looked cool as a cucumber.

"Cool bus!" said Damien. "But it sure feels weird in here." He looked around. The cabin was oblong in shape, with curved couches against the long walls. Mia and the two cats were still strapped into their seats on the couches. At the center of the space, in front of the two couches, there was an adjustable table which could be extended to different heights according to the need: a table for eating or a desk for studying, a coffee table, or just something on which to prop up their feet. It could also sink down into the floor to be entirely out of the way, which is how it had been stowed for takeoff. At either end of the capsule the two couches were separated by a narrow hall. At the back end was a hatch that led down to the toilet and ozone shower and the storage area. At the front end, above their heads, another hatch led up to the control room. The walls encircling the main cabin curved into a domed ceiling above them. Latched cabinets were fixed above the couches and covered with an upholstered finish made of spider silk. The tiny, windowless room had a cozy feel.

"Cool bus," Damien repeated. "So, where are we

going?"

"Um… you mean you don't know?" asked Shane. It dawned on him that in all the excitement he had forgotten to mention this detail to Damien.

"A lot was going on," explained Damien. "I guess I must have missed it."

The others looked at each other apprehensively, not knowing exactly how to break the news.

"We're going to Meta," offered Mia quietly.

"Oh, cool! Yahoo! I'm going to Meta!" was the unexpected response. "I've always wanted to travel to another planet! Wait till my father finds out!" He suddenly got quiet. "Oh, yeah, he's gone. I forgot. How am I going to find him now? He doesn't even believe in Meta."

"Don't worry, Damien. Our dad won't stop looking for him," encouraged Shane.

"Yes, if anyone can find him, Dr. Rockwell can," Cyril agreed, "– and he will, too, just you watch. We'll find a way to let him know you are safe with us."

"Yeah, I guess you're right. Thanks for rescuing me, guys. How long does it take to get there?"

"Two months," answered Shane.

The reality of their situation was finally beginning to sink in. "I want Mommy and Daddy," sobbed Mia.

"Yeah," said Shane, fighting back tears himself, trying to be brave. "Now we're all kind of in the same boat, without our parents."

"I believe you all will see your parents again," comforted Lyric.

"Ouch!" exclaimed Damien as his head hit the ceiling. He had been slowly drifting upwards since he had crawled out of the trunk. Mia probably would have laughed, but she was too upset at the moment.

"Weightlessness," declared Shane. "It's hard to control where you are going." He pushed himself away from the wall and somersaulted off to the other side — spinning into Mia who was still strapped in her seat.

"Stay out of my space!" she snapped, pushing him aside. Shane smashed into the wall and then bounced back into Mia. When he finally got himself under control she was glaring at him. "This space around me," she said, drawing an invisible line with her finger, "is my space. Stay out of it."

Damien lazily drifted down and deliberately stuck his finger on Mia's line. It was a good thing Lyric reacted when she did. She pounced in between the children and dug her claws into the couch so that she wouldn't bounce away. Glaring at Mia, Damien and Shane, she ordered them into their seats with their seat belts on. "And you will stay there until you can prove that you can get along!" she hissed, glaring at the kids until they had backed into their seats.

"Let's eat," said Cyril to get the children's minds off their squabble. "There's nothing like food when you're hungry, I always say." So everybody turned their attention to eating. Cyril pushed a button next to his seat with his nose and with a quiet hum the table steadily rose to its full height. Then he gravely passed out packets of pills, some hard-tack flat bread and a small bottle of Tang each.

"This is breakfast?" asked Mia in disbelief.

chapter thirteen

The children learned to endure dehydration, as water had to be conserved. They learned to ignore the feeling of being a little hungry. After a while their stomachs even seemed to forget that it wasn't normal not to be always full.

The passengers settled into a daily routine regulated by the clock. They woke up in the morning according to the time of their distant home. The first order of business was to refresh and change in the ozone shower. After a brief breakfast they would settle down to their studies. These were conducted by Cyril and Lyric, with the help of educational software in the on-board computers.

They concentrated especially on studying the Metan languages – not because they actually expected to find anyone still alive who spoke them, but because all their lives Mother had insisted they should learn them. Lyric took up the task of drilling Mia and Damien in the basics of Medaryan. Mia already knew a little bit of the language, and tried to help Damien with her superior knowledge. The results were not always successful. Cyril and Shane, who already spoke Medaryan quite well and could carry on entire conversations in it, studied the more advanced manuscripts.

Some of these writings contained short passages in another language called the "forest language". It used the same alphabet as the second inscription on the Sumerian Rune Rock, but with one difference – the meaning in the manuscripts could be worked out. This language puzzled and fascinated Shane. Its complex grammar bore absolutely no resemblance to Medaryan, and the only clues to its pronunciation were cryptic references to "singing" or "whistling" or "clicking" or "rustling". It took work, but he was beginning to be able to read bits of it.

Lyric and Cyril pressed the children to study until lunchtime. After lunch they would exercise to keep their joints limber and muscles active, doing stretching routines and zero-gravity calisthenics. This was followed by music lessons. Wooden flutes and recorders of various sizes had been packed on the shuttle for the family's use. Shane and Mia always looked forward to this time – there was something very satisfying about making music and harmonizing together. Damien, however, had never learned to play an instrument before and found it frustrating because he could never get it to sound right. After music lessons they would play games – computer games, card games, board games, chess tournaments, and other kinds of competitions. It was quickly discovered that Damien excelled at games of strategy. Neither Shane nor Cyril could beat him at chess. Even Mia could not outwit him, though she could be a very crafty opponent – Damien always caught on to her tricks.

After supper the time was usually less structured, and they would close their day with various activities: individual reading, reading aloud, discussions about some interesting topic or other, storytelling, or more games. Shane used this time to keep up on his journal.

One evening after a dinner of capsules, rye-tack and beef jerky, Cyril had Shane pull out the copy of the map of Medarya that he and Mia had been keeping in their treasure chest – the chest which Cyril had, at the last minute, rescued. Shane carefully placed the map on the coffee table in front of them and secured it with magnets so it wouldn't float away. For a long time they stared at the map of Meta, as if the knowledge of its reality and their arrival there was something told to them in a dream. All their lives this place had formed the backdrop of their consciousness. They had learned about it and pretended about it so many times, but it had always been like a faraway fantasy. How could they now be speeding towards its reality?

"It is important that we all become familiar with the layout of the land," Cyril began in an expository manner. He pointed with a claw as he indicated the places marked on the map. "The research colony is here. It is situated on more or less open ground at the edge of the Great Plain, which extends far eastward. As you can see, the ancient Cliff City lies a little to the north, within full view of the colony. In front of the Cliff City, facing the plain, is a series of large terraces or small plateaus, probably used for farming at one time. These would have provided an excellent place to land, except for the fact that we would be seen by all eyes in the colony.

"Now, this gap in the mountains to the west of the colony, where the river flows out – this is where the Enchanted Forest begins. The large valley beyond the opening is covered by the forest which, as of the most recent communications from the colony, remains unexplored. It has proven to be a most treacherous place. Besides the dangers, it is also thickly overgrown and provides no good landing spots that we know of.

"There exists, however, a decent-sized clearing at the edge of the forest near the cliffs, behind this ridge. It is neither in direct view of the colony nor actually in the forest. This is where we have chosen to land. We wanted to be as close to the Cliff City as we could without risking immediate discovery. We are scheduled to arrive shortly after nightfall, but before moonrise, to provide the cover of darkness and allow as much time as possible to find shelter before morning. After sunrise it is certain that the colony will come looking for the cause of the previous night's disturbance."

"Won't they come looking for us immediately?" asked Damien.

"Oh, no, I think not. There is a strict policy in place at the colony that no one is to go out beyond the gates at night, and no one is to venture into the forest even in the daytime. Over the years they have lost a number of individuals and several exploration parties – even those accompanied by an armed guard – and they can't afford to lose any more. It is difficult enough to transport people back and forth, but it becomes even harder to recruit new researchers when the stories of such disappearances get back to Earth. No, we should be safe enough from prying eyes until morning."

"Do we know what we are going to do when we arrive?" asked Lyric.

"Only in general terms. We still need to come up with an exact plan."

"Well, we should have enough time for that," observed Shane.

"The first thing we need to do is find a hiding place for the shuttle. There is supposed to be a large enough cave in the cliff right here, close to where we land, that is meant to suit this need After we secure shelter – well, I don't know exactly what to do next," Cyril admitted.

"Once we've hidden the shuttle and found shelter, I would like to see the throne room of the ancient Cliff City," stated Shane.

And so the evening discussion continued until bedtime as they made plans for their landing.

chapter fourteen

Back at the estate the investigation began at daybreak. The CIA had satellite photos of something that looked like a large flying cat, but the image wasn't clear enough to be decisive. They had contacted the Center for Metan Research and requested an exhaustive and detailed inventory of all material brought back from the planet. Everything must be accounted for. The investigation was to involve all the scientists, but especially the Rockwells who were closest to the sighting.

The director at the CMR was not having a good morning. He found himself at the downtown law offices of Pfneudl, Wiefels, Bickerstaffe & Snook, in a lively consultation with his attorney.

"Where do those goons come up with their cockamamie ideas, anyway? They sit in their ritzy offices, with their black wingtip shoes propped up on their oversized desks, making UFOs out of every little birdie that flies in front of their satellite cameras! Then who do they blame? The scientists!"

As far as the director was concerned, the Government was on a witch hunt for flying saucers. He was adamant that none of the great cats had been brought back, and considered the whole notion preposterous.

"Just how do they think we would have transported one of those savage beasts? Kept him in a big metal cage in the luggage compartment, and fed him another astronaut every few days so he wouldn't starve?"

It took some humoring and coaxing by his attorney, but eventually he calmed down enough to agree that the most prudent action would be to give the CIA a careful and complete inventory, in order to prove the good will and innocence of the Center. So with the grim authorities watching their every move, they began a meticulous tallying and accounting of everything in Jerrod's laboratory, with careful explanations of every experiment and its results. On the basis of sufficient cause, the Court granted a search warrant for the Rockwell house and grounds, and by that afternoon there were official-looking men swarming over the property, poking into every corner and broom closet in a forensic search for what wasn't even supposed to exist.

The investigators were not allowed to take any evidence off-site because, as the CMR authorities did not neglect to emphasize, the risk of contamination was too great should the environment of Earth be exposed to the extraterrestrial life forms in Jerrod's laboratory and the estate grounds. So the CIA set up a portable forensic center in the Rockwells' living room and conducted their investigation from there. Every time they entered the residence, the detectives and forensic technicians were required to scrub down with anti-bacterial soap and change into freshly laundered clothing. They were issued latex gloves and carbon filter masks which were to be worn at all times. At the end of the day the decontamination process was repeated, and the gloves and masks were deposited in a bin labeled "☠ **HIGHLY TOXIC** ☠" and subsequently destroyed.

Thanks to Nanny's meticulous housekeeping, no evidence of any winged cats – or large animals of any kind, for that matter – was found in the house. A thorough search of the estate grounds was delayed for almost a week as the earlier cloud cover had developed into a drizzle by mid-morning, followed by steady rain and then a downpour which lasted on and off for days. By the time the inspectors were able to scrutinize the grounds, any evidence that Lyric and Cyril might have left behind had long since been washed away. The results from the Center's examination of the laboratory were equally disappointing – they found no winged cats. All they found was that Jerrod had been performing top-quality research, the results of which had contributed greatly to their understanding of the extraordinary alien world of Meta.

In spite of their failure to find a smoking gun, the Government continued to insist that the evidence must be there somewhere, and given just a little more time they would find it. The attorneys devised strategies and conducted negotiations, they filed motions and declarations, petitions and objections with the Court, they held conference calls and hearings with the judge, they did all the things that lawyers do. Days stretched into weeks, and weeks stretched into months.

Meanwhile Jerrod and Serena endured as patiently as they could. Once the Government took over it was out of their – and anyone else's – control, and matters simply had to run their course. They were not allowed access to their house while the investigation was going on. The Director of the Center apologized profusely for the inconvenience, but they knew as well as he did that he was powerless to do anything about it. They took some comfort in the assurances of Jerrod's colleagues that the animals in the laboratory were being well taken care of. Jerrod and Serena were provided with temporary accommodations which were comfortable enough, but neither of them seemed to be getting much sleep. Their faces took on a haggard look, and there were dark circles under their eyes.

"I miss my lab" was Jerrod's regular complaint, to which Serena would always reply, "I miss my manuscripts." Neither of them dared voice what they were really thinking: "I miss our children."

It seemed like an eternity, though in reality it was only about two months, before the good news finally arrived. The Government had exhausted every legal excuse to keep the investigation open and had still come up with nothing, so the judge threw out the case for lack of evidence. Jerrod, Serena, and the CMR were cleared of all suspicion and the Rockwell estate was vacated by the authorities – somewhat worse for the wear, but not irreparably damaged.

"We are so relieved it's all over and we can go home," Jerrod confided to the Director of the Center.

"Yes, now we can all return to our work," he agreed. But secretly he was not so sure it really *was* over. The Government, he suspected, had already concluded the Rockwells' guilt, and although thwarted for now, it was not likely to roll over in defeat – not yet.

A plan began to form in his mind. Unless or until the Government brought more charges, the Rockwells were free citizens – free to come and go as they saw fit, even free to leave the country if they wished. And the Center was also free – free to conduct their business as they saw fit, even free to send Jerrod and Serena to Meta if they wished. There was plenty of research work they could do on Meta, and on Meta they were more likely to be out of harm's way, if it came to that. The Board of Directors of the Center agreed to his plan, and thus it was that Jerrod and Serena and their household – which was Nanny – were scheduled to depart on the next official shuttle to Meta, due to launch in less than a month.

Jerrod and Serena began their preparations for a lengthy departure, Jerrod making sure all the precious plants and animals in his lab would be well taken care of, Serena gathering the books and papers she would need to study the Medaryan writings on-site. Once they left, it would take another two months before they actually arrived. They hoped they would find the children and cats okay. Jerrod spent an inordinate amount of time grilling Joe on the safety of the craft on which he had trustingly loaded his children, and Joe continually assured him that the ship was sound and the children were fine and that he also would be joining them at Meta as soon as accommodations could be made.

Remembering his promise, Jerrod also tried to make inquiries into the whereabouts of Damien's father, but could get no further information than the official statement that his whereabouts were unknown. Reading between the lines, Jerrod felt sure this meant that his whereabouts really were known, but only to certain people, and the Government intended it to remain that way. He was not sure whether this was reassuring or not.

Jerrod had not seen anything of Damien since the children's departure. This puzzled and worried him at first. He even made a couple of visits to the chateau next door, but to no avail – nobody ever answered the bell. Eventually he contented himself with the conclusion that Damien must have been sent away to the academy during the time that the investigation was in progress and they were not at their house.

chapter fifteen

One morning about three weeks into the journey, Mia was reciting her Medaryan verb conjugations while doing slow somersaults in the air. Suddenly she stopped and asked, "What's a *paw fussy*?"

"I've never heard of a paw fussy," said Shane, deep in concentration about something else.

"But Mommy said! She said there was supposed to be a paw fussy with my stone knife," insisted Mia.

"With your stone knife?" Now Shane was looking up.

"I want to find the paw fussy for Mommy and put it with my stone."

"Your stone was found under the throne in the Cliff City. We could look there, but I don't know what we would be searching for," said Shane. "I've no idea what a paw fussy is."

"I think it had something to do with words written underneath the throne."

"You mean the throne runes will tell us where to find

the paw fussy? Actually, we have the writings that were at the throne. It's among the manuscripts Mother gave us just before we left."

Shane floated over to one of the cabinets and rummaged through the papers and folders it contained. There was an envelope marked THRONE. He pulled out its contents and laid them on the table, securing them with magnets so they wouldn't float away. He looked at a drawing of Mia's stone which showed all of its intricate symbols and carvings along with a written description of the throne and the compartment underneath. The only thing found in the compartment was the stone and an inscription carved on the compartment itself.

By now Damien was looking over Shane's shoulder, starting to get interested.

Shane took a closer look at the hand-drawn copy of the writing inscribed on Mia's stone. "The words etched on your stone were translated by Mother. And here beside the translation, she has scrawled in quick writing, 'Could this be connected with the prophecy?'" The truth suddenly dawned on him. "Mia, the word is not *paw fussy*, its *pro-phe-cy*. A prophecy is something that predicts what is going to happen in the future. It's written before it happens. Go get your stone. Let's take a look at it."

Mia rummaged through her stuff and brought out the prized stone.

"See this?" he said, drawing attention first to the carvings on the handle of the stone and then to writing on the paper. "Here is the Medaryan script on your stone. And below it is the translation:

> Queen Ryall, bequeath this stone
> to Princess Ryall 'til she's grown –
> from royal daughter to her own.
> The princess who shall hold this stone
> is heiress of her gate and throne.

"That's very interesting," mused Shane. "Remember how Mother said that she is genetically related to the people who were entombed at the Cliff City? She, a distant daughter of Ryall, has passed the stone on to you, and in that way Mother has obeyed the directive on the stone to 'bequeath' it. She must really take this seriously."

"Yeah," said Damien, "but that's not a prophecy. It's just an instruction that your mom followed."

"It *could* be a prophecy," Mia insisted hopefully.

"No, Damien's right," Shane said, sounding a little disappointed. "The inscription only tells what the stone's purpose is and what should be done with it."

The next sheet of paper had a sketch of the plinth under the throne and the well-concealed compartment where the stone knife was found. "This diagram shows that there was also some writing on the inside of the compartment," Shane pointed out as they studied it. "Maybe this is your prophecy, Mia. Mother took a rubbing of it. Here is her translation:

> Revenge of mage, by his hand sown:
> the plague will rage, the death drums drone.
> Cease the age, and end the throne,

as lore by sage and seer has shown.
Our people cease – that much is known.

Arise, young son of King Shane-Torh,
from ashes and from tombs of yore,
reborn the flesh and blood and bone.
The blight that brought the end – Atone.
Your hand again your realm restore.

Read this prophecy; learn this lore:
To find the maps and keys of yore
the king has stored below the throne:
The hand that owns the princess' stone,
strike the blade, cross center score.

"Whoa!" said Damien. "That's deep."

"But what does it mean?" wondered Mia.

Meanwhile Shane was examining another piece of paper. "Wait! There's more to it. Or, at least, there is something else written below, but it doesn't actually seem to be a part of the prophecy. It isn't in verse. Mother translated it, too. It says:

I, the last king, have passed on this
prophecy, but know not its meaning.
If you, my child, find my writing and hold
the key, then understand.
May the prophecy guide you to bring back
our kingdom.

"Do you think it could be talking to us?" asked Mia in a hushed tone. "That's kind of creepy," she added with an excited shiver.

"Hmm," said Cyril, "I believe it may very well be speaking to you. You and Shane could be described as 'reborn'. I don't think they would have had the concept of cloning."

Shane began thinking out loud. "The last king wrote: *If you, my child, find my writing and hold the key, then understand.* I think we should try to understand the prophecy. After all, in one sense at least I am the heir of the last king, and I have his writing. I don't know if I have the key to the prophecy. Still, if I am the *young son of King Shane-Torh* reborn, then the prophecy is talking to me, and I have to do what it says."

"*The hand that owns the princess' stone* – that's me!" chimed in Mia. "Mommy gave me Ryall's stone!"

"That's right. So you are supposed to *strike the blade, cross center score* (whatever that means)."

"I don't know about all this," interjected Damien skeptically. "I mean, a prophecy is supposed to predict something that is going to happen, right? But if you do what it says because you know you're supposed to, then it's not foretelling the future any more, it's just telling you what to do. My dad calls that kind of thing a 'self-fulfilling prophecy', says it isn't really a prophecy at all."

"The king thought it was real!" retorted Mia, her eyes as big a saucers.

"Yes, but that doesn't mean it really *is* real!" argued Damien. "It just means *he* believed it."

"Then how did the prophecy know we would be reborn?"

"It *didn't*. That's just the point! Your parents read the prophecy and that's what gave them the idea to clone all of you guys. And now *you* are going to try to do what it says, too, and when it happens you'll say, 'See? The prophecy foretold it.' When really it just happened because you made it so – that's all."

"But, Damien," Shane addressed him in a reasonable tone, "how can we make something happen when we don't even understand what it says? For example, we don't know how or why Mia is to *cross center score*. But if we find out what it means, and it leads us to *find the maps and keys of yore the king has stored below the throne*, then we didn't make it happen, did we? It was the prophecy."

Damien glared at them defiantly. He was outnumbered but not defeated. "I still say it's an instruction, not a prediction," he insisted resolutely.

Lyric, who had been watching the whole exchange, was just about to intervene when Cyril spoke up. "You may have a point there, Damien," he said with a conciliatory purr. "We mustn't simply assume that it is true without proof. Still, will it hurt anything if we try to see whether these instructions lead anywhere or not?"

"No, I guess not," Damien admitted a bit sulkily.

"On the other hand, it might help us understand better what happened to the last king of Medarya."

"Maybe if we were actually there and saw the inscription and the layout of the throne room for ourselves, we could figure it out," suggested Shane.

"You know what?" said Damien, brightening up. "Maybe the maps and keys will show a us place to live."

"That's an interesting idea," said Cyril.

Lessons were forgotten for the rest of the day as they continued talking over the meaning of the prophecy.

chapter sixteen

The days and weeks wore on with the children fidgeting and fighting more and more in their cramped space. Mia began asking, "Are we almost there yet? When are we going to be there?" several times every day until the others were fairly sick of the question. But secretly Shane and Damien, too, were wondering if the trip would ever end.

Late one morning Shane drifted down to his luggage and retrieved a large metal cylinder from which he dumped a great glob of purple slime onto his writing tray. It was some sort of purple polymer.

Damien, who was desperately bored, stopped rolling his pencil over the Medaryan sentences he was attempting to write and looked up interestedly at Shane's glob.

"Hey, can I have some?" he asked.

Shane carefully divided his glob in half. Then he sectioned it again and handed Damien a piece about the size of a grape. "Here, taste it."

Damien popped the blob into his mouth. After all, he'd gotten used to slug-fruit jell-o – this couldn't be worse.

He swallowed it just before Mia shrilled, "That's primordial ooze. Don't eat it!" But it was too late.

"Jerk!" exclaimed Damien, grabbing half of Shane's glob and flinging a piece of it at him with his pencil. Shane threw some back at Damien – but it missed, bounced off the wall and hit Mia in the face. Now it was all-out war. It was Mia's idea to mix tissue into the polymer and soon they and the cabin were a splattered mess.

"Enough!" roared Lyric from under the table where she'd taken cover. Damien and Shane were now wrestling. Wrestling without gravity and covered in slime is messy business. Lyric quickly restored order among the children, but the cabin was in shambles. It took quite some time before they had scraped the place clean. Mia was in the worst shape, because she had it not only in her hair but also in her feathers. She stretched out her wings and rustled the feathers to dry.

"Will you get out of my face!" snapped Shane, pushing her wing aside. He drew an imaginary line between them and said, "Don't cross it."

"You're the one who covered me in primordial ooze," said Mia, stretching her wings even more demonstratively.

"Does anyone know any spooky stories?" asked Damien, trying to distract them from another scuffle.

"I do," said Mia brightly.

"Oh, this ought to be good," said Shane, settling in a more comfortable spot. "Mia's good at stories."

Mia began:

A long, long time ago, when the Kings of Medarya were powerful and brutal lords, they demanded the princesses dance the dance of princesses before the throne at midnight under the full moon whenever both moons were full. The dance of the princesses was an ancient ceremony and could not be left undone, or else the spirits of the land would screech in anger and devour all the little girls and boys of the realm. No matter how horrible the dance was, they had to do it, for the consequences of not doing it were even worse. And besides, the kings were powerful and brutal lords, so they liked the dance.

It was always the princess who was to be the next queen who was required to lead the dance, and so she would lead all the other princesses in their white, flowing dresses to glide and twirl around the throne. The princess who was to be queen would hold the queen's stone above her head and whirl around 'til she was dizzy and so were those watching her. Only then would the guards drag in a struggling man, bound and chained and pleading for his life. The princess would slash the razor-sharp stone closer and closer as she danced toward the sacrificial victim – nearer and nearer...

"Mia, that's enough!" commanded Lyric.

"But its true!" insisted Mia. "It's in the sagas Mommy translated."

"It is not. That's nonsense."

"Is it true?" asked Damien

"Of course it is," said Mia. "Why do you think we brought you?"

"I said, that's enough!" repeated Lyric severely. "Your mother says you have too much imagination for your own good."

Mia's face took on an innocent look as she sat back quietly, and she smiled at Damien like a cherub.

Cyril decided it was time to change the subject. "Now, what was it we were planning to do again after we land?"

Shane pulled out the map of Medarya, and they all gathered round. Cyril led the discussion again. "As we all know, we shall land – here – shortly after dark. The first priority will be to hide the craft before daylight comes. Even at night the colony is likely to spot our descent and will be sure to find where we landed in the morning. So we must find the cave shown on the map and hide the shuttle in there."

"But what will keep them from finding our tracks to the cave?" asked Damien.

"We have a number of net root seeds in our supplies. We shall plant them in the ground behind us. They grow exceptionally fast, so our tracks should be well covered."

"Are we sure the cave is big enough for the shuttle, and accessible from the clearing?" wondered Shane.

"It is big enough. Whether or not there is still open access from the clearing, we cannot be positive. Your father and Joe found it 18 years ago. If the cave proves unsuitable, the other solution, I think, will be to pull the ship deeper into the forest and hope the searchers will be afraid to investigate too far. But that is only a backup plan. We cats are fierce enough to protect you from most wild things, but there is no point in deliberately exposing ourselves to unknown dangers."

"But is the cave safe? There could be wild animals in there," Mia said hesitantly.

"Lyric and I will make sure there are not."

"Are we going to try to hide in the city?" asked Damien. "Don't people from the colony go there?"

"Yes, they do, so we shall have to hide in the cave with the shuttle."

"Only in the day, though," asserted Shane. "We should use the nighttime to explore the city and the throne room."

"Yes, we will have to do our exploring at night. The cave is near the Cliff City, so we won't have to go very far."

"I want to see the throne room right away, after we have hidden the ship. I'll even go by myself if I have to."

"I'll go with you," said Damien.

"We'll all go. We must stay together," said Cyril. "But we can't take more than a couple of hours. We must be hidden well before daybreak and we must cover our tracks."

Mia bit her lower lip. She hadn't considered that they would have to do everything at night. But then she thought of their all going to the throne room of the ancient kings under light of the moon, and her mouth curled into a naughty little smile – this was going to be perfect.

"What are our long-term plans?" Lyric wanted to know. "Are we going to take up permanent residence in the cave?"

"I'm afraid we can't make firm plans yet, my dear, beyond the first day or two. Once we have landed we shall have to take stock of our surroundings and the options open to us, and go on from there."

For the first time, the gravity of their situation began to sink into the children's minds.

The final weeks of the trip passed slowly. They struggled to understand the cryptic prophecy, but it still wasn't clear. The king had stored some maps and keys beneath the throne, and they were to find them. But just where were they hidden? How were they to find them? And why were they important?

PART 3

Medarya

1. The Dwarf Caves

chapter seventeen

On the ship's radar, the tiny speck that was Meta drifted closer to the center of the screen and, imperceptibly at first, began to grow bigger. Soon it filled a large portion of the radar screen. Cyril spent a good deal of time in the control room as the landing day drew nearer, checking and double-checking the flight path and making last-minute calibration adjustments to the navigation computer according to Joe's instructions. Just before their launch Joe had told him what would need to be done, and had also left detailed written directions in the control room.

Finally, on the sixty-third day of their journey, they settled into orbit around Meta, circling at an altitude of 120 miles. Everything was secured; luggage was stowed under the seats; cupboards were latched; even Moogkey was tied down.

Two hours later the autopilot announced that it was time to prepare for landing. The passengers strapped themselves into their seats. There was a nervous calm and nobody spoke for the longest time. The landing was the most dangerous part of the journey. If the calculations were not perfect, they would not live. Or – an equally disturbing thought – they might land safely, but somewhere other than the intended target and they would be lost forever on the strange planet. And what if they landed in an ocean by mistake – if there were any oceans?

It was a little after eight o'clock p.m. Meta time when they broke from orbit and started their descent. The nose of the ship tipped slightly down toward the planet until they were spiraling in at a shallow angle. Compared to the vacuum of space, the surface of the atmosphere would be like the surface of a pond, and their ship like a flat rock thrown at the pond. If the angle was too shallow, they would skip off and bounce back into space; but if it was too steep, they would slam into the atmosphere with such an impact that all aboard would be instantly killed – if the shuttle itself even survived.

The smooth, silent flight of outer space began to be replaced by a mild vibration as the craft began to dip into the planet's upper atmosphere. At the same time, the effect of gravity began to come back, so that it was no longer just their straps that kept them in their seats. Both sensations, gentle at first, increased steadily as they descended into the ever-thickening layers of atmosphere, until at the worst it felt as if they were flying through a hurricane with elephants on their laps. But soon the shaking and suffocation began to ease up as the ship's fall slowed, and it was almost as if they were back on Earth once again. Heaviness was a sensation they had nearly forgotten. It felt almost oppressive, yet somehow there was security in it, too. At this point the reverse thrusters blasted, then the parachutes were released, and the ship drifted gently toward the surface. The landing gear deployed and the autopilot began its controlled touchdown.

Cyril was out of his seat and in the control room again, springing up through the hatchway as if there were still no gravity. There was not a lot he could have done if the landing went awry, but he felt better being able to see that everything was all right. It was. The computer had calculated their coordinates on Meta and had flawlessly maneuvered the craft to their landing spot. At eight-forty, with a gentle thump, they settled on the ground.

Nobody moved until Cyril spoke. "Well, we're here – safe and sound. Quietly, everyone. Let's disembark."

Mia was the first to stir, but Damien and Shane beat her to the door, scrambling and stumbling on legs of jelly which had forgotten how to support their weight. Shane undid the emergency latch and swung the hatch door open. They were greeted by a cool, damp darkness and the sounds of night and the lush smell of an unfamiliar forest, spicy and aromatic. Mia and Damien elbowed each other, both trying to get out of the door first.

Cyril squeezed past, nearly knocking them over in the process, and turned to face them. "Mia and Damien, get on my back," he ordered. "Shane, you may ride Lyric. We're going to fly above the tree line for safety and survey the area. Keep your eyes open for the cave where we plan to hide the shuttle."

Mia and Damien willingly clambered onto Cyril while Shane swung his leg up over Lyric's back and buried his hands in her fur. Momentarily they stood in a large clearing, listening to the chirping and croaking and howling of the forest around, feeling the fresh moist air on their faces, gazing at the eerie beauty surrounding them. The night was misty and neither moon was out yet, so they could see little clearly. The ground was covered in grass and moss and tiny herbs, wet from the heavy dew that had fallen just a couple of hours before. Dimly they could make out the dark forms of huge trees draped in grey mosses which gave them the appearance of grotesque robed giants reaching over them. Once or twice they heard a soft rustle and thought they caught the glimpse of some blacker shadow moving within the murky darkness – or was it just their imagination?

Then a ripple of powerful muscles tore them from this strangely enchanting carpet and launched them into the air, wings surging upward. They didn't have to fly very high before they broke out of the fog. Above the blanket of low-lying clouds they could see a whole new world. The sky was clear, the stars twinkled brightly overhead, and the first moon was just beginning to rise in the eastern sky, slightly larger than Earth's moon. They could see the tops of the trees clearly though the ground itself was obscured by the soft grey haze. A steep, craggy ridge rose up beside them, with sheer white cliffs and broad ledges, and many black holes cut into the rock face, especially toward the top. These were too evenly shaped and regularly spaced to be natural, and it took them no more than a moment to realize what they were viewing. These were dwellings of some sort, carved into the mountain – part of the Cliff City.

They could see the advantageous position chosen for their landing spot. The clearing lay nestled between the forest and the cliffs. This was at the back side of the Cliff City. According to the map, the main part of the Cliff City should lie on the other side of this ridge – as should also the research colony. That fact, combined with the fog cover which effectively blocked a view of the sky from the ground, would certainly have hidden their approach, and – except perhaps for the noise – it was likely their landing had not even been detected. They flew in circles over the clearing for several minutes, scouting the area as the light from the rising moon grew brighter.

"I think I see the cave!" Shane suddenly announced in Lyric's ear, spotting a dark place in the cliff wall almost hidden in the haze. Lyric dipped back into the cloud cover and Cyril followed. They settled near the shuttle once again. The cave was just on the other side of a jutting outcrop of jagged rock.

"I'd better go investigate," said Lyric. Shane slid off and Lyric ducked into the cave. Cyril stood protectively with the children outside the entrance, listening for any noise from the darkness. They heard nothing until she returned. "There was the scent of some animals I don't recognize in there, but it is quite old. I think the cave is safe enough. It's very small and ends immediately – no more than a hole, but I think the shuttle will fit."

"Okay, let's get the shuttle into the cave. Shane, can you drive it?" asked Cyril.

"I don't know. I've never driven before," said Shane dubiously.

"Well, just do your best. Joe assured me it isn't difficult, and you will only be moving a few feet per second. We will guide you from the ground to make sure you don't get turned around and end up in the forest." There was a hint of amusement in his voice. "Lyric, what is the floor of the cave like – is there any slope to it inside the entrance?"

"No. It's pretty flat, only a bit bumpy," she answered.

The path from the shuttle to the cave was mostly clear of obstacles. Shane had to drive over a couple of small saplings which bent as the vehicle passed over them and sprang right back up when it had passed. It took some tricky maneuvering to get the shuttle into the cave without scraping the sides. The space was cramped, but Shane managed the job without any mishaps. Afterwards the five stood at the entrance looking at each other, considering what to do next.

"Can we go the throne room now?" suggested Shane.

"Yes, let's!" agreed Mia with a sparkle in her eye – it wasn't a double full moon tonight, but it was close enough as far as she was concerned.

"We are lucky to have the cloud cover tonight," agreed Cyril. "Once above the clouds we can fly anywhere we want without being seen." In fact it was not luck that brought the cloud cover, as they were to learn over the following days and weeks; nighttime fog was normal this time of year.

"Are we *flying* there, then?" asked Damien.

"I don't know how else to get up there," replied Cyril.

"I'm game," said Lyric. "Hop on, Shane."

"Hold on a minute – I'll be right back!" Shane disappeared into the shuttle again and returned a few minutes later carrying a rucksack. "I got some flashlights," he explained. "I figured if we're going into the caves we may need them. The cats might do okay seeing in the dark, but not the rest of us. And also a couple of ropes, because – well, Damien and I can't fly, so if we get stuck or something..."

"Good thinking, Shane," said Cyril with approval.

The children clambered back onto the backs of Cyril and Lyric, and the two big cats soared up above the clouds once again. The sight that met them as they rounded the point nearly took their breath away. Towering above them were the most magnificent white cliffs they had ever seen, shot through with gold veins that glinted in the moonlight – the Cliff City of Medarya. It was a vertical city, carved out of the solid white granite, splendid and proud in its gold-marbled elegance, but sad, too, it seemed, standing there so empty and silent.

"Incredible!" gasped Damien in hushed awe. Mia's sparkling eyes drank in the alluring scene as if it quenched a thirst.

Rising out of the fog below them were a grand staircase flanked by a majestic colonnade of ornamented columns which led diagonally up the cliff towards the top. At intervals the stair rested at a landing which was

ornately decorated with scrolls of carved leaves and flowers as if in celebration of nature, or with statues of winged people dancing or taking flight. The whole face of the cliff was honeycombed with a grid of dwellings, neatly aligned loggias opening to the air. Some entrances were grander then others. Some led to family dwellings and others to more official-looking structures. The largest were near the top, including the grandest of them all, the throne room. Cyril and Lyric alighted on a ledge that was announced by a triumphal arch elaborately carved from the glistening white stone. The arch led them into a vast gallery flanked by statues of noble winged guards, and a colonnade of caryatides lined the promenade on left and right, leading into the cave, directing them towards the throne. Along the back wall of the cave they could see more doors, secondary entrances; but the main entrance was behind them, from the sky.

It was obvious where the throne belonged. It was meant to sit solitary on its grand dais, flanked by the colonnade of statues. But it wasn't there. All that remained was the large plinth, about ten feet by ten feet and two feet high with four steps cut into its front side. Mia climbed off Cyril and flopped herself down on the edge of it. "What a disappointment," she said with annoyance. "This ruins everything!"

"They filched it!" exclaimed Damien with disgust. "Now what do we do, Shane?"

"Well, we can't exactly go to the colony and ask them to put it back." Shane laid down his rucksack and looked around. "It is peaceful up here, though."

By now both moons were up in the eastern sky, casting double shadows from the statues and columns. Below them was a soft grey blanket of fluffy clouds.

"Both moons are out tonight, and they look pretty full," Mia announced pointedly.

"Yeah?" said Damien.

"So, I think we still have to do the sacrifice, even without the throne. It wouldn't do for all of us to get eaten by spirits on our first night here, would it? Not when we could prevent it."

"You're not making sense, Mia," declared Damien.

But this rebuke did not stop Mia. She began to sway. She took a step forward and back, and a step to the side and back. She undulated with the wind and began to twirl and jump and leap to the rhythm of her heart and to the pounding of her feet.

It was Lyric who caught on first. "No more, Mia," she commanded. But Mia only danced more wildly. Then she began to chant:

The hand that owns the princess' stone,
strike the blade, cross center score.

As she did so, she pulled out her stone knife from
where she had been hiding it in her clothes. She swung
the blade from right to left, then crossed up and down,

closer and closer towards Damien.

"That's enough, Mia," said Damien, catching her arm with one hand and effortlessly taking the ceremonial knife away from her with the other. Mia collapsed in a heap of giggles. When she had finally got herself together enough to look up, Damien was sitting on the throne plinth running the stone across it distractedly, making patterns in the dust.

"Did you like my interpretive dance of the riddle, Damien? Oh, don't be so stuffy, Lyric – I was just joking, honestly. May I have my knife back, please?"

But Damien wouldn't give it back to her. "I don't agree with your interpretation," he said.

Shane came and sat down beside Damien. "Mia only said the last two lines of the prophecy:

> Read this prophecy; learn this lore:
> To find the maps and keys of yore
> the king has stored below the throne:
> The hand that owns the princess' stone,
> strike the blade, cross center score.

"*To find the maps and keys of yore…* The question is, *what* are we to strike cross center with the blade?"

"Maybe we are to strike the compartment under the throne where Mia's knife was found," suggested Damien. By now he was tapping the stone against the floor of the platform he was sitting on.

"Hey," said Mia, "give me back my knife! You're going to break it!"

She started to reach for it, but before she could do so the stone caught in a rut and slipped out of Damien's hand. "Ouch!" he exclaimed, scraping his knuckle. Mia hardly even realized the knife was free from his grasp before he had seized it again with a lightning-quick movement. He held it away while Mia struggled vainly to get it from him.

"Stop it, you two! Look at this!" Shane commanded, inspecting the ridge in the stone platform where the knife had momentarily caught. "Maybe there is writing here." He started to brush at the surface they were sitting on. Immediately Damien started scraping with the stone in one hand, keeping Mia away from it with the other. They did find an indentation running the length of the plinth, but it was just a straight line – not writing. Shane and Damien were both disappointed – and so was Mia, who still had not succeeded in wresting the knife back from Damien..

"Hey, here's another groove running the other way!" said Damien, still chipping away at the caked dirt. He was now near the middle of the dais in his efforts to evade Mia. The second furrow was short – just a shallow slot about six inches long and an inch wide.

Shane was next to him in an instant. "The lines cross in the center. Of course! How could we be so dense? This would be right *below the throne*."

Damien tried working the tip of the stone knife into the cleft where the two cracks intersected, but got nowhere. The bottom of the groove was hard.

Mia was watching him like a bird, waiting for her

opportunity. In the moment's distraction, while he was busy working at the groove and not paying full attention to Mia, she saw her chance. She jumped forward and grabbed the knife. Her hand closed on the handle, and the force of her lunge struck the point of the blade forcefully down into the slot.

With a crack the bottom of the groove gave way, crumbling and disintegrating like an old, brittle membrane. The knife plunged into the slot until the blade was fully embedded. It came to a stop with a *thunk* as of stone against metal. A whirring sound followed as some mechanism was engaged, and the floor shifted.

All three children jumped away with a start and watched open-mouthed as the platform parted down the middle with the sound of stone scraping on stone. The two halves parted to reveal a narrow stone stairway leading down.

"Don't go in," Lyric cautioned urgently. "This is like an Egyptian crypt. There may be traps. Or at least throw something down first. Do be careful!"

"Um, why don't you go first?" Damien suggested to Shane.

"No, you found it, you go first," said Shane.

"Actually, *I'm* the one who found it," Mia corrected proudly.

"Yeah, but that was just a fluke," Damien retorted. "*I* was actually looking for it."

"We were *all* looking for it—" began Shane.

"Mia wasn't!" Damien argued hotly. "She was just trying to get her stupid knife back."

"That may be. Still, the prophecy does say *The hand that owns the princess' stone*, so I suppose it was really Mia's to do anyhow."

"Hmph!" was all Damien replied.

"It's creepy," said Mia, peering into the opening. "I'll go first." But Damien was not about to be outdone by her. He started to push past her – not too gently – when they were both stopped short by a sharp roar from Cyril.

"Hold it right there!" he ordered. "Neither of you is going first. Let me by, please, and I will see if it is safe." He sniffed the musty air rising from below and then carefully placed one large paw on the first step. Nothing happened. He took another step, then another, and cautiously descended the narrow stair followed by the others. It opened at the bottom into a small chamber, in the center of which they discovered a large, square, raised object – they bumped into it.

"It's probably a casket," said Mia in the dark.

But it wasn't a casket. Once their eyes adjusted to the dim light from the pale stream of moonlight falling down the stair, they could see that it was a table in the center of the room. On the table was a stone box and next to it some stone slabs. Shane lifted the lid of the box, but it was too dark to see what was inside. He wasn't about to reach his hand in.

"I left the flashlights upstairs," he said. "I'll go get them."

He was back in an instant with his rucksack, a flashlight already in his hand. He switched it on and shined the beam inside the box. There they saw seven more knives just like Mia's.

"They're not knives," said Shane. "They're keys. *To find the maps and keys of yore the king has stored below the throne.* It's simple, really. And now each of us will have our own stone key."

The other items on the table were indeed maps. One of the slabs was a map of the immediate area, carved in relief into the pale grey stone. Another one was larger and showed the whole land of Medarya. The most fascinating map was in layers, all intricately carved and placed one atop the other to form a three-dimensional model of the Cliff City in depth. It also revealed a second system of caves that extended deep into the mountain. Shane cautiously tested the top slab to see if he could move it and was surprised to find it was light enough for him to lift easily.

"It looks like pumice," observed Cyril. "It's a volcanic rock, full of microscopic holes so there is a lot of air trapped inside. These stones might even float in water."

Only one thing on the maps was not carved from the whitish stone. A meandering line of little red jewels was embedded in the surface, glinting as the light hit them. The line ran along the grand stair they had followed up the mountain, leading down and around the point to where there appeared to be an another entrance to the caves.

"They're tiny footprints," remarked Shane in amazement as he observed them closely, "and there is something written by that cave entrance. It says *Gwin èl Pórt* – that's Medaryan for 'Queen's Gate'. I think the map is telling us to go to the Queen's Gate. The king who left us these maps and the keys must have wanted us to go there."

"You're clever," said Cyril, "and I think you are right. But before doing anything else, I think we should take these maps back to the shuttle for safekeeping. We'll carry back what we can on this trip and return to get the rest. After that we can look for the Queen's Gate. Who knows? Maybe there will be a better place for us to hide than in the shuttle's cave."

"How are we going to carry the stones?" asked Shane.

"Weight won't be a problem. The rock is very light. But carrying them while flying – well, that does pose a challenge. Lyric, might you and I be able to carry a slab in our paws as we fly?"

"I don't think so, Cyril."

"Why don't we just strap them onto us with the ropes?" suggested Damien.

"And I could carry another one in my rucksack, along with the keys," added Shane.

"Excellent idea!"

It took two trips to tote all the maps back to the shuttle. On the last trip up the steps Damien remembered to retrieve the stone key which was still embedded in the stone platform. As soon as he withdrew it the two halves slid together again, converging with a boom that echoed through the large room. Cyril had them brush dirt back into the crack and cover their tracks as much as possible.

Once the task of transporting the maps back to the shuttle was done, they stood outside the cave entrance and took their bearings. According to the map, the Queen's Gate should lie just a little farther along the same mountain face, at about the point where the forest began. There was no path to it and the underbrush was thick with net roots. In fact, at the spot where the Queen's Gate ought to have been there was only a covering of net roots so dense that it was like a gnarled wall.

"The gate has to be under all of this brush," said Shane. "But how are we going to get to it?"

"We could burn it away," suggested Cyril. "On a night like this, we don't have to be too concerned about the smoke attracting the research colony. Nor, I think, should there be any great danger of its getting out of control. In fact, our biggest difficulty may be in keeping the fire going. But I don't know any other way to get through five thousand years' worth of net root growth."

"I think we should try it," said Lyric, who wasn't keen on living in the cramped cave where the shuttle presently sat. They collected matches from the shuttle (and fire extinguishers, too, just in case), then trampled over the uneven carpet of net roots to where they hoped the Queen's Gate lay deep behind the thick growth. Shane lit the first match and held it to a vine stalk. The plant seemed to shudder a little as it began to smolder.

"I can understand why Joe never wanted to burn the net roots away from our pool," said Shane. "They do seem a bit too alive."

The three children lit more vines. There were no flames as the shoots burned, only a vivid red glow and a lot of acrid-smelling yellowish smoke as the fire smoldered its way along the pithy wood. Where it came to a fork, the fire would continue up both branches of the split, and in this way it ate its way through the entire complex maze of roots. Soon there was a gaping, smoldering hole four feet into the side of the cliff and several feet in every direction.

The net roots burned amazingly quickly despite the soggy weather, and everyone was surprised and alarmed when the fire started to spread out of control. It took some frantic work with the fire extinguishers to halt its rapid progress along the ground back toward the shuttle cave.

Their battle on the rock face was not so successful. They were unable to stop the fire from advancing up the vertical cliff out of reach. Cyril tried taking Damien up on his back with a fire extinguisher, but they could not get close enough to the smoldering vines to put them out effectively. At one point Damien leaned out to far and slipped. Cyril dove for the ground while Damien scrambled to stay on his back – dropping the fire extinguisher in the process.

"Hey, watch it!" they heard Shane exclaim as the plummeting canister narrowly missed him. The cat and boy crash-landed in a clump of dense undergrowth twenty feet away. Fortunately, the fern-like shrubbery contained no thorns or brambles, and they were not much hurt. Mia begged to fly up by herself to fight the fire, but Lyric would not hear of it. They could only stand below watching helplessly as it continued to spread.

As it turned out, Damien and Cyril could have spared

themselves the bruises and scratches, for nothing else caught fire. It appeared that only net roots would burn on a damp night like this.

The sickly yellowish smog hung heavy in the air for some time afterwards. When it cleared enough to see the cliff wall, they could make out a carved stone arch with an ornately fashioned, arched door engraved with runes announcing the Queen's Gate. Under this name there was another inscription: *MIL KANDA-SOR EY, DOWANI WILEY KHOER' ES OM OWPERI GWAOLD' EO DHAN DU^{H}TIYA* 'To my lady, a gift from Sir Wiley, lord of the Dwarves'. Damien, who still had Mia's stone in his pocket, pulled it out and began working it into the key slot beside the door.

"Hey, *I* should do that," claimed Mia stoutly. "It's my knife."

"Is it a knife – or a key?" asked Damien pointedly.

"It's… well, okay, it's a key," admitted Mia slowly.

Damien looked at her narrowly. "Tell me you're sorry."

"I'm sorry," said Mia mournfully, "…for being such a good actor."

"Are you really sorry, then, or just acting?"

"Okay, I'm acting," said Mia in a small voice. "But I did say it – sorry!"

"At least you're truthful," said Damien, giving up and handing her the stone key. Mia lustily took the stone and with much ceremony inserted it into the slot that Damien had dug out. They heard the catch of metal on metal and the whir of a mechanism. Then the gate slid upwards to reveal an opening like a gaping mouth leading into a cavernous throat. They shined their flashlights into the darkness.

The stone walls of the grand entryway arched away from the gate, outward and upward into a ribbed groin vault above their heads. Along the walls of the cavern curving out to the right and the left ran two arcades of smaller vaults, flanked by rows of beautifully ornamented columns. A series of pointed arches opened onto a vast central room, the ceiling of which soared far above their heads in a high and elaborate dome. Once over the threshold of the gate, the floor was level and smooth.

"This will do perfectly," purred Lyric. "And the shuttle will fit through the gate, too, without any problem. We should bring it in here right away. Then assess the damage to the foliage outside and see what we can cover and repair of the net roots."

It was hard for the children to tear their eyes away from the wonder before them, but there was a lot of work to be done yet. Back outside, they surveyed the damage their fire had done. Net roots were still smoldering in several places high up on the mountain side, but no other plants seemed to have caught fire. On the ground they saw the black, still-smoking trail where the net roots had burnt partway back towards the shuttle cave. With some further controlled burning – a bit more carefully this time – Cyril figured they could make a path wide enough for the shuttle to pass. Soon Shane was able to back the craft out of the smaller cave and drive it slowly down to the Queen's Gate.

Under Lyric's supervision, Damien and Mia

immediately started planting new net root seeds in the ground everywhere the shuttle had left tracks. The new shoots began to spread like moving fingers in all directions, crossing and crisscrossing over the whole clearing, covering all evidence of their presence. Once the shuttle was safely parked inside the large cave, they also planted a few seeds outside the entrance.

"Net roots grow very fast," instructed Cyril. "We should have a new ground cover by light and with luck the gate will be covered as well." He wrinkled his nose. "I'll bet the smell of this smoke is keeping all the animals away. It would definitely keep me away if I were a dumb brute." Lyric looked at him but said nothing.

Everybody was exhausted by the time the foliage repair was finished and they had shut the gate behind them. They crawled into the shuttle to sleep.

chapter eighteen

Mia awoke hours later to the sound of laughter and splashing water. At first she thought she was dreaming – how could there be water in space? For that matter, how could Shane and Damien be outside the ship? Then the landing and night's adventure came back. Mia rubbed her eyes and sat up, swinging her legs over the ledge-bed. It was strange to feel gravity pulling her downward again, and her legs felt as awkward as they had the previous night – except now they were stiff, too, from unaccustomed exercise.

Mia peeked out of the spaceship and was almost blinded by the glare – the exterior lights of the ship were on. When her eyes adjusted, she saw that she was in the entryway of a most wonderful cave. The white walls and dome had been polished until they shone. The vaulted ceilings of the arcades were supported by metal ribs which gleamed silver in the light. It looked like the inside of a cathedral – or perhaps more like a mystic grotto.

The sound of her brother and Damien's laughter echoed from somewhere off to the side. Mia followed along the arcade and came through a pointed archway into another sort of room, where underground streams collected in a big pool. Multiple rivulets, running down the walls of the cave for millennia, had cut deep troughs into the stone. Damien came sliding down one of the troughs, landing in the pool with a big splash and soaking Mia.

Not one to be outdone, and considering she was already wet, Mia climbed to the highest trough she could manage and plummeted head first into the water below. After the ordeal of dehydration and not having a normal bath for two months, the water felt delicious.

They stayed inside the cavern all that day (the few hours that were still left of it) and set up camp. After looking around the caves a little, everyone selected a suitable place to sleep where they could stretch out and not be in anyone else's way. This was a very welcome change. They brought their personal belongings out of the shuttle along with other supplies they thought they might need. When that was done, they sat down to eat some dinner and discuss their plans.

So far there had been no indication that the colony was aware of their presence, but, Cyril reminded them, it would not pay to be careless. They could start cautiously exploring their surroundings, but they should not stray too far from the shuttle until they had a better idea of their situation. There was still plenty of freeze-dried food in the ship's stores, so while they were all sick to death of the taste of it, at least they knew they wouldn't starve.

Now it was getting late by their watches, and Lyric insisted that they turn in for the night. Exploring could wait – right now they needed sleep so they might adjust to the local time as quickly as possible.

Mia was very unhappy about having to go to bed again so soon – she had just gotten up only a few hours ago. She wore a petulant scowl the whole time she was getting herself ready, and afterwards she lay in her bed thinking sulky thoughts. She didn't feel at all tired – bored, yes, but tired, no. They had spent all this time to get to Meta, and now that they were here they couldn't even stay up and explore. It just wasn't fair…

They next thing Mia knew Damien was prodding her awake. "Get up, lazybones! Let's go exploring," he tempted her.

"Oh, of course," sighed Mia, "how could I sleep?"

"It's morning," said Damien. "You've slept late."

Mia looked at her watch – almost nine o'clock in the morning. After two months on the spaceship her body seemed to have no clue what time of day it was. The fact that there was no daylight inside the cave didn't help, either.

Moogkey, too, seemed to have been waiting for Mia to wake up. As soon as she sat up he hopped onto her head with a satisfied spark.

"Here's some lichen, Mia. Eat it – it's not too bad." Damien handed her something that looked like bark, whitish-grey on one side and brown on the other. She sat up and took it. The texture was like cardboard, but the taste really was pretty good.

Outside the shuttle Mia found Shane with Lyric and Cyril huddled around a carved stone table studying something. The stone table and chairs looked just the right size for Shane, but rather too small for the cats.

"Must be dwarf-made," Damien commented.

The trio was studying the stone tablets they had retrieved from below the throne. There were four maps in all, laid out on the table in front of them: the larger tablet containing the map of Medarya, the smaller one of the area surrounding the Cliff City, and the layered map depicting the Cliff City itself and the adjoining system of caves. The fourth map they couldn't decipher.

It was the three-dimensional map and its second mass of caves on that they were examining now. This was something completely new to them. Jerrod and Serena had known nothing about it, and no reports of it had ever come out of the research colony. Up until now, no one seemed to have had any inkling that anything other than solid rock lay in the heart of the mountain.

They could now see that this was really another city, and to judge by the map's scale it must be enormous – at least as big as the Cliff City, probably bigger, but lying below it and deeper within the mountain. It was evidently an independent municipality, entirely separate except for three access points: a large entrance on the major thoroughfare, and two smaller portals, perhaps reserved for privileged individuals. All three entrances were sealed off with sturdy stone gates. They could also see where this city connected through gateways and stairways to the little cave they were now in – at least, it appeared little on the map.

"According to the map, the Queen's Gate is a dwarf-built cave," Shane explained to Damien and Mia. "In fact, the whole of this complex is called the Dwarf City."

"There are dwarves here?" asked Mia, her eyes growing big.

Lyric answered, "It doesn't seem as though anybody has been here for hundreds – maybe thousands – of years."

"There's got to be at least bugs in here," said Damien.

"No," said Cyril, "we have not even found any bugs. It seems as though this place was completely sealed off many years ago by the net roots we burned away. Once a net root takes possession of a domain it can last for a very long time. They are tenacious plants. It looks as though they were even blocking the water source because when we first got here the water channels were dry, but now they are completely open and flowing. It also must have opened up some ventilation shafts – otherwise we would eventually be asphyxiated."

"What's *fixiated*?" asked Mia.

"*As*phyxiated. It means dying from not getting enough clean air," answered Lyric. "As it is, there is water and air, and even a few dry mosses on the rocks."

"Let's go look around," said Damien, tossing Mia a flashlight. They scanned the cave. The large dome where they stood was centered on the exterior gate where they had entered. To the right of the entrance an arcade of metal-ribbed groin vaults followed the curve of the wall and led to the underground pools and spring that lay at the right-hand quadrant of the circle. To the left another arcade of vaults curved around the opposite wall, forming a hallway with a row of doors – smallish doors. Straight ahead, where the far wall of the domed room should have been, was an immense gaping blackness. When they went to investigate, they came upon an intricately fashioned railing perched on a ledge that overlooked a vast, unfathomable expanse. The air was clammy and deathly still, and the darkness was so black and so deep that it seemed to Mia and Damien to have neither bottom nor end.

"I don't think we should try to go this way. Maybe we should start by exploring the row of small doors back along the side," suggested Damien.

"I'm game," answered Mia.

"Wait!" said Cyril who had quietly stalked up behind them. He shot off and disappeared into the ship, and when he came back out he had a ball of kite string in his mouth. "Tie one end to the ship and unravel the other as you go. When you reach the end of the string, don't go any further. And stay together. If you get lost we might never find you."

Damien obligingly tied the string to the shuttle and he and Mia set off toward the shadowy outer edge of their large space. They decided first just to look at the smaller rooms that came off of the main room where the shuttle was. At the first metal-framed door Damien peered into darkness beyond the small opening and hesitated. Mia, gawking at the arches overhead and not watching where she was going, slammed into him, knocking him into the room and tumbling after. He bumped against the vertical stone slab of the door, which must have been on a pivot because it slammed shut behind them, sealing off the room with a resolute thud. The ball of string remained on the other side of the door.

"Can you watch where you're going?" snapped Damien.

Mia gave a little squeak and pointed, wide-eyed, at the door. Standing between them and any possibility of escape through the tightly shut door stood a goblin-like creature, swaying back and forth and leering at them, a gnarled hand stretching out toward them.

"It's just a statue, numbskull," said Damien as he reached for the hand to still it. It came off in his grasp. This time it was Damien who yipped.

Mia giggled nervously. The statue was attached to the back side of the pivoting door in such a way that it would rock back and forth whenever the door was opened or closed – the clever design of an ancient jokester.

Totally creeped out now, the children began to cast their flashlights about the room. The walls were curved and cave-like. The only furnishings were a small bed and nightstand, and a table and chairs, all carved out of stone and just their size. Mia sat down at the table. "Perfect," she said. "Do you think a kid lived here?"

"Shane said this was a dwarf city. Maybe they were our size."

There was a hearth in the corner with a smoke escape which tunneled through the stone above as far as they could see. There was even a cauldron hanging above the fire pit and a pot that looked a little like a teapot. There were metal bowls and plates and spoons. On the nightstand beside the bed was a very old book which fell apart when Mia tried to open it.

"Let's go look somewhere else," said Damien.

"Why?" asked Mia.

"It's the hand on the floor – it gives me the creeps."

Mia took a closer look. "It's hollow," she said, gingerly picking it up. Something fell out, something metal – or some things metal. "They're keys – I think." They were oddly shaped, but were arranged on a ring like keys. She tried one in the hole in the door. It fit easily. They heard the lock click and then it jammed. "Oh, no!" cried Mia, wiggling the handle and pushing at the door. Both remained firm.

"Oh, great!" said Damien looking warily at the statue which seemed to be grinning at him. "We weren't locked in before. Why did you have to lock it? Now how long do you suppose it's going to take Shane to chisel us out?"

Mia looked up and noticed for the first time that with its one remaining hand which was folded across its chest, the grinning statue was pointing off to the side. They hadn't noticed it before, but there in the adjacent wall was a very well-concealed door. Mia unfastened the ring from the stuck key and tried several of the others in the second door. One clicked. She pushed at the door and with a groan of stone grinding on stone it swung open.

"I'm not going where that statue says to go!" said Damien.

"Fine then. I'll go myself, and you can just stay here. I

hope the statue doesn't eat you!" Mia stepped over the deep threshold into a shallow tunnel with crudely hewn walls. It wound down and around and came to a fork. Mia took the right tunnel which also forked. She went right again.

"Hey, slow down. You're going to get us lost," panted Damien behind her.

"Well, you're the one who dropped the string on the other side of the door," replied Mia.

"I dropped it because you bumped me... And you're getting us lost," Damien repeated as Mia came to another fork and quickly turned right.

"No, I'm not. I'm taking all rights. So to get back we just have to take all lefts."

They came to a slightly larger area that looked as if it were a kind of basin. The walls around were full of holes, small tunnels slanting upward and larger tunnels slanting down. The ones going down were big enough for a kid to crawl through – which is what Mia did, with Damien following her.

"This wasn't what I had in mind when I asked you if you wanted to go exploring," grumbled Damien as he caught up to her. The tunnel made a sudden bend downward, and Mia paused. Damien slammed into her – and she lost her footing. They went sliding faster and faster past a myriad of interconnecting tunnels until they landed, jumbled in a heap, in another basin-like chamber at the bottom. Moogkey had gotten dislodged in the tumble but quickly regained his perch on Mia's head and sat there cowering.

"I think... we're lost," said Damien, "...in the sewer."

"Well, if you hadn't bumped me and made me fall, we wouldn't be," said Mia self-righteously.

Damien just looked at her, exasperated, and then focused on the walls around him. There were doors in this part of the tunnel network. "Maybe they're service doors," he said, scratching his head. It was caked with dust. "Probably five-thousand-year-old sewage," he muttered.

Mia was trying the doors with the keys she still had clutched in her hand. Several of them opened. They took the far right one. Rough-hewn steps took them up a flight to another door which wasn't locked at all. This one opened onto a narrow street. On either side of the street were homey looking doorways that led to smallish cave dwellings much like the one they had left with the laughing statue.

"Wow, cool!" exclaimed Damien.

The beams of their flashlights could not reach to the ceiling above them. The space was so vast that – except for the thick blackness – you could easily forget you were underground. They were now down in the dark pit that they had looked out over from the balcony above – the main cavern of the Dwarf City.

They walked for a long time, following the street. There was nothing to tell them which direction they were going – even if they had known which direction they *wanted* to go. They just continued on. The houses – if that's what they were – got larger and grander as they proceeded, with more elaborate stone carvings embellished with decorative metal.

Soon they came to a cross-street that looked like a main boulevard. They turned and followed it to the right. It was wide and lined on both sides with statues holding lanterns. These, it turned out, were real lanterns, and, amazingly, many of them still worked. They seemed to be triggered by motion, because they would flicker on as the children neared a statue and flicker off again as they left it. Moogkey sparked every time another one lit up.

It was a relief to Damien and Mia to have more than just the light from the flashlights. They switched them off to save the batteries. Now they could see the buildings and the streets much more clearly. They had never imagined anything like this underground city. They followed the line of funny dwarf statues – some men, some women, others children, all bearing different sorts of comical expressions. As they moved past one statue after another, the buildings grew less homey and more official-looking. The boulevard crossed several major streets. The children counted them as they passed, but did not turn onto any of them. They continued following the funny statues. These, too, seemed to be growing more serious as they proceeded; some were even getting fierce and daunting. "I wouldn't want to meet up with that guy in a dark alley," observed Damien, pointing to a larger-than-life dwarf with his sword raised.

Now they came to the end of the boulevard. It opened out into a wide open area which must have been the city's center. It could not exactly be described as a town square, because it was not square – it was round. It was more like the hub of a large wagon wheel, with boulevards and streets radiating out in all directions like spokes.

"I like that building!" Damien said. Directly ahead of them, at the center of everything, stood an imposing edifice with enormous square pillars and a carved square triumphal arch encasing the largest and grandest doorway they had come across yet – big enough for two shuttles to drive through side by side, with two more hovering above them.

They climbed up the majestic steps to the solid and elaborate doors so huge they would be impossible for a child – or a dwarf – to open.

"Mom would love this," said Mia, looking at the runes carved into the doors. She pulled out her stone key from where she had tucked it in her boot and tried it in the key slot. Nothing happened. "Shucks," she said. "How about yours?" She grabbed Damien's stone from his pocket and jammed it into the slot. This time they heard the whirring of the ancient mechanism and the crunch of massive stone shifting after thousands of years in one spot. There was the thunderous rumble of stone grating over stone as the door parted in the middle and slid into the walls. Mia smugly handed Damien his key. Then a blinding light hit them in the face.

When they could see again, the sight before them dazzled even their wildest imaginations. The opening of the door must have triggered an automatic lighting system that flooded a vast room, bouncing and glinting off thousands of metal weapons: swords, spears, knives, shields and armor. They stepped inside and the great doors closed behind them with a sturdy thud that made them jump.

"We found the city's armory!" Damien cried out, stunned. "Thanks, Mia, for getting us to fall down the sewer!"

Mia was excitedly looking at a weapon which resembled some type of mechanical crossbow. She fitted a dart in position and pulled back the lever until it cocked. She released the trigger and the arrow whizzed through the air with frightening force, ricocheting off the walls several times before finally coming to rest somewhere to her left.

"Wow! I want this," she exclaimed as she ran off to find where the arrow had gone. Damien meanwhile was looking over the dwarf-sized swords. He had left the main rack of swords and was gazing at a special one hung from the wall. It was sleek and black. The handle glittered with encrusted purple jewels. He swung it around. "This one suits me," he said, studying the intricate rune-work on the hilt and handle.

There was another jewel-encrusted sword on the wall, slightly longer, with a thin, sharp, two-edged silvery blade. He took it down. It, too, had runes on the handle and a large light blue center diamond. Damien swung it around, testing its weight. It was nicely balanced, but a bit long for him. "I'll take this one back for Shane," he announced.

He began striding up and down the isles, taking stock of the armory as if he owned it. At the very middle of the square room was a large round table. Circular aisles ran in concentric rings around the central table. These rings were pierced by an aisle which traversed the room from the main door through which they had entered to another door on the opposite wall, and by another aisle perpendicular to the first. The table stood where the two large aisles crossed. Smaller aisles also radiated out at regular intervals from where the table stood.

Damien walked up to the table and saw that it held a map of the dwarf city in relief. He realized that the organization of this main room of the armory mirrored the plan of the city. Two large boulevards, including the one they had come up, crossed at the city center. Smaller streets also radiated out from the center, and still others ran in concentric circles around it. At the focal point of everything stood the armory.

As he studied the map more closely, he saw that there was also writing inscribed on it. At the armory in the middle there was a bold red ☒ and the rather unnecessary message *KÍRI TÈ^H UT^{H}A* – 'YOU ARE HERE'. There were numerous arrows leading from the smaller streets onto the main boulevards and then continuing outwards from there to the edges of the table. At many points throughout the city there were other labels containing various symbols, words, and even whole paragraphs of instructions.

"Hey, Mia, come here and look at this! There's a map of the Dwarf City carved on this stone table. I think it's an evacuation map. It shows which areas are to be evacuated through which city exits." When Mia was beside him he pointed out a circular structure at the outskirts of the table. "This must be the Queen's Gate, here. See? It's labeled *Gwin èl Pórt*. And it shows our path to get back to it. We follow along this main boulevard until we reach the… let's see… the *seventh* intersection. Then we turn right, pass two smaller intersections, turn left onto the third one, and follow that street until we get to this place." He pointed out where the avenue ended at a long flight of stairs which switched back and forth up the side of the steep ascent leading to the Queen's Gate. "It's a long climb. But at least we're not lost anymore."

They continued looking around the armory until they were sure they had seen everything there was to see, then decided it was time to start heading back.

They thought it would be a good idea to bring back the armor and weaponry they had found – as much as they could carry, at least. They chose the two swords that Damien had picked out and Mia's crossbow and darts. In a section that seemed dedicated to cat armor, they found some battle claws for Lyric and Cyril. There were also some full outfits made up of layers of small metal platelets – a type of plate mail that looked a lot like the pictures of Sarmatian horse armor Mia's mother had shown her. "Cyril would love this," she exclaimed. So Damien draped the heavy mail across his shoulders. He thought he could carry at least one suit.

They went out by a different exit from the one through which they had come in. These doors had trouble working and it took several tries with the key before they opened even partway. Once outside the children saw the lights go out automatically and heard the mechanism strain to close the doors behind them. At first nothing happened; then there was a shudder, an ear-splitting screech, and the doors slammed together with a boom that echoed across the whole city.

Just before he stepped through the doorway, Damien had noticed a plaque on the wall by the exit which carried a copy of the relevant portion of the evacuation map. *These dwarves seem to be very warlike,* he thought. *They put their armory at the center of their village, and have the escape routes and evacuation instructions all planned out ahead of time. I wonder if all the buildings have an evacuation map by the doorway – or, at least, all the public buildings.* Further investigation confirmed his hunch – that every public building had an evacuation plan posted near the exit.

As the two heavily laden children began to follow the belanterned statues away from the armory, the lights sprang to life as they approached and winked out after they passed, Damien reflected soberly, "So far we have been very lucky. Life isn't always that way."

"What do you mean?" asked Mia, a little annoyed by his gloominess, for her life had always been easy. She had never been taught to fear, never had a feeling of failure, never had need or want for anything. This, probably more than anything, had formed Mia's character.

chapter nineteen

Shane stood at the railing overlooking the vast, dark expanse, his mood reflecting the blackness in front of him. He had found Damien and Mia's unused kite string and had felt a pang of irritation at their carelessness. Now they had been missing for hours while Lyric, Cyril, and he had been searching and calling for them in vain.

He turned as the two cats padded up behind him. "It's not your fault," said Lyric soothingly. "You can't hold them back. They've been cooped up for two months, and now that they're free again, they hunger for adventure. If we said they couldn't go, they would probably sneak off anyway when the rest of us are asleep."

"Yeah, I guess you're right," said Shane.

"Mia has always been bold and undaunted," she went on tartly. "But when you get the two of them together, Mia and Damien, they are practically irrepressible."

"We'll keep looking for them, and we are certain to find them eventually – if they don't find their own way back first," Cyril reassured him.

"I know that. But this just comes on top of something else that has been bothering me," said Shane.

"What's that?"

"I have been worrying about the old prophecy on the compartment under the throne. So much of it has held true. Listen, I've memorized it:

> Revenge of mage, by his hand sown:
> the plague will rage, the death drums drone.
> Cease the age, and end the throne,
> as lore by sage and seer has shown.
> Our people cease – that much is known.
>
> Arise, young son of King Shane-Torh,
> from ashes and from tombs of yore,
> reborn the flesh and blood and bone.
> The blight that brought the end – Atone.
> Your hand again your realm restore.
>
> Read this prophecy; learn this lore:
> To find the maps and keys of yore
> the king has stored below the throne:
> The hand that owns the princess' stone,
> strike the blade, cross center score.

"Having seen this city, dead and deserted like a ghost town, I think I can sort of understand the first stanza. Life in Medarya was completely wiped out, the prophecy says by a plague. The last stanza told us where to find the maps and keys to this civilization. It's the middle stanza that troubles me. I am a clone of King Shane-Torh, reborn, in a way, so I think it must be speaking to me: *The blight that brought the end – Atone. Your hand again your realm restore.*

"Then there is that Sumerian riddle on the Rune Rock in our peppermint garden at home. Remember? The original was found in the Medaryan throne room. I can't help but think that it is connected. It, too, mentions an inexperienced king and a plague:

> Thee, neophyte king, awaits my rancor.
> Drink with me my bane of canker.
> Plague, spring forth! For fools can't hold
> The molten rock to burn the gold –
> Though song from yonder ledge be told.
> Lead, firegrasses! Path behold!

"*Thee, neophyte king* – that certainly describes me, doesn't it?" he said wryly. "So – the epidemic that wiped out Medarya is waiting for me, too, and yet somehow I am supposed to rectify the destruction it caused and restore the kingdom. I don't know how!"

"We will just have to wait and see how the future unfolds," said Cyril.

"But I'm supposed to unfold the future," Shane insisted with urgency.

"Maybe," said Cyril.

"And now Damien and Mia go missing on us and we can't find them. And I'm feeling responsible somehow, of things I have no control over – things I don't know how to deal with. It's all too much."

"Now, remember, King Shane-Torh," said Cyril kindly but very deliberately, "everything does not rest on your shoulders alone. Your parents charged me with the care of you children—"

"And me, too," interjected Lyric.

"—so the burden is ours as well. We will come up with a plan of action together."

Just then they were startled by a high-pitched, metallic screech that echoed up from somewhere down in the darkness, followed by a resounding boom. They watched and wondered at a flicker of light that moved far below. For a while it followed a straight line, then turned once, and then again, snaking in their direction.

"That plan of action can wait," Cyril suddenly spoke up. "I believe we have found our wayward scamps. The first order of business is to go down and get them."

Shane felt a wave of hope, relief, and a something else – he wasn't quite sure what it was, except that he was a bit angry at Mia and Damien for their own good. Cyril must have felt the same way, because as he and Lyric took off and plunged toward the light below she pleaded, "Please don't be too upset with them."

They found the two exhausted children near the bottom of the stairway. Damien had abandoned the heavy cat armor halfway up the avenue. It had been a struggle to carry it even that far, but when he had caught sight of the innumerable steps rising up, up the rock face that loomed ahead of them, and the shining balcony of the

Queen's Gate hundreds of feet overhead, he had given up – but he still clung to the two swords. "Can we go back and get the armor?" he asked with weary hopefulness. Cyril agreed. So while Lyric carried Mia up to their lodgings, Cyril flew back with Damien to retrieve the suit of mail. Thus the two hungry, exhausted and gift-laden explorers were brought home.

After hearing the young explorers' adventures of the day, Lyric and Cyril insisted that they study and memorize the map of the underground city before they ventured off again. Damien and Mia began by trying to trace the path they had followed. Shane meanwhile seemed a bit sour.

"What's the matter, bud?" Damien asked. "It's really not very easy to get lost, you know. There is an evacuation map at the exit of every public building in the city. You can always find the way out."

"Yes, but you didn't know that until after you had gotten yourself lost."

"True enough. But look on the bright side – if we hadn't stumbled onto the armory, we would not have found you a sword."

"Well, I do like the sword," Shane admitted.

While Shane and Damien were still sparring, Cyril came strutting out in his cat armor like a war veteran showing off his medals. He strutted about with an important air, his battle claws clicking smartly on the stone floor.

chapter twenty

One evening about a week later, Shane asked Cyril if he would accompany him to the Tombs of the Kings. They had discovered an alternate route into the Cliff City, a winding stone stair that led to a private gate at the rear of the city. It tunneled through the mountain so there was no risk of detection from outside.

By now they were pretty confident that their presence on Meta had not been detected by the research colony. If any disturbance had been heard the night of their arrival, it had not led to their discovery. They felt their secret was safe as long as they stayed in the dwarf caves during the daytime. They only visited the Cliff City at night after the colony had shut its gates, and then one of the cats always came along in case they met up with any wild animals.

That night Cyril and Shane made their way up the winding stone stairs. When they arrived at the gate Shane took out his stone key and inserted it into the lock. By now they had discovered that the royal keys were masters that opened all the official locks of the city. There was the familiar whir and the stone ground open. They stepped into a long gallery of arches and vaults carved into the polished white stone. They followed the gallery out into the moonlight. It was a clear night above the clouds that blanketed the plateaus below – miles and miles of clouds.

"It's sublime. This is what people think of as heaven." Shane spoke in a hush. "But we're here to find the tombs." Breaking himself away from this vision, Shane followed the map in his mind which led them through several passages to another grand and solemn arched entrance. Once inside, when their eyes had adjusted to the shadowy chamber lit by clerestories high above, they could see the niches – rows and rows of niches, each one housing one or two or several stone coffins. On the lid of each casket was a carved sleeping statue in royal regalia of the person it entombed – the Tombs of the Kings.

Shane walked past the likenesses of the kings and queens, generation after generation of them peacefully reposing there for thousands of years, as he proceeded deeper and deeper into the chamber. He passed hundreds of niches before he came to the very last one. This is what Shane had come to see. There in the dim light were the carved sleeping images of a man and a woman lying on a double sarcophagus. Even in the half-light Shane could tell that the faces were exact likenesses of himself and Mia, only much older. The man looked to be about fifty and the woman – his queen – about forty. Below the figure of the elderly Shane was a Medaryan carving that read *Shane-Torh, King of Medarya*; below the adult Mia was carved *Mia-Ryall of Shane-Torh, Queen of Medarya*.

Shane stared, rapt, at the statues, so lifelike and so lifeless. It was as if he stood outside of time and reality, a stranger, gazing upon his own future and death so long ago – and his sister's, too, who in this surreal world was somehow no longer his sister. He reached out to touch the serene faces, trying to find some reassurance there, but the coldness of the smooth, hard stone struck him with a barren chill, and he wished he hadn't done so.

The prophecy of King Shane-Torh's return drifted across his awareness and he felt the weight of it even more keenly. It was his to create the future, to resurrect the past – a past that was his own, yet of which he had only read and had no recollection. Now he felt even more alien and alone.

"Don't tell Mia about this just yet," Shane said solemnly to Cyril. "I'm not ready for her to know." Silently, the two walked back to join the others.

chapter twenty-one

A good night's sleep seemed to have lightened Shane's spirits a little. "Let's all go exploring together," he suggested. "The maps say the Dwarf City is supposed to have a library. I would like to find it – there will be books there."

Mia rolled her eyes at Damien.

"Sure, mate," said Damien agreeably. The three of them set off to the library, Shane at the lead.

"Umm... how is it exploring if we already know how to get there?" protested Mia. But she still followed them out to the ledge that overlooked the Dwarf City. They started down the steps that Damien and Mia had ascended the evening before Three flights down they reached a landing that led off to the library.

The library was on a level all its own, carved into the rock and extending all the way around the city. From below it would have looked like a ring of uniform columns encircling the city from above. From inside it was like a vaulted gallery that curved away in both directions with an open colonnade on one side overlooking the city below. On the opposite side was a wall into which were set many doors, variously decorated with carvings in the white stone. Shane chose a modest-sized door and pushed at it. It swung open easily enough and the lights flickered on to reveal rows and rows of racks with stacks of ancient writings, rolls and scrolls stowed in slots, and books lined up on shelves.

"They'll just fall apart when you touch them," said Mia.

Shane stood speechless. He was so much like his mother in that this was his vision of a candy store. He walked up to the grandest-looking shelf and stroked an ancient leather book as if it was the most sacred thing he had ever touched. It didn't crumble in his fingers. He gently pulled it off the shelf and set it flat on a nearby table. Then he slowly opened the cover. He read *Rüigis òm Dóllizhᵇa – Chronicles of the Kings.* "I can't believe it," he said under his breath, turning the thick vellum leaves. "This book is still whole. They must have treated the books in the library with the same chemicals they used to embalm the kings." He went to another shelf and saw more titles: *History of Invention, Dwarf Ships through the Ages, The Era of Conquests.* He moved on, scanning the shelves. "We must be in the history section," he remarked as he came back to settle down with the first volume of the *Chronicles of the Kings.*

"I thought we were going to explore," complained Mia.

"I *am* exploring," said Shane, starting to be drawn into his book. He was hopelessly gone, Mia knew.

Damien motioned Mia aside and whispered in her ear. "I have an idea. Let's go bring some armor up here, and then wait until Shane steps out. When he does, we'll set it up like a statue with me inside. Then, after he comes back and gets completely absorbed in his book again, I'll suddenly start moving and walking towards him. We'll scare him out of his wits!"

Mia nodded enthusiastically and the two wandered away, looking as nonchalant as possible. Once out of earshot of Shane, they ran at a breakneck speed down the stairs, along the avenue, and down the boulevard to the armory. Now that they knew the way, it didn't seem nearly as far as it had the week before. Still, it was several hours of exhausting work to carry the armor up piece by piece. They hid it in a small room in the library next to where Shane sat reading. Every time they checked on him, he looked as if he hadn't moved – in fact, he even forgot to eat and they had to pull him away at the end of the day.

All the way back to the Queen's Gate Shane was recounting the things he had learned that day. "The Medaryan kings protected this whole continent and kept it safe. They organized the different societies and maintained peace between the winged people of the Cliff City and the plains, the dwarves who lived under the mountain, and the keepers of the forest. They established law and kept out the goblins."

"There are goblins on Meta?" asked Damien.

"Yes — or at least, that is how we translate the word *érguk*. I don't know what they are exactly. From the way they are described, we don't have anything like them on Earth. But they're supposed to be pretty beastly."

They were back at the Queen's Gate by now and Lyric joined in the conversation. "The goblins are mentioned quite a bit in the lore, your mother says. They are described as a constant problem, always pushing at the borders and always having to be driven back. I imagine when the winged people died out they probably overran the forest."

"Yeah?" said Damien. "That would explain why it's such a dangerous place. You do realize we're going to have to go out in the forest to hunt pretty soon. We can't live on shuttle supplies and fried lichen forever."

"Yes, and we don't want to wait until the supplies actually run out," she agreed.

"I'll organize a hunting party," offered Damien.

"Do you know how to hunt?" asked Cyril.

"Oh, yeah. I'm pretty good at it. My dad has taken me hunting and fishing in Alaska for moose and duck and salmon. We also went on a safari in Africa once. Dad has trophies all over the walls of the den and his library. Step-mom hates them, but I think they are pretty cool. We've done all kinds of fishing, too, and I know how to clean a fish and skin a deer. Dad usually tries to only get animals we can eat, though. He says it is wrong to kill an animal just to kill it, but it's okay if it's self-defense or if you're hunting for food."

"Cats hunt for food," said Lyric quietly. "We are made

for hunting."

Cyril weighed the matter. "We will have to hunt during the daytime, and that is risky. If anyone happens to see us, a human boy will attract more attention than two winged cats. Still, as long as we remain under the cover of the forest, there is little risk of being seen. It's settled, then. Damien, Lyric and I will do the hunting. We must stay in the woods, and must always go out in a group, never alone, for safety's sake."

"I want to hunt, too!" piped in Mia. Lyric looked at her sternly but said nothing, and the group set themselves to preparing another meal of lichen and freeze-dried food.

chapτεκ τωεΝτγ-τωο

Shortly after Jerrod and Serena's shuttle left for Meta, the Government moved to reopen their case.

No fault had been found with the Center for Metan Research's detailed inventory and exhaustive report of their research, so they were off the hook. But new evidence was purportedly discovered near the street in front of the Rockwell's estate – long white hairs and large paw prints that they claimed had been clumsily erased, so the Court granted a reopening of the investigation. The CIA was startled when the Rockwells could not be served with a summons because, it was explained, they had left the planet for the research project on Meta. The Government decided to try them *in absentia*.

One forensic expert for the defense insisted that the hairs and paw prints found near the residence were really only those of a Samoyed husky owned by the neighbors down the street. The Government lawyers quickly attacked the man's credibility and succeeded in having his testimony thrown out.

The Secretary of Defense, Dominic Dumsford, had taken a personal interest in this case. Although the alleged evidence, found only outside the house, was circumstantial at best and did not prove that any cat had ever belonged to the Rockwells, the Secretary was livid that he could not bring the Rockwells in for questioning because the CMR had sent them out of reach.

This fact may have had some influence on the subsequent announcement that the Secretary of Defense himself would be taking a trip to Meta. It was well known, of course, that other countries were expressing interest in the establishment of a presence in the new world, and the Government was to host some wealthy foreign guests with political influence on Meta. Why exactly this job fell to the Secretary of Defense was less clear. When questioned about this by reporters, Dumsford responded, "The planet of Meta is of utmost strategic importance not only to our country, but to all civilized nations that value democracy and liberty. If the resources of Meta were to fall into the wrong hands, it could pose a serious threat to the entire free world, not to mention the spread of democracy through the solar system. It is in our nation's self-interest to make sure that Meta remains neutral."

The Secretary's trip was to take much less time in transit, so he would be arriving only days behind the Rockwells even though he had left weeks after them. He intended to deal with the situation personally and with finality – for he had already adjudged their guilt in his own mind and was bent on proving it.

chapter twenty-three

The morning after Damien and Mia had hidden the armor in Shane's library, they woke up early and mumbled an excuse to others that contained the word "exploring", then sneaked off to the hidden armor. They dragged it out to an alcove near Shane's reading table – the recess had a statue of a scholarly looking dwarf cast in some type of metal. Together Damien and Mia pulled the statue out of its niche and hid it. Then carefully they put the coat of plated mail on Damien, and he tucked himself into the nook. The job done, Mia flew up to the top of the nearby book stacks to hide, and they waited for their victim. They had guessed right. They didn't have to wait long before Shane showed up, selected the same book as yesterday, and settled down at his comfortable reading table.

Soon Shane was so engrossed in the *Chronicles of the Kings* that he didn't even see the suit of armor take a step toward him. He didn't look up when the armor tried to take another step but the plates, stiff from so many years of disuse, locked up and it froze, one foot in mid-air. He didn't hear Mia start to giggle high above him on the book stacks, nor did he notice even when the suit of armor started to wobble dangerously on one foot. He did look up when it crashed to the floor.

"Ow!" it said, wiggling around trying to get up. "Mia! Help!"

"Damien, what are you doing lying on the floor inside that suit of armor?" asked Shane, unruffled. Just then the armor flopped over on its stomach and crashed into the book stacks that Mia was peering over. Losing her balance, she and the contents of the shelf came crashing down in a heap of feathers and books on top of Damien. Thankfully he had the armor on.

Shane put his hand on his head and closed his eyes. "You guys are not taking our situation seriously," he chided, "and the books you dumped over – those are priceless!"

"We were just playing," whimpered the suit of armor. "It was for feeding me to the sharks at the feeding rock."

"Things have changed now," said Shane. "We have to survive."

"It's *you* who have changed!" accused Mia. "We have a perfect adventure and you're ruining it!"

Shane reflected back. It was true; they hadn't done anything he wouldn't have done a few months ago. But things *had* changed, and he was having to change with them.

"Look, Mia, there's more to adventure than play. This

is real, and the consequences of what we do or don't do are real. I've been reading the *Chronicles of the Kings*. They believed that the state of the whole country depended on what type of leader the King of Medarya was. If he was wise and virtuous, the whole country prospered, but if he was corrupt and unscrupulous, it suffered.

"Furthermore, they took the prophecy that the last king left to us very seriously. They believed their society would end by a plague – and it did. But that's not all. They also believed that it would be restored – which is why we have been given the keys to the Cliff City and the Dwarf City. The last king gave us the maps and the keys for this very reason. Remember what he said? *If you, my child, find my writing and hold the key, then understand. May the prophecy guide you to bring back our kingdom.* I want the realm restored, and by my hand it will be – if it is within my power!

"But there is another threat at hand: I believe the plague that destroyed the Kingdom of Medarya is also to return for us. We have an enemy, a very dangerous enemy, who killed our ancestors and is coming back to kill us. I am trying to learn all I can to prevent that."

"I'll be by your side fighting anyone we must fight!" cried Damien. He had finally struggled out of the armor. "After we put the bookshelf back together, I'll go find Cyril and Lyric, and we'll go hunting and scouting out the lay of the land. We'll be in before dark."

"Me too!" said Mia.

"No, Mia!" Shane barked out sharply. "This is a job for the cats and Damien, not for a little girl like you. It's too dangerous!"

"That's ridiculous!" Mia shouted back. She stamped her foot and flew off in a huff.

2. The Enchanted Forest

chapter twenty-four

Mia took the long way back and crept past Cyril and Lyric. She sneaked into the Shuttle to retrieve her crossbow and some fishing line. She put on her strongest pair of leather boots and tucked her stone key-knife into the right one, then put on a cloak.

Mia checked on Moogkey who had taken a fall the day before and suffered a scratch. Mia had set up a little hospital in the shuttle. She had wrapped Moogkey in gauze and Band-Aids like a little mummy and laid him in a small puffy bed. The sucker anemone was mortified and tried repeatedly to get up, but when he found he couldn't move, after a while he gave up struggling and accepted his fate. "I'll be right back and then we can change your bandages," she whispered and quietly tiptoed out the door.

Lyric and Cyril were deep enough into the caverns that they didn't hear the stone door slide open and shut again. Mia faced a web of net roots hanging over the doorway, too dense to cut through easily. She found, however, that by pushing outward she could make a space enough to move sideways along the cliff. She quickly reached the end of this heavy curtain of net roots and slipped out from behind it into the bright sunlight.

The forest was exquisite in the daytime. It had lost all its eeriness of the first night, and what remained was sheer delight. There were great trees draped with sage mosses, their huge limbs arched overhead, providing a canopy of heart-shaped leaves. Purple ivies, exotic flowers and tiny herbs and grasses carpeted the forest floor. Ahead of Mia, beams of sunlight shone dreamily through breaks in the trees, revealing pathways between clumps of herbs and underbrush, beckoning her onto the spongy carpet and into the forest. The air was fresh and alive; a light breeze rustled the leaves and flowers, whispering to her to follow. A small spotted deer-like creature with long spiraling horns darted into the underbrush when it saw Mia. Mia recognized a number of plants from their estate: the gnarl vines which she knew how to avoid, the blood suckers and net roots, the cooker plant and the frostmints and the globbybulbs. There were giant yellow and pink and orange flowers as large as she was. There was a clump of snapdragons whose tentacles could sense a heart beat, for they reached in her direction with loud clacks as she passed. Mia giggled and dodged one, which gulped a few glowbugs instead. She swallowed some raw slugfruit that squirmed on the way down and thought about what everybody else holed up in the caves was missing.

A bright blue fuzzy creature about the size and shape of a tennis ball bounced out of the underbrush and nearly smacked into Mia, then skidded away between parting vines. Mia followed it for a little while. She sang and skipped and took to flight. Way, way, up she flew, as she had never been allowed to fly before, through the crystalline air and shimmering light bouncing off the clouds. She could see the mountains surrounding the forest and the seven large terraces that skirted the cliff city. And then the plain where the colony sat – a complex of rectangular wooden buildings surrounded by a defensive log palisade, it looked like nothing more than a military outpost from the pioneer days of the American West, entirely out of place in this strange and wondrous new world.

Mia looked back at the forest. Further in she caught the shimmer of a large pond. She dove down until she was hovering above it. Flying was wonderful when you had all the space in the world. She had never realized what she was missing and now knew she could never go back to the little world of their estate where all her childhood she had been hidden, flitting outside beneath its trellises or inside the enclosed aviary, or caged up in her own room with just her little perch to fly to.

Mia sat down on a flat warm rock that jutted out into the clear water. Silvery fish were darting around the lily pad stalks and hiding in the shadows. They were shaped like saucer sized sand dollars with bulgy pinkish eyes. Mia remembered that she was there to hunt and thought it would be a grand scheme to bring back a dozen small fish for dinner. She would have them all prepared and cooked before the others even returned from their hunting. Then they'd be sorry they told her she couldn't go hunting with them!

Mia selected a dart from her quiver and carefully tied it to a stretch of fishing line with the fisherman's knot that Damien had taught her. Then she tied the other end of the line to a branch that bowed overhead. Carefully she set the dart in the crossbow and sat as still as possible. When she had got her aim at a slow-moving fish, she pulled the trigger. The arrow whizzed into the water and struck harmlessly a few inches beyond the startled fish, which disappeared in a flash. Mia tried again and again without success, until it dawned on her that for some reason she needed to aim to the near side of the fish if she wanted to hit it. She had never heard of *refraction*, and she did not know that light waves bend as they pass from air into water, making objects in the water appear to be where they are not; but once she learned to adjust for it, she started to catch some fish.

Another thing Mia did not know was that there were eyes watching her as attentively as she was watching the fish.

chapter twenty-five

Back at the caves, Shane and Damien were trudging back to the shuttle deep in conversation about a creature called Gwar. Gwar was mentioned in the writings of the dwarves – an ancient, crafty, and dark enemy, a beast of some kind. He had been the companion of a wicked sorcerer.

"Do you think Gwar could have something to do with the danger that awaits you?" asked Damien.

"I'm not sure. How could he possibly still be alive? Can anything live that long? Of course, the net roots did. After so many years, they still sealed off the Dwarf City."

"If it *is* possible that this Gwar is still alive, then I should hunt him before he hunts us," said Damien darkly.

"Indeed," agreed Shane as they returned to the queen's cave. They came upon Lyric and Cyril snoozing in front of the shuttle.

"Is Mia with you?" Lyric asked Shane.

"Well, she was, but she got into a huff and came back

here. Isn't she with you?"

Damien ran to Mia's cave and then to the shuttle and looked inside. "Moogkey's still here, but she's not," he called out.

"When did she leave you?" asked Lyric.

"Earlier this morning," answered Shane miserably. "I think we had better search for her."

"Could she have gone back to the armory?" suggested Damien. "Or worse – hunting in the forest? She wouldn't have done that, would she?"

"I'm afraid she might," said Shane, a pit forming in his stomach. He should never have snapped at her and forbidden her to go. To Mia, that would have been a challenge. Why had he been so careless? "In fact, I'll bet that's exactly what she did do."

"Lyric and I will search for her outside," said Cyril. "We need you two to stay and wait for her here in case she turns up."

"I'd like to help look for her, too, if I may. An extra set of eyes wouldn't hurt. Can I come with you, Cyril?" asked Damien.

Cyril considered. "You were going to come hunting with us anyway. If Shane is willing to stay here by himself, then you can come, Damien."

"I'll stay and hold the fort," said Shane.

The other three left quickly. It was evident where Mia had slipped behind the net roots. They followed to where she had stepped out into the open. After the large cats had squeezed their way through, there was a good-sized tunnel between the net roots and the rock wall. Now any of them would easily be able to go in and out of the Queen's Gate through this passage. Yet from the outside the opening was almost invisible. Even a close inspection would have revealed only a dark hole that resembled nothing more than the opening to some large animal's lair.

Outside Damien studied the ground. "Look, her tracks!" He pointed to a trail of footprints that led into the forest. They followed it for a few minutes until the tracks abruptly vanished in a small clearing. "She definitely stopped here."

"Yes," said Cyril. "Her scent disappears."

Damien looked up to the opening in the trees above their heads. "At this point, I think she started to fly." He climbed onto Cyril and the three took off into the late afternoon sky.

chapter twenty-six

Mia was so engrossed in her fishing that she was completely unaware of all the eyes watching her. The sun hung low on the horizon dancing with orange flames on the mirror of the lake. Mia was humming to herself as she collected up her string of fish. "They'll make a fine dinner," she said to herself. "I should also pick some slug fruit."

"Hello, little human," said a very polite voice with a strange toothy accent.

Mia was so startled that she almost fell into the pond with the fish. There a few feet away stood a very pale – in some spots bluish grey – dark-haired, shriveled little man. *He's awfully hairy*, thought Mia, *and he has bat-like wings. Yuck!* But still, Mia was used to human-speaking animal-like things. "Hello," she said. "How is it that you speak English?"

"I learnt eet from my last meal... er, I mean... male... er, I mean... man, yes, d'he last *man* I met. You know, d'he sv^weet people in d'hat nice leettle colony at d'he edge of d'he v^wood?"

"But, I was told that no person who ever came into the woods ever left alive," protested Mia.

"Oh, ees d'hat so?" said the creature. "Such a pity. I v^wonder v^what happened to d'hem? Perhaps d'hat ees v^why I meet so few humans d'hese days, now I have grown so fond of d'hem. I v^would be most gratified to have you over to my humble cave for a bite... er, of tea and cake, you know."

Mia didn't want to be rude, and she was curious about this courteous, ugly little man, so she decided she should accept. She just wouldn't stay too long. When he grinned at her she saw some very pointed teeth and she wondered what he needed pointed teeth for. She also noticed that he hobbled awkwardly on his short haunched legs.

"Shall v^we fly?" he asked. "V^walking ees so hard on my feeble old bones."

"Sure," said Mia agreeably. "Is it far?"

"Oh, no, eet ees just on d'he od'her side of d'he hill."

The two were about to launch themselves into flight when a dark shadow suddenly spread over them. Mia felt it touch her head and arms – it was scratchy and stiff and left welts where it hit her. Then she realized it wasn't a shadow at all but a net of rough twined rope which tightened cruelly around her. Through the netting Mia could see her captors: wrinkled and fanged creatures with bald heads and long gnarled fingers. They had pointy ears and piggish noses and were chattering and snorting at each other.

"Goblins," said the very polite man as two of the hideous creatures pinned them to the ground, sitting on them to keep them from moving while the others gleefully produced two long, sturdy poles. "D'hat ees how d'hey carry d'heir prey – how do you call eet, pig-tied?"

"Hog-tied," corrected Mia wretchedly.

"Ah, yes, of course. But *pig* and *hog* – d'hey are d'he same animal, no?"

Mia didn't bother answering. What did that matter? She watched as the gloating goblins snickered and snarled at each other.

"You see how pleased d'hey are? Eet has been a lucky catch for d'hem – you and me, and a string of fish. D'hey are very bad at fishing."

With snarls and cackles the goblins organized for their march, punching and pushing into place. Mia was heaved into the air as two goblins picked up her pole, one on each end, and hoisted it onto their shoulders. She dangled a foot above the ground. Then they began to march, and the goblins' foul voices settled into a rhythmic grunting – barbaric and almost musical – in time with their oafish footfalls.

Next to her, suspended between two other goblins, the little man swung politely. "Eet ees all the v^worse for you, you know. I v^was only going to drink your blood. Now you v^will be roasted."

The meaning of his words sunk in. "Drink my blood?" she asked, astonished. "You mean you were going to kill me?"

"Oh, but it v^would have been painless," said the little man airily. "I v^would have anesthetized you first. V^we v^would have had plenty of time to talk, as you v^would have lasted for several meals. And my English v^would have been much improved by d^the end."

She stared at him incredulously. As he hung there upside-down, tied to the pole by his claws and feet, Mia realized now that he looked more like a bat then a man.

"You're a vampire!" she blurted.

"*Vampire?* Ah, yes, of course. D^that ees v^what d^the od^thers called me."

Mia felt sick. She had never heard anything so horrible in her life. Hanging there upside-down tied hand and foot to a pole, jouncing as she was carried along, she had time to reflect. The ropes cut into her wrists with each bump. Her captors were ugly and vicious brutes, squabbling among themselves. She could see greed and hunger in their eyes. Every once in a while one would come so close to her she could see it drooling and smell its putrid breath, until it got clubbed away by another goblin who seemed to have the job of guarding the catch.

For the first time in Mia's life, she felt fear – real fear. It pierced through her bones and heart and made her tremble. Shane's serious face flashed into her mind, followed by Lyric's, kind and full of concern. Along with them came a pang of something else that was new – regret. Now she understood why they hadn't left the safety of the caves. Shane and Lyric were not being spoilsports as she had thought. They were just trying to protect her. Oh, why hadn't she listened? She had stamped her foot like a spoiled child and run off in a huff. And now she would never see them again.

Maybe Shane and Damien and Lyric and Cyril were out searching for her right now. But it was too late. They would find her crossbow by the lake. They would find her tracks – and the vampire's, and the goblins'. They would try to follow her and rescue her – and then maybe the goblins would get them, too. And it would be all her fault. Tears streamed down her face and she shuddered at the thought of their all being roasted.

Mia was jolted from her horror by a terrible screeching roar. Before anyone knew what had happened, an enormous beast swooped from the air and snatched Mia. Its massive tail smote in the middle of the goblin pack, sending a dozen of their lifeless bodies flying, and the rest scurried into the bushes with hideous howls. Mia felt herself lifted into the sky to the beating of mighty wings, but all she could see were the horrible hand-like claws that held her in their clammy purple grasp, and the scaly underbelly of the beast, glinting and cold. On they flew with the large, gold-red sun hanging low in the sky behind them, threatening soon to drop from sight. Mia shook all over from fear and chill.

Then out of the corner of her eye, she saw a flash of silver and white speeding up towards her. *Lyric!* The big cat swept in from the left and agilely swiped at the beast with her claws. Then she dropped back for an instant, and darted in from the right. By her third strike, Mia's captor was ready. Still holding Mia with one claw he lashed out with the other as Lyric passed, opening a deep gash in her shoulder and flank. Lyric screeched in pain and faltered, but recovered quickly and lunged in for another attack. Like a shot, the whip-like tip of the purple tail struck Lyric, swatting her effortlessly from the sky.

Lyric went tumbling to the ground. Mia cried after her. The limp body plunged into the thick forest below and disappeared; it was the last Mia saw of Lyric before she passed out.

chapter twenty-seven

Cyril and Lyric had decided to split up to look for Mia. Damien went with Cyril. Thus it was that he and Cyril witnessed it all from a distance. They saw the huge dragon plunge into the forest and rise again, clutching something in its front claws. They watched Lyric attack, and knew what the monster held. They saw her tumble to the ground. Then the massive purple-and-black beast flew over them and away to the southeast, Mia dangling limp in its claws.

"Cyril?" It was Damien who spoke first. "I think we should split up. I'll go after Mia and you go after Lyric."

"I can't let you face that monster alone," said Cyril.

"I will be all right. But not Lyric. If she is still alive, she will be eaten unless she is protected. See to her first, and then you can join me. I'll climb the mountain to where the dragon landed. See? He is still visible on the ledge there. With your wings, you won't be far behind me."

Cyril still hesitated. The choice seemed impossible.

"Cyril, we must hurry!" said Damien with urgency. "Don't worry about me – I'll be fine. See you at the dragon's lair," he called over his shoulder as he dashed off.

Cyril knew it would be useless to try to stop Damien now. Shaking off his indecision, he whirled around and leapt into the air, taking wing toward the blood-red sun suspended over the horizon.

Damien turned his face towards the cliff into which he had seen the dragon disappear. Now he was glad for his cross-country running training. He clenched his jaw and felt the hilt of his sword. With stealth he hadn't known he possessed, he began his run through the forest.

As Damien rushed on, his heart pounding, he could hear the sound of creatures following him out of sight behind the undergrowth. Without slowing his pace, he drew his sword from the sheath and held it at the ready. Then, without any warning, a goblin jumped into the path directly ahead of him, its teeth bared. Before he even had time to think, Damien struck it with his sword, catching the creature in full swing. In a leap he was over the falling body before it even hit the ground, and it lay quivering behind him, the severed head coming to rest a few yards away. No more goblins attacked after that, though he could still hear them tracking him, keeping under cover.

They stayed with him until he reached the edge of the wood where the forest ended and the barren rocks rose up in front of him. Winded as he was, he did not stop to catch his breath, sensing that if he paused even for an instant, the goblins would be on him in a flash, overwhelming him with their numbers. He began to scramble up the rocks, and was relieved to see that he was not followed. No goblins showed themselves even when he was still low enough that they might have caught him. Perhaps they were afraid to leave the cover of the trees, knowing what dwelt in the crags above.

With the last sliver of sun dipping below the horizon, Damien began his treacherous climb to the dragon's lair.

chapter twenty-eight

When Cyril finally found Lyric, she was lying in a twisted heap on the ground. He alit beside her and cautiously sniffed the motionless form. There was still life. He leaned over her face and gently licked her forehead. Lyric stirred.

"You're alive," he said softly. "I was afraid I'd lost you, too… the way I've lost Mia and Damien."

"Mia?" said Lyric weakly.

"The dragon took her. And Damien has gone to fight it, alone. And you have also nearly been killed. I fear I have failed all of you, and I've failed Serena and Jerrod. It was my responsibility to look after the children, and to protect you. I have succeeded in none of this."

"You should leave me and go after Mia and Damien," said Lyric. She tried to struggle to her feet only to collapse again.

"I won't leave you," said Cyril. "But you need to try to walk." Lyric strove to rise again, but could not. The dusk was beginning to close in like a shroud, and Cyril sensed they were being watched hungrily. He could hear soft rustlings in the brush, and the occasional rasp of a ravenous breath; now and again he saw the glint of eyes from the shadows; but most of all it was the unclean stench that wafted on the breeze and assaulted his keen sense of smell. In desperation and despair, Cyril roared out at the unseen eyes peering at them through the underbrush, but it did not seem to frighten them. If anything the eager excitement in the air increased.

Then he heard another sound. It was the sound of marching – or was it a stampede? No, it was definitely marching. The creatures in the shadows heard the sound too, and fled. The rhythmic tramping grew nearer, then quieter and more stealthy until it disappeared. There was a new smell in the air now, not foul but wild and unlike anything Cyril had ever encountered before. Nor could he tell whether it was friendly or not.

"Can you get up, Lyric? We must hide!" he whispered loudly in her ear. But Lyric was still, and Cyril knew that they were already surrounded. Strange man-like creatures emerged on all sides from the wood, and the circle began to close like a noose. In front of Cyril men appeared with a lions' heads; to his right were men with eagles' faces; to his left, the men had faces of oxen; and behind him were more men – who were men, but also lions, and eagles, and oxen. Then he realized they were all the same kind of beast, and all had four faces – none of which looked friendly. They stood around the two cats in a regimental square, and Cyril saw that they were well armed. He stood over Lyric and growled.

Suddenly he heard a soft twang and felt a sharp pain in his right side. He turned with a snarl toward his attacker, but as he did so there was another twang and another pain in his left haunch. With a roar he spun around, only to receive another dart in his left shoulder, and then a fourth one... Now he was becoming confused... there were too many attackers... all around... and their faces were starting to swim. Darkness was closing in – not the darkness of night, but a strange, sickening blackness. The world was spinning... the men and lions and eagles and oxen melding into one... Then the darkness overwhelmed him and Cyril knew no more.

chapter twenty-nine

Mia awoke to find herself still tied up, but the goblins'
pole was now gone. She was half-sitting, with a rope
wrapped around her, pinning her arms to her sides. Her
feet, too, were bound. Looking around she saw that she
was in a huge gaping cave, propped up in a corner against
a wall – else she would not have the strength left to sit. It
was dark outside, and a chill breeze blew in from the
broad opening. There was a long, low hearth on the
opposite side of the cavern that ran the length of the wall.
Whole trees were blazing in the hearth, giving off a
welcome heat. A massive black and purple reptile the size
of a small house lay the length of the hearth, basking in
the fire's warmth.

One of its yellow eyes opened to survey her. *"ʔGir-ʔgắr
utʰa nùw, ù pếtʔyu-màghwi,"* the dragon snorted, blowing a
smoky bluish ring from its nostrils – "You are awake
now, winged child." It spoke in perfect Medaryan with a
deep, dark, gravelly voice that rumbled from its throat

and echoed off the stone walls.

"*Kórum suli^b vòy méy ʔis tu*," whimpered Mia, responding in Medaryan without being conscious of it – "I hurt all over."

"*Mìya-Ryáll kha tsúw* – You are Mia-Ryall," stated the dragon, lifting its great head to look at her directly.

"*Né'm, Mìya wu ni ^bélyi* – No, just Mia," said Mia unhappily.

This odd conversation continued in Medaryan. "You're speech is strange – yet I know your voice. How did you come to be here again after so long?"

Mia didn't know how to answer such a strange question. "Please… I've never been here before. We just arrived a few days ago."

"Yes, I know. I have been watching the Queen's Gate since you and your companions hid there."

"You knew we hid in the dwarf caves?" asked Mia.

"I miss very little that goes on around here. I have been watching, and waiting. You left the cave this morning – by yourself, foolish child. No thought of the goblins and vampires and flesh-eating plants and other predators in this accursed forest. I saw it all. You were nearly a meal for a vampire and then almost roasted by a pack of goblins. If they hadn't gotten you, that cat would have."

The mention of vampires and goblins brought Mia's mind back to the horrible events of the day. At the mention of Lyric, tears welled up in her eyes. "You killed Lyric," she sobbed.

"*Lyric?*" snorted the dragon, as soot-black smoke

issued from his nostrils. "A gentle name for a deadly beast. Was that wretched tiger a pet?"

"She wasn't a pet," wept Mia weakly. "She was… she was like a mother… She was…"

"A dumb brute like all the other dumb brutes around here," interrupted the dragon in a disgusted tone.

"Oh, no," said Mia earnestly. "Lyric was very smart and could speak and has been with me all my life…"

"Interesting," growled the dragon, narrowing his eyes.

"…but now she's dead, trying to save me – and you killed her! Murderer!" Mia shouted with the little strength she had left.

The dragon swung his monstrous head close and scrutinized Mia, an unreadable expression in his eyes.

Mia cringed under his piercing gaze. "Why did you rescue me from the goblins? Are *you* going to eat me now?"

The dragon turned away with a soft snort. "You are Mia-Ryall," he repeated, as if that explained everything.

There was silence for a time after that, while Mia cried softly and shook pitiably and the dragon brooded in his dark reflections. Finally he spoke again. "I have seen no winged people or talking cats in Medarya for five thousand years, since the great plague. Where have you come from?"

"Earth," she replied simply.

The dragon narrowed his eyes again, as if weighing a new thought.

"I, too, am from Earth." His voice was a whispery growl, not quite attaining the gentleness he was apparently trying to affect, and for the first time he spoke in English.

"You can't be from Earth," sniffed Mia, "There are no dragons on Earth, and the dinosaurs died out ages ago."

"So it's true, then. They did succeed in exterminating us." There was a tinge of unmistakable sadness in his voice.

"But there never *have* been real dragons on Earth."

"No? Then they even succeeded in eradicating our memory!" This time there was bitterness like steel. "Still," he muttered shrewdly, after an ominous pause, "there are no winged people or winged cats on Earth, either. Yet now here you are. Perhaps dragons can return, too."

While he was speaking, Mia caught a movement out of the corner of her eye. Damien had pulled himself up onto the cave ledge and now pressed himself against the cave wall by the entrance.

Mia thought to distract the dragon. "How is it that you know English?"

"The tunnels of my lair run deep beneath the human research colony. I've been listening to them for years trying to get news from Earth, to know if there are any of my kind left. Now I know there are not. Vile race that destroyed my ancestors and wiped out my species! I have found out what I wanted to know. Now I shall wipe out the colony in a single breath!"

Mia could see Damien's hand move to his sword, readying for an attack.

"How did you know that I am Mia-Ryall?"

"You are Mia-Ryall – your face and your voice, and

most of all your scent tell me so without any doubt – but you died in the plague thousands of years ago. And yet you live again, and are a child again, and come from Earth, and have no memory from before. A creature of my years sees very little that is new. Yet this is new. So be it – I will explain."

Although he addressed her as he spoke, Mia could not be completely sure he was really speaking to her. He seemed to be musing aloud, talking rather to himself than anyone else. But now he spoke directly to her.

"I knew the former Mia-Ryall when I was a baby and she was a little girl. She was the only one who has ever been kind to me. She used to save her dessert from the king's table and share it with me as the evening set in. I would meet her at the Queen's Gate, for that is where she lived: she was to be the next queen. Every evening we would eat her dessert and she would talk to me and... scratch my nose."

"Were you purple and fuzzy then," asked Mia, "like it says in the sagas?"

"I would like that humiliation forgotten. It took two hundred years for me to lose my baby down, for a dragon ages slowly. The mage who brought me here did not understand that, and he made me ashamed for it. I was always a disappointment to him. He had expected me to grow big quickly so he could ride me and strike fear in the hearts of all who saw, so they would revere him here as he had been revered on Earth. But I was ever a hatchling, never big enough for him to ride, never old enough to breathe fire and consume his enemies." Again the dragon seemed to be talking to himself, as if reliving those bygone days. His voice began to grow in bitterness and rage. "He had saved me from sure destruction on Earth. He was the first to feed me when I hatched. He was like a mother to me. Yet he did not love me. He expected me to grovel before him and serve him like a mindless brute, a tool for his twisted designs. He hated me for being a baby, and treated me worse than a dog – until he died, insane, deformed, a fitting meal for the filthy goblins!" He let out a tremendous roar, and bright red flames exploded from his terrible mouth.

Mia was frightened by his unbound fury, yet she also felt compassion for his torment. In her mind's eye she could see the little animal, cute and purple and fuzzy, cowering in a corner with fear and confusion in its big eyes as the enraged mage cursed and kicked at it in his madness.

"I am very sorry you were treated badly by my people," she said softly. "I would share my dessert with you again, if I had any."

"I know." With a sigh the dragon suddenly grew calm again. "But you misunderstand me. It was not *your* folk who did me wrong. You were a friend. I do not forget that. And the others – they feared me perhaps, and shunned me, but only because I belonged to the mage. How can I blame them for that? He was an Earth man, like all other Earth men – a cowardly race of wanton butchers. *They* are the ones who are guilty. I am Gwartấr Wirtir éts ề, and I will have my revenge!"

Mia did not know what to say to that. She had never

considered herself different from other people. What about Mother and Father? Or Nanny and Joe? Or Damien?

"But now," said the dragon with a cunning voice, "I believe one of your companions has come for a visit. A human, from the smell of him. He has overheard a great deal – I am surprised he did not flee in fright."

Damien had been standing motionless, sizing up the situation. His suspicions were confirmed when the creature said his name – this was Gwar, the ancient dark

enemy written of by the dwarves. Now he stepped forward, his sword drawn. "If Mia was always nice to you, why do you hold her prisoner? I am an Earth man. Release her, and let your quarrel be with me."

The reptile reeled around to face the intruder. If it is possible for a dragon to smile, this one did. "A child? *You* have come to fight *me*?"

"I will vanquish you, or die trying," said Damien fearlessly. He began attacking with the slashes and jabs that he had learnt in fencing class.

The dragon actually seemed amused. Casually he raised a pinky claw to parry and block the blows. "Too regular, too rhythmic. I can see your next move coming a mile away. You need to vary your attack, cut and thrust, pause then lunge in with more speed. Do what I don't expect." He was obviously intending to fluster Damien and wear him out, but Damien responded with greater focus and discipline and with increased viciousness.

"Damien, please don't hurt him!" Mia cried.

Gwar tilted his head to look at Mia. "Little fear of that, I think."

Damien took the opportunity of the dragon's distraction to attack with all his might, stabbing at the dragon's heart. The point did not even penetrate the thick, scaly skin. It merely tickled the beast, and a puff of lavender smoke poured from the black nostrils. "Stop that!" the dragon snorted, easily picking Damien up by the scruff of the neck between a clawed forefinger and thumb and dangling the boy above him for a closer inspection. "You are very brave, little fool. I admire bravery. Perhaps all humans are not cowards?"

Damien knew struggling was useless, so he tried a different tack instead. Something Gwar had said when he first arrived on the ledge came back to mind, and he suddenly had an idea. Looking the dragon in the eye, he said, "King Shane-Torh has returned to restore the kingdom of old. Mia-Ryall has also come back, and so have the talking cats. If it were possible for the king to bring back the dragons, too, would you and your sons agree to serve the king of Medarya with me and my sons? As captain of his army, I would be more honored to have you as an ally than as an enemy."

Gwar's eyes blazed and he roared with indignation, "Me, serve man? My ancient enemy? If you were not a child, I would have reduced you to ashes for such a suggestion!"

Damien was not as frightened as he might have been, however. Gwar's reaction had told him that the disdainful dragon was beginning to take him seriously.

"No, you would not serve man. How could I propose such a thing after all the wrongs you have suffered? But

King Shane-Torh of Medarya is not a man. It is him you would serve, *alongside* men. You would be our equals – you and your sons – with all the honor due your noble species."

Gwar turned to Mia. "Does King Shane-Torh trust this captain of his army?"

"Shane trusts Damien with his life," said Mia with conviction, "and so do I. Please don't hurt him, Gwar."

Without warning the dragon dropped Damien in a heap and turned toward the huge fire, his eyes narrowed to yellow slits glinting in the dancing flames. Here, too, was something new to him – a human of uncommon bravery, who thought of others before himself, who had come to rescue a friend of a different heredity, even if it spelled certain doom for him, and who had offered the hand of friendship – no, even honor – to one who was an ancestral enemy. "A human boy with the heart of the sons of Torh," he rumbled into the flames. "And dragons to live again. How can such things be?"

Damien picked himself up, recovered his sword, then went over to Mia and cut her ropes. She was bleeding from the welts on her wrists and ankles.

Gwar suddenly rounded on Damien again, who instinctively gripped his sword tighter but didn't raise the weapon. "Does King Shane-Torh really have the power to grant me sons?"

Damien decided it was best to be forthright. "Of himself, no. It was others who brought him back, and Mia, and the cats. They will be following after the king. It is they who have the knowledge."

"And they would do as the king bids?"

"I believe they would, if it meant gaining your allegiance."

Gwar's intense gaze bored through Damien, his expression as inscrutable as ever. "I will consider your words," he rumbled after a few moments, and turned back to his consultation with the fire. "In the meantime, there is food in the corner."

Damien brought Mia over to a basin of water and helped her drink. There was some dried meat hanging up and some watercress along with a pile of branches that had berries. Clearly the dragon had prepared to bring Mia here. Damien insisted she eat.

Mia seemed to recover a little. Every time Gwar stirred Damien jumped to his feet and faced the dragon, his sword hand at the ready.

"Settle down," said the dragon. "I will not harm Mia-Ryall, and I will not harm you, either – as long as she wishes it, and there is the promise of sons."

Damien relaxed a little.

Finally the dragon spoke. "Before I give my answer, I have a condition of my own. I must meet your king in person and receive these assurances from his own mouth, not that of his deputy. While no doubt your intentions are true," – Damien was not positive whether he was being sarcastic or not – "a place of honor in the king's court is only his to offer.

"But that can wait until the morning. You two will need your rest, and after so many millennia, what is a few more hours to a dragon?"

chapter thirty

The strange beasts with four faces strapped Lyric and Cyril to separate stretchers. Rearranging their marching formation with the two great cats in the center, they began their retreat through goblin territory.

During the long march back to the creatures' camp, Lyric sank deeper and deeper into delirium as infection set into her wounds. She mumbled and twitched the whole trip through the untamed vegetation. The beasts moved with stealth as if they were traveling through dangerous land. Finally they reached their camp and set the unconscious cats down. The two creatures that carried Cyril untied him from the stretcher and shackled his rear legs to a post near one of the bonfires. After making sure he would be comfortable once the tranquilizers wore off, they joined the other creatures at the next fire who were working over Lyric. Masters of herb-lore, they began to mix ingredients in a cauldron that was set atop the fire. Another beast was preparing a poultice. Yet another one was sterilizing tools. While they worked the creatures talked quietly in their own language – an odd combination of clicks and hisses like the rustling of leaves, accompanied by tones that were reminiscent of wind flutes.

They cleansed Lyric's wounds and anointed them with pungent-smelling salve, they stitched shut the large gash, wrapped her in poultices, and set her broken front leg in a splint, then they forced some dark liquid down her throat. All the while, others soothed her with a mesmerizing tune played on a strange kind of instrument. Her restlessness eventually subsided and she fell into a tranquil sleep.

By early morning, however, her fever had flared up again and she began muttering in her delirium. "Mia… can't save Mia. Dragon… map to Shane…" The four-faced creature who had been set to guard her looked up. He peered more closely at Lyric with his human face and listened attentively. He roused the others and they conferred amongst themselves.

"It is clearly speech. The cat speaks."

"Is that possible?"

"It is told in our legends and folklore."

"But this cat is no folk tale."

"Where did she come from?"

"What is she saying?"

They fell silent so they could hear Lyric's continued mumblings. "Mia… fly…"

"These are words in the language of Garrt. Hooth, Tlispirr, go get Garrt quickly! Maybe he will know what we have here," ordered the one who had been guarding Lyric. Immediately two of the other creatures set off into the woods, and the others set to work re-dressing Lyric's wounds.

"You say the cat talks?" called an enthusiastic voice through the forest half an hour later. "In English? Could it be? Cats made. Cats three. Made to speak. To speak like me!" A man came into view, dancing a little jig and singing. He went up to Cyril and lifted the cat's right eyelid. "Cyril, I presume?" Then with a start and a high-pitched whoop he jumped back. The eye didn't close.

Cyril stirred and opened his other eye. "Jerrod, I have failed you," he said heavily. "Lyric is dying and Mia has been stolen by a dragon..."

"Lyric I know. But Mia? Who's she?" asked the man.

Cyril looked confused. "It's Mia, Jerrod – she was captured."

"Mia Jerrod? Can't say I know her."

"Jerrod..." Cyril repeated tiredly.

"Not Jerrod. Garrit. We must get these things straight you know. Wouldn't do at all if I called you Lyric, now, would it?"

Cyril looked unbelievingly at the Jerrod gone mad.

"Lyric (or Cyril, if you prefer it that way) is well cared for. She is in the keepers' hands of the forest – er, in the forest's keepers' hands – I mean, in the hands of the forest's keepers – that is, the hands of the keepers of the forest. (Never can keep the order straight. It changes on you every time you turn your back.) They are excellent healers."

"Are the keepers of the forest the ones who have killed me?" asked Cyril.

"Oh, but you're quite alive," Garrit pointed out to him. "See? They really *are* marvelous healers."

Cyril's understanding began to unfog. "Could it be? Are you Garrit – Jerrod's twin?" he asked.

"Yes, yes, the one and only one and the same – like two peas in a pod. Gave you to Jerrod when you were but a cub, I did. Named you, too – named you two – both you, and Lyric, too."

Jerrod Rockwell had always been infamous for his zany sense of humor, but it was nothing compared to this. Cyril could always tell when Jerrod was joking even if he kept a straight face, but Garrit appeared to be entirely in earnest. Cyril found himself vaguely uneasy about the man's sanity.

"We all thought you had been executed."

"The report of my death was an exaggeration."

Cyril sighed sadly. "I think we have some catching up to do, then." He began recounting the whole story, about the children and the shuttle and the dwarf caves, and Mia and the dragon and how Lyric had tried to save her.

"Uncle Garrit, I am, am I?" said Garrit. "We'll just have to save Niece Mia. But first, let's ask the keepers of the forest for their opinion. Have you met them yet? I suppose not – introductions are always awkward when one of the parties is asleep." Uncle Garrit called out some words in the strange language of the unusual creatures. He was amazingly good at imitating the clicks and rustling sounds and tune-like wind-tones.

Three of the creatures approached, answering Garrit in the same language. Cyril could see them more clearly in the broad daylight. In addition to the four faces he had noticed the night before – an ox's face, a lion's face, an eagle's face, and a man's face – they had four arms that looked like human arms and four wings that stretched above their heads. Beneath their somber brown robes could be seen four hooves which moved together in pairs as they walked, giving them a giraffe-like gait. If they wanted to change directions, there was no need to turn their bodies – the face on the side now became the forward face, and the hooves paired up the other way.

"Prepare yourself, Cyril, old boy," Uncle Garrit advised confidentially in a loud whisper as the creatures came up. "Four-faced beasts have eyes on the back of their heads. And the face that answers you may not be the one you're looking at. But no need to be concerned – they may be four-faced, but they are not two-faced. A truer and kinder lot you will never find (if a bit on the gloomy side – *I* have been trying to get them to crack a smile for years). I call them seraphim, except without the wheels."

The creatures respectfully pretended not to hear Uncle Garrit, even though his exaggerated undertone was clearly audible as far as the next campfire. They waited gravely in silence until he finished. Then one of them, a tall one that carried itself with authority, stepped forward and graciously bowed, one arm folded across the waist and the other three spread out in a gesture of welcome. He wore a solemn expression on all four faces, and spoke English in an odd-sounding manner, with a soft musical lilt. "Honorable Garrt, I was told that we have guests who are your friends."

"Honorable Tsargahn, hello. I introduce to you Cyril. He is a talking winged cat, like those of long ago. Cyril, this is Tsargahn, chief of the keepers of the forest. He is a four-faced beast."

Tsargahn stepped forward with his lion face and bowed. Then he stepped back.

"And Irdor," introduced Uncle Garrit. "He is also a four-faced beast."

Irdor stepped forward and bowed. Then he stepped back.

"And Raugus. He, too, is a four-faced beast."

Raugus also stepped forward and bowed, but instead of stepping back he bent over Cyril and released his shackles. "Please forgive us. We did not know that you were a talking cat," he apologized.

Tsargahn explained, "Occasionally a winged cat from the Great Plain will wander into the forest by mistake. But we know of talking cats only from our ancient lore. We are most honored to meet a living one, and apologize most profoundly for your ill-treatment."

"I'm very pleased to meet you, too," said Cyril, bowing to the three of them, "for I have never met four-faced creatures before. You have treated me most humanely, under the circumstances. But I should like to ask your advice concerning these circumstances under which we have met."

"Of course. We will offer what wisdom we may."

Cyril explained again about Mia, the dragon, Lyric,

and Damien. Tsargahn and the other two seraphim listened thoughtfully.

"Your story clears one mystery. Our lookout witnessed the fight in the sky and reported what none of us could easily believe: that the dragon had carried away a winged child. The watchman himself doubted his own eagle eyes. It was also extraordinary to us that a winged cat would attack the dragon. They roam the plains but rarely venture into the forest, and it is unthinkable that one would attack the dragon unprovoked. We organized a march immediately to find where the cat fell. What we found now raises more questions than it answers – but perhaps these questions must wait for another time. What is the advice that you wish to ask of us?"

"We must attempt to rescue Mia – and Damien, too, for he cannot have succeeded in rescuing her alone. I do not ask you to help fight the battle with us, but I wish to learn what you can tell us about this reptile and how he might be defeated."

"I feared this is what you would ask. And I fear you will not find our counsel very useful or comforting. This creature called Gwar is very ancient – his beginnings are unknown to us – and he is very intelligent and crafty. He dwells in the mountains and roams the forest unchallenged, for all fear him and none can withstand him. He is a great meat-eater, although we have no knowledge of his ever having eaten one of our kind. We have always avoided encountering him, and he has always left us alone. How to confront him – much less defeat him – we cannot say."

"We must try, at least. There is no other choice. Before we go, may I see Lyric?"

"Of course," said Tsargahn, leading the way to the bonfire where Lyric lay. She was surrounded by several of the four-faced creatures who were playing a haunting melody on instruments that looked remarkably like bagpipes.

"They are talking to the herbs with their music," whispered Garrit, "telling them to release their medicines." Lyric didn't stir now but slept peacefully.

"She will not wake for many more hours. But our doctors believe she will recover completely," offered Tsargahn.

"Thank you," said Cyril. "I know she is in good hands. We must, then, put our minds to rescuing Mia."

"Time to face the dragon," said Uncle Garrit. "Beard the dragon in his den. Take the dragon by the horns. A crafty dragon deserves a crafty foe. Ready my steed!"

Uncle Garrit put two fingers in his mouth and blew a piercing whistle, then scrambled up to the crest of the hillock that was the backdrop of the seraphim camp. There, leaning precariously out over the cliff edge stretched a lone tall tree on which hung a strange contraption. No sooner had Uncle Garrit unhitched the dangling contraption than Cyril heard a humming coming towards him from behind. Instinctively he ducked, just in time to be missed by a large green flying thing. It was shaped like a jelly bean with two drooping ends, though in consistency it was more like a jellyfish. It was mostly air inside. Its two giant oval eyes were too big for its face.

It actually resembled the small creatures in Jerrod's laboratory that were riding the air currents of the heating and cooling vents and feasting on dust motes, except that this one was huge and had a green fringe of feathery hair along his underside.

This curious flying animal wobbled its way to Uncle Garrit who had climbed out onto the tree limb. "Here, Shimmer, old boy," Garrit called, holding out what looked like a harness to the huge jelly thing which seemed to float on the air the way a jellyfish floats on the water. Uncle Garrit managed to cinch the saddle-like contraption onto the hovering Shimmer, then he swung himself into the harness. He hung below the creature as if he were dangling from a hang glider.

"Hi-ho, Shimmer, away!" yelled Uncle Garrit. "Mush!"

Cyril took off after the wobbling and bobbing jelly glider, shaking his head.

3. The Riddle

chapter thirty-one

Shane was alone in the dwarf cave holding vigil with several volumes of the *Chronicles of the Kings*. He hadn't slept the night before and, exhausted from searching the caverns for Mia, he had decided to keep himself awake by reading, so he had brought up from the library a few tomes of the ancient set of books.

Shane's head snapped up when he heard the stone of the gate grating open. Mia burst in and flung herself around Shane's neck. She sobbed, "Oh, Shane, I'm so sorry. I'm so sorry to have caused so much trouble. I'll never do it again. Because of me Lyric is dead. Where is Cyril? Hasn't he come back yet? Oh, dear. And Moogkey – is Moogkey okay?" She ran off to find her neglected pet.

While Shane was trying to sort through this torrent of words, he saw Damien enter, walking confidently and followed by a huge purple and black head – Gwar's head and flexible neck were able to fit through the net root tunnel, but that was all.

"Your Majesty, the dreadful and peerless dragon, Gwartár son of Wirtár, requests an audience with the king," he proclaimed in a loud and what he hoped was official-sounding voice. He had been working out an appropriate introduction for Gwar since he awoke that morning.

Shane was rather taken aback by the sudden appearance of the huge beast and Damien's announcement. He did not feel very kingly at the moment, and supposed he did not look it either, dressed in his normal Earth clothes and with no crown. Nevertheless he opened his arms toward the large animal in the manner that he had read about in the Medaryan chronicles and said, "Welcome, Gwartár son of Wirtár."

Gwar dipped his head and replied, "Greetings, your majesty, King Shane-Torh." Then regarding Shane with keen eyes, he remarked dryly, "It is indeed King Shane-Torh I see, though he seems to have misplaced his wings."

"Do you know me, then, dragon?" asked Shane, not to be put off by Gwar's disparaging comment.

"I knew you when you were a child, thousands of years ago," said the dragon. "You are still but a child."

The dragon seemed to be trying to nettle him, to bruise his pride and make him angry. Shane refused to take the bait. Instead he replied with grace and poise, as befits a wise king. "Then you are very old indeed. I am honored by your introduction. Do you come as a friend, or as a foe – or simply out of curiosity?"

"I am neither friend nor foe, yet. Where my allegiance

will lie in the end, remains to be seen. And my curiosity could be satisfied by watching from afar. No. I have requested an audience with the king to discuss in person the bargain offered by your delegate, the commander of your army."

This was news to Shane, but he showed no surprise. "Of course," he replied. "I see you are shrewd." He turned to Damien. "Damien, please brief me on the exact details of our offer."

Damien summarized the discussion he and Gwar had had in the cave.

"Do you find these terms unreasonable – allegiance in exchange for a place of honor in my court and the return of your species?" Shane asked Gwar.

"The terms are not unreasonable." Gwar's yellow eyes were cold and calculating. "But I do not trust men. And perhaps even winged people may prove unreliable."

Shane again felt that Gwar was testing him. He decided that two could play that game. If Gwar was a danger, he wanted to find out. He answered carefully. "This is true. Trust must be earned; and once lost, it is very difficult to regain. Yet I have seen that not all men are evil, just as not all winged people are reliable. Dragons do not have the best reputation on Earth, either. So you see, I, too, must be prudent before striking a deal with you. Tell me, Gwar, where do you come from and how did you come to Meta?"

A glint came into Gwar's eyes, as if he was satisfied with Shane's answers. "You also speak as Shane-Torh," he remarked. "He was a good king and did not deserve the evil that befell him and his son and their people. I will explain."

By now Mia had returned with Moogkey sparking happily on her head. They all settled down to hear the dragon's tale.

"Dragons are not native to Meta. We are from Earth. It is said that once a dragon gets the taste of man, he desires no other kind of meat, but becomes a man eater. Few dragons ever actually ate humans, but for the handful that did, men vowed the extermination of all, and slew the dragons big and small. My father was Wirtár, the Protector, a chief among dragons. Although he had never harmed a man, he was the first to be slaughtered, by a leader of men called Índara."

"Gwar!" exclaimed Shane, with sudden understanding. "Pardon me for interrupting, but I have heard of your father. He was Vritra, the dragon slain by Indra."

"How do you know of him?"

"It is told in the Vedic hymns of Earth's antiquity," answered Shane, "in the hymn to Indra:

Áhann áhim párvate śiśriyāṇám
Tváṣṭāsmāi vájram svaryàm tatakṣa
á sāyakam Maghávāḍatta vájram
áhann enam prathamajám áhīnām
áhan Vṛtrám vṛtratáram vyàṅsam
Índro vájreṇa mahatā́ vaḍhéna

He slew the serpent lying on the mountain;
  the Craftsman fashioned his roaring weapon
    for him.

The Generous one took his missile, his weapon,
    he slew him, the firstborn of serpents.
Indra slew Vritra, the greater hindrance, the
    broad-shouldered,
    with his great and deadly weapon."

"No doubt he was thought a great hero for this murderous deed," said Gwar.

"Actually... he was made into a god," said Shane.

The smoke that poured from Gwar's nose was thick and black. "Why am I not surprised?" he growled.

"I am sorry to be the bearer of such news," said Shane. "But please, continue your story."

Gwar resumed his account with a bitter scowl. "Thus all of my kind were mercilessly annihilated, and their killers were proclaimed great heroes and gods. My mother was one of the last to die. She tried to hide her eggs from destruction, but while she was away concealing the first one, her nest was discovered and the others smashed. When she returned, she too was killed. I was the one egg she managed to hide.

"It was my fortune to be found by a young man who did not wish to destroy me, but hid me and watched over me until my day of hatching. He was a mage, a mystic priest who served in the White Temple of Uruk in the land of Sumer.

"In those days some winged people from Medarya had traveled in a ship to Earth, and they ruled men and were honored as gods at the White Temple. The mage who found me served them. He was a very gifted priest, trained in the sciences of nature and astronomy. Because people did not understand his science, they called him a magician and sorcerer, a great and wise man. They feared him and he became very powerful.

"There was a terrible disaster that befell the Earth in those days. The climate shifted and warmed and the glaciers melted. The wells of the earth burst forth and the rain in heaven fell and the waters rose. All of the land and its peoples and animals were drowned in a deluge, as the ancient civilization of Earth sank into the sea.

"When the waters began to rise, the winged people who dwelt at the White Temple escaped in their sky ship. The mage, with me still in my egg, stowed away secretly on their ship, and thus he escaped from Earth and came to Meta.

"That is how I came to be here. I hatched in the days of King Darael-Torh, when Mia-Ryall and Prince Shane-Torh were children. I was raised by the mage. He was my teacher and guide. From him I learned the history of Earth and of my kind, who my parents were and how they died. I have never seen Earth myself. But I have long harbored a hatred for Earth's men, who brought about the extinction of my race and banished me to live alone for five thousand years, an outcast with no hope of there ever being another one of my kind."

"But surely this mage was a different sort. After all, he saved you from death and took care of you. He must have been a good man." Shane did not really think so, but he did want to see if the dragon thought so.

"So I believed at first. I thought the mage had rescued me out of mercy and kindness, and that he was different from other humans. But I was young and naïve. All he desired was power. He had saved me, as I later found, only because he thought he could gain for himself a greater standing in the sight of others, if he could control and ride a great and dangerous beast. When I did not grow fast enough to be useful to him, he began to mistreat me and kick me around. I began to think that he kept me around only to provide a vent for his anger. What I suffered, however, was nothing compared to the others. In the end the outrage he committed was as great as that of all his kinsmen together, if not greater.

"He had devoted himself to learning about this world. He was fascinated by his new environment and strove to master the forest and the wind and the fire at the center of Meta, to become great and respected here as he had been on Earth.

"The one thing that distracted him was the princess, Mia-Ryall, with whom he fell in love (if such a man can truly be said to be capable of loving anyone but himself). He sought her for a wife. He was denied, of course, for Mia was destined to be queen. The mage returned to his sciences of sorcery in bitterness. It was a bitterness that grew and warped him. It began to eat away at his flesh, rotting his ears and his nose and his fingers.

"When young Shane-Torh became king and Mia-Ryall became queen, the mage went mad. Instead of being revered as he felt he deserved, he was shunned. He became a disfigured and terrifying outcast, and I was cast out with him. He blamed the royal family for his troubles, and began to plot revenge on them. Shane-Torh and Mia-

Ryall both died, suddenly, before they grew old. I do not know what killed them, nor whether the mage had anything to do with it. But he saw their son become king – the son he thought should have been his, and his hatred swelled to encompass all of Medarya.

"Over the decades the mage became obsessed with finding a way to control the bitterness that was eating away his flesh. He changed it by breeding it in dead flesh and by adding various substances. He learned how to slow down its progress, though he could never stop it completely, and he learned how to make it advance faster. For his experiments he caught and caged talking cats on whom to test his poisons. He would take the carnage to an underground volcano and offer it as a sacrifice to his god of fire, to which he prayed for power. He was very confused, deranged.

"The mage had read a Medaryan prophecy which predicted that the civilization would end. He formed the idea that he was the one destined to fulfill the prophecy to cause the peoples of Medarya to cease. He set himself to find a way to make it happen. He worked at it until he had bred a variety of his disease that killed the cats within days of contact and would spread from cat to cat.

"Finally, the mage unleashed the disease that he had cultivated on the Cliff City… They all died – both the cats and the people. He laughed at how he had fulfilled their own prophecy of the great death."

"That is horrible," said Shane. "But you did not share his mirth." This was worded as a statement, though there was a question behind it.

The dark flush that spread over Gwar's face at this suggestion and the fire that ignited in his eyes gave Shane the answer before he even said a word. When he did speak, there was a deadly menace behind every syllable. "The mage was a vile, despicable, and depraved man. His mirth rose out of the venom that consumed his mind. Had I laughed, I would have become as contemptible as he!"

The silence that followed was so thick it almost felt as if you could reach out and touch it. Gwar glowered and fumed in the doorway and smoke swirled around him while Shane considered what to say next. Damien and Mia kept quiet as mice.

It was Gwar who finally broke the silence.

"Do not underestimate the determination of the mage. His hatred was not even satisfied in death, for the prophecy also indicated that Shane-Torh would return and reestablish the kingdom. This troubled him greatly, and haunted him after he had committed his genocide. He became obsessed with it.

"One version of the prophecy said that after five millennia of turns around the sun, Shane-Torh would return. The mage came up with a plan to stop this from happening. He found a way to contain a cultivation of the disease in mulan wood. It eats through the wood at a set rate. He calculated the years and the thickness of the wood and how long it would take for the disease to get out. He combined it with a combustive substance that explodes on contact with gold, and encased the wooden capsule inside a golden sphere. His plan was that at the set time – the time of your return, young king, which is now – the disease would eat through the mulan wood, the sphere would explode, and the air and water would again be contaminated. In so doing it would bring the return of the great death."

"Did the mage not tell you where he hid the biological bomb?"

"No," said the dragon sadly. "He made sure even I did not know that. He always blindfolded me so that I would not know the way to his lair and the underground volcanoes where he tested and hid his work. I never could find the sphere, though I searched. He died in madness, leaving me only impossible riddles which I have not understood these five thousand years."

Shane reflected on all that Gwar had said. "Your dealings with people have been few and evil, Gwar, and the ill will you bear them has been well earned. But one thing still confuses me. You do not consider me an enemy. Why don't you hate me the way you do other humans?" Shane, like Mia, had never considered himself different from other people.

Now it was the dragon's turn to be confused. He had never considered the winged people and Earth's humans to be the same. "Your majesty," he said levelly, after a slight hesitation, "your people were never my enemies. Your kin, like mine, died at the hands of Earth's men. The enemy of my enemy is my friend."

Shane nodded slowly. "I believe you are a worthy friend, and free from guile. Therefore I am prepared to offer you a place of honor in my court, if you will accept it. But there are some things you must know. First, you would be serving alongside humans from Earth, such as Damien whom you have already met. You would be allies, not enemies. For I have lived among humans all my life, and while I know of the evils that some men are capable of, I have also seen great kindness and self-sacrifice by others – not just for their fellows, but also for strangers and even for helpless animals who have no way to repay."

"You were ever the peacemaker," observed Gwar. "I will not serve man, but if there are men of good heart who serve you, I would serve *alongside* them."

"Very good. That is what I ask. Second, the cloning of sons is a matter we must return to at a later time. It requires the special learning and skill of a scientist, which I do not have. The one who does have this knowledge is the one who brought Mia and me to life – our human father. He is coming, but has not arrived yet. When he does arrive, we will discuss it together. That is all I can promise in honesty, for now."

Gwar's eyes narrowed and his voice grew slightly colder. "But you do not deny that it is possible."

"It can be done. It has never been done to dragons before, of course, but it has been done to many other creatures. It is risky, and the outcome is not always knowable – for example, in my case the wings did not come through with the rest of me, but in Mia's case, they did. You must be aware of this risk, and your decision must be made in the full knowledge of it."

Gwar weighed this intelligence for several minutes before answering. "I have seen that even in the normal course of things, a new birth is not without risk. So be it. But the promise of my full loyalty must remain conditional until I have my final answer on this point. For when a dragon makes a pact, your majesty, he does not break it."

"Fair enough," replied Shane. "And may you never find my good faith worthy of suspicion or doubt."

The children and the ancient dragon sat in silence for a while until Damien spoke. "Your majesty, there is still the matter of Cyril and Lyric that needs our attention. We should organize a search party."

"Agreed," said Shane. "And, Gwar, if you are willing to help, your knowledge of the area and your wings would be of great assistance."

Gwar regarded Damien critically. "The lack of wings is indeed a handicap (begging your pardon, your majesty). Very well. I may take you upon my back again, unless you would rather I hold you in my claws."

"On your back would be good," Damien assured him.

"Just remember that you are not in charge, young human," growled the dragon.

"Neither are you," retorted Damien.

"Mia, I think you should remain here," said Shane, "and I do hope that doesn't upset you."

"I'll stay," said Mia meekly.

Shane then turned to dismiss Damien and the dragon. "After you return, Gwar, I would like to speak to you more about the riddles the mage left to you."

When they had left, Shane turned to Mia. "Whew! Well, that's over. Do you think it went okay?"

Mia was all admiration for her brother. "Oh, yes. You were very kingly. How did you learn to talk that way?"

"It comes from reading," said Shane. "That's how kings always talk in the books."

Changing the subject, he said, "Mia, do you remember the Rune Rock in our peppermint garden back home? There was Sumerian cuneiform cut into the rock, and Mother always wondered what it was doing on Meta near the king's throne. Gwar's story clears up that mystery, I think. It must have been written by the mage from Sumer, after he had killed all the people here on Meta. Do you remember what it said?"

"No," said Mia. "I just remember it was some weird riddle."

"Yes, but I think it makes better sense now. It said:

> Thee, neophyte king, awaits my rancor.
> Drink with me my bane of canker.
> Plague, spring forth; for fools can't hold
> The molten rock to burn the gold –
> Though song from yonder ledge be told.
> Lead, firegrasses! Path behold!

"*Neophyte* means new, like a beginner – new king, that's me. *Rancor* is hatred or anger – his anger awaits. A *bane* is something that causes death, and *canker* is a kind of open sore, a disease – I think the mage must have had something like leprosy, which developed very slowly. So he wants me to die from the same disease. According to the dragon, he set up a biological bomb with his disease encased in gold. I think the *molten rock* refers to the hot lava in the underground volcano that Gwar mentioned, which of course would be hot enough to *burn the gold* – or destroy it, and the bacteria as well. I think I understand that far."

"Then there were the strange symbols underneath the riddle," added Mia. "Mother never knew what they meant. What do they have to do with a disease?"

"I don't know," admitted Shane. "But maybe we can find something here on Meta that will tell us."

chapter thirty-two

Gwar and Damien flew low just above the reach of the trees and scanned the forest floor where Lyric had gone down. There was no sign of the cats. They searched the skies and the cliffs, and were still looking when the sun set. The two moons cast their double shadows on the uneven earth which shifted with life. Small deer hopped through the glades and loons nestled in the rushes along with many creatures that Damien had never seen before.

After the darkness had completely fallen Damien spotted something in the greenery at the side of a huge lake. It was glowing a light green.

"Down there," said Damien to Gwar, "let's have a closer look." Gwar, flying low, made a silent landing ten yards away. Damien slid off and began to creep towards the lake where he could see the minty greenish glow.

"Don't go any closer," whispered Gwar suddenly. "That's a pixie. They are nocturnal, and very dangerous. Come back away from there."

But Damien, fascinated, crept in for a better look instead. It was a girl slightly smaller than a human child his age – about two-thirds his size. She was sitting on a rock, washing her light green and bright blue glowing hair under a small waterfall. Her luminous mint-green dress seemed to grow off of her like leaves, casting an eerie light on the water around her and brightening the clearing. She had bright blue wings like a huge dragonfly. A glowing blue flower grew from her dress and another one from her hair so that she looked part plant. She softly hummed a hypnotic tune while she squeezed the water from her hair. Damien was entranced. He'd never seen anything so lovely in all his life. He crept so close he could almost touch her.

Then the pixie saw him. She gave a terrified squeak and buzzed off out of reach. She perched on a rock and giggled and fluffed her hair and fluttered her wings and her eyelashes at Damien. She made a noise in a high-pitched voice that sounded like *veque-xi*.

"Is that your name?" asked Damien. "Veque-xi?"

"Damien, we must leave!" he

heard Gwar say as if from a long way off. Gwar grabbed Damien, firmly stuck him on his back and prepared to leap into the air. But before he had a chance to do so, the

pixie fluttered over and also jumped on Gwar. She shook her dragonfly-like wings, powdering Damien and Gwar with a bluish dust – pixie dust.

Pixie dust is a powerful drug. Damien was no longer in his right mind, and even Gwar, big as he was, was affected. He became compliant and was now willing to fly wherever the pixie wanted him to.

Veque-xi led them to a shallow lagoon where lotus plants grew at the edge of the water and partway into the shallows. The lagoon was hidden by gnarled trees and strange lumpy walls covered in bark and drooping moss flecked through with orangey-red aromatic flowers. Frogs croaked and hoppers chirped and a ten-legged snake, startled out of its reverie, slid into the water from the little mossy patch where Gwar touched down. It was like a spongy carpet.

The lotuses were white and sweet-smelling, with a heady aroma almost like vanilla. Veque-xi showed them how to eat the fragrant plants, and they ate until they had all eaten as much as they could. Damien and Gwar in their lotus-induced stupor forgot all about their search mission and those who were relying on them. They lost all desire to return home to their caves. All they wanted was more lotus. The pixie flitted happily about, poking at her prisoners to make sure they stayed on their thick mossy beds and didn't fall into the water.

Gwar and Damien didn't wake up from their trance until late the following day as it was again settling into evening. Veque-xi was nowhere to be seen. Damien couldn't remember much except that he had almost touched a pixie; after that his memory went fuzzy. He did know that he wanted more lotus.

"Look, its getting dark. Let's go back to the lake and see if we can find Veque-xi again," said Damien dazedly as he climbed up on the dragon. "Then we can bring her back here to share some more lotus with us."

"Veque-xi!" grumbled Gwar. He was in a foul mood, with a dragon-sized headache – but at least he was more lucid the Damien. Because of his great size, the pixie dust and lotus didn't have the same hold on him. They took off, but the dragon did not go to the lake. He flew back to his lair, taking Damien there by force.

"Pixies are not human," lectured Gwar. "They hatch from eggs that grow from spores – like a mushroom. They are a type of mushroom. They are not capable of speech or relating as intelligent creatures. So get Veque-xi out of your mind!"

chapter thirty-three

When Cyril and Uncle Garrit had found Gwar's lair empty and no sign of the children or the dragon, they returned to the outpost of the keepers of the forest. Now they were making their way by foot back to the dwarf caves. Lyric was being carried on a stretcher by two of the seraphim. Two others walked behind and two ahead of the party, playing their pipes to the trees and underbrush which parted before them and closed behind them. Other then the music, they marched in silence with only the sound of the moving trees and crunching of leaves underfoot. They solemnly wended their way to the ancient dwarf gate.

Shane heard Cyril yowling at the gate and rushed to open it. "Father!" he said in surprise. Hearing this, Mia came running out of the cave and flung her arms around Uncle Garrit's neck. "Daddy!" she squealed.

"Whoa, now, hold it there, young 'uns! That's a mighty warm reception, and I do appreciate it, but it's better reserved for your father than for your Uncle Garrit!"

Mia withdrew and looked at him doubtfully. Then she saw Lyric lying on the stretcher. "Is she alive?" Mia asked under her breath. She plucked up her courage to ask one of the strange creatures with four faces, "Is Lyric all right?" It was the eagle she asked; she gave a little cry when the face on the other side, the ox, answered her.

"She lives," it replied.

"Yes, I'm alive," said Lyric. "I'm just a little weak and sore. Mia, we thought *you* weren't alive."

Mia gave Lyric a hug, but gently lest she hurt her more. "I'm so sorry, Lyric, for running off like that," she sobbed. "I caught some fish, but then I was almost eaten by a vampire, and then almost roasted by goblins, and then the dragon took me…"

Emotions were running so high it took some time for the confusion to settle. The reserved seraphim stood by the whole while and resolutely refused to enter the cave. Dwarf caves were not a favorite place of the keepers of the forest.

"Oh don't be such fuddy-duddies," said Uncle Garrit to Raugus.

Irdor had been eying Mia and Shane in silence. Now he stepped forward. "Our chief would be honored to meet you. Could we set up a banquet in your honor in a week? We will come here to escort you to the outpost."

Shane graciously accepted the invitation. Garrit seconded the acceptance, nodding enthusiastically and shaking all the creatures' right hands – which took a while, as every face had a right hand and each beast had four faces. Uncle Garrit made a little circle around each one. The four-faced beasts took this little ceremony in stride as though they were used to it. When he was done, they began to unload some food and supplies which they had brought for the children.

"Our noble commander-in-chief Tsargahn has sent a gift for the young king," said Irdor. He handed Shane something folded up in a decorative cloth. Shane unwrapped it to find an exotic instrument, exquisitely fashioned out of ivory. It resembled the chanter of a bagpipe, but much more elaborate, similar to those that the four-faced beasts had played as they marched through the forest. "It is a very old instrument, and one of the finest we have seen. But we do not use it because the legend says that it was made by a mage who came here from Earth. He lived long ago when the winged people still lived. We do not know how our people came to have it, but we long have wished to return it to its rightful owners."

"Thank you," said Shane. "I look forward to meeting your commander-in-chief, the Honorable Tsargahn, in a week." Everyone bowed.

That said, the creatures made haste to retreat to their camp, and the people went in to the safety of the dwarf caves.

Shane stood looking at the instrument, turning it around and around. "Mia!" he cried suddenly as recognition hit him. "Come look at the symbols carved on this chanter! Remember the rock in our mint garden back home – the runes that Mother couldn't decipher? They're the same symbols, a different one for each tone and mode of the pipe. I'll bet that's not the forest language written on the Rune Rock – it's music!"

"Doesn't the riddle says something about a song?"

"Yes, of course it does! I don't know why we didn't think of that before. That must be the song the riddle mentions, written right there below it."

"A song for your chanter?" asked Uncle Garrit. "Excellent! You should try chanting it to the forest. It isn't named the En*chanter*ed Forest for nothing, you know. When the keepers of the forest chant their songs to the forest, it obeys. I have, for a long time, been trying to master this art of the forest music."

"Is it magic?" asked Mia hopefully.

"Oh, no," chuckled Uncle Garrit, "not magic. In a way, it's like a Venus flytrap or a sundew plant, which responds to touch – when a fly touches the plant's hairs, it tickles the plant and it folds up. The principle is the same but much more complicated. When certain sounds or resonances touch some of the plants in the forest, they react to the frequency of the sound waves. It tickles them and thy move. The four-faced beasts have learned which plants react and how, so they know how to play their chanters and pipes to make the forest move the way they want it to. They even have words in their language that can make some herbs move."

"So then, if I have a particular song and I play it right, it has a particular effect on the plants – like a command?" asked Shane.

"Something like that. But it's not magic. It's completely scientific. Sorry to disappoint you, little Mia. Your father is a scientist, and I am, too. Wouldn't do at all to teach his kids to believe in magic, now, would it? No such thing, unfortunately. All this about mages, and magic, and what-not. Next thing you know, we'll start believing in purple dragons! People here need to realize that they are very lucky we didn't bring them dinosaurs."

"But we *do* believe in purple dragons," protested Mia.

"Speaking of dragons – where is Damien?" asked Cyril.

"*Where* is Damien?" asked Uncle Garrit. "*Who* is Damien? *What* is Damien? Is Damien a dragon?"

"No, Damien's a boy. He's *with* the dragon. They flew off two days ago to look for Cyril and Lyric," Mia blurted.

"What?" gasped Lyric, lifting her head for the first time. Her eyes were suddenly alert. "The dragon who tried to kill me and eat you? Damien is out riding him?!"

Shane cringed. He had hoped to explain the situation to her gently.

Mia bit her lip, realizing she had been rash. She looked at Shane but he showed no sign of coming to her rescue. Mia bit her lip again and then began slowly, "After I ran off, a vampire found me and was planning to eat me. But before he could do that, a pack of goblins caught both of us and were planning to roast us. But before they could do that, the dragon flew in and rescued me. His name is Gwar. He thought you were wanting to eat me, too, Lyric. I'm sorry – this was all my fault!"

Lyric was aghast. "His name is Gwar? Mia, dragons are not creatures to befriend. They are untrustworthy beasts. They are not safe!"

"A dragon is safer if he considers himself an ally then if we treat him like an enemy," stated Shane pragmatically. "With all reasonable creatures I aim to make friends. This is not to be a time of war. Furthermore, the dragon has asked for a place in the realm – he does not wish to be an outcast. I prefer this to his enmity."

Lyric was silent.

"There's wisdom in that," agreed Cyril.

chapter thirty-four

It was several days before Damien showed up again – or more accurately, before Gwar brought Damien back. (At least, he brought Damien's body back; his mind was somewhere else.)

"The captain of your army has returned," Gwar announced sardonically from the cave door. "I had to bring him back. He ate lotus." Gwar hid the part about the pixie. "He is not in his right mind and must be watched. I have had a time keeping him from running off to get more lotus. He has also developed the habit of walking into walls."

"You know, if you eat the roots as well as the flowers, it takes months to wear off," quipped Uncle Garrit.

Gwar looked at him with glowering eyes. He did not seem amused – but then Uncle Garrit did not seem to be joking, either. Shane vaguely wondered how Uncle Garrit knew this.

Lyric was glaring at Gwar from her bed through

narrowed eyes, her ears flattened against her head and a low growl rumbling from her throat. It was a good thing she was still unable to walk, or there might have been trouble. Gwar turned his head and inspected her.

"You are alive," he said. "That is just as well. Your attack was very brave, and equally foolhardy. I did what I did to protect Mia."

"And I did what I did to protect Mia," Lyric retorted fiercely.

"It is ironic that we were fighting each other, then," said Gwar dismissively.

Lyric was not appeased by this observation and was about to shoot back an angry response when Shane intervened.

"Gwar is right. You were both wrong – and yet you were also both right. Each of you mistakenly thought the other was out to harm Mia, and you acted as the situation demanded: you fought to protect her. Neither of you had any way of knowing the other's intentions, and there was no time to ask questions. But now that you know better, it is important that you both recognize this and pardon each other. It may be a hard thing to ask, but I do not want continuing enmity between dragons and cats. Lyric, is this possible?"

Lyric gave a silent nod and wearily laid her head back down on her pillow.

"And Gwar?" asked Shane.

"It is no more than what I desire," said Gwar. "I hold no enmity against the royal cats, your majesty."

"That is good," said Shane. "Now, Gwar, I have been

waiting to ask you about the riddles the mage left you. I would like to know more."

There was a tense pause before Gwar spoke again. "Hmmm," growled the dragon darkly, and a yellow light began to smolder in his eyes. His voice was low, and seemed to be addressing the cave wall behind Shane. "Mine alone for nearly five millennia. And now, just like that, am I to have someone else open its secrets? And a mere child, besides? – But no, not a mere child; rather, the noble King Shane-Torh!"

Blackish grey smoke poured out of his nose as he dialogued with the stone. Mia began to cough and Shane tried to clear away the smoke in front of his face with his hand. "Gwar! Enough, please! We can't breath."

Gwar lowered his eyes to look directly at Shane again. "You understand my reluctance, I trust, your majesty. I inherited this riddle from the mage as a whelp, and have brooded over it most of my life. If I hand it over to you to solve, it would mean my failure and your glory."

"I have no desire for glory," said Shane, "but I do wish to live. And I suspect that your riddle is a key to my survival. If my solving it means your failure, then know that I myself have also failed. For I, too, inherited a riddle from the mage, one which has taunted me for as long as I can remember. You already helped me towards understanding its meaning, when I could not help myself. Perhaps I can return the favor."

Gwar considered this in silence. Finally he said, "So together we may achieve more than each alone, is that it? Very well, then. I will tell. The mage said, 'To solve the riddle, you must ask a riddle of a riddle.' This advice in itself was a riddle that amused him greatly. He snickered smugly as he continued:

Ask the guardian of Pharaoh's tombs
by what the death at future looms.

His chuckle grew into a cackle and he began to laugh insanely. His mirth overcame him and he fell to the ground clutching his sides as he repeated it over and over, gloating in his own cleverness. And for five thousand years I've sought to solve his grand joke of the guardian of Pharaoh's tombs."

"*Ask the guardian of Pharaoh's tombs by what the death at future looms,*" Shane intoned. "Your mage left you an unfair riddle, for Pharaoh's tombs are on Earth. Only someone who knew about Earth, like the mage himself or some of the winged people he had already destroyed, would have known the answer. Yet the joke was on him, for he could not have foreseen that King Shane-Torh would return from Earth. So I can help you with the first part.

"*Pharaoh* is the term for the ancient rulers of Egypt, one of the great early civilizations of Earth. The guardian of pharaoh's tombs is a great stone sphinx, a mythical animal with the body of a lion and the head of a man. There are also legends that this monster would ask riddles of all who passed, and would kill and eat any who could not answer correctly."

A look of triumph spread over Gwar's face. "I know

of such a beast! He descends from an ancient dynasty that is as old as I am, and even older. From father to son they pass down their riddles."

"Where can this beast be found?" asked Shane.

"He dwells at the farthest edge of the forest, two days' flight from here. He guards the pass through the southern mountains."

"Will you take me to him," asked Shane, "so that I may ask him *by what the death at future looms*?"

"Only against my better judgment. This beast is deadly, and if you cannot answer his riddle, I cannot save you. The poison in his teeth and claws can kill even a dragon."

"Yet if I do not ask this riddle of the sphinx, the mage's doom will not only kill me, but all of my companions as well. I see no other choice."

"I will come with him," said Cyril.

"If there are two," said the dragon, "you will each be given a different riddle. If Shane cannot answer his riddle himself, you cannot save him."

"No, I will go by myself," said Shane with finality.

"Then I will take you," said Gwar, "but only to within walking distance of his den. You will have to face the monster alone."

chapter thirty-five

Shane and Gwar left early the next morning for the mountain range that lay far away to the southwest. At first they flew close to the treetops, low enough so as not to risk being seen but high enough so as not to be snarled by gnarl vines and other hostile plants. After an hour or so they were able to increase their altitude. When evening drew on, they stopped and set up camp for the night. There were goblins here, too, for they had overrun the whole land, but Shane feared no attack as long as he was with the dragon. The air had grown drier and colder as they headed south and Shane was glad he had brought a coat and gloves.

In the afternoon of the second day they stopped to build a fire and cook some food they had caught. They touched down at the safest place they could find within sight of the border where the mountains rose up out of the forest. These mountains were higher than the ones into which the Cliff City had been carved, though not as steep. There was less vegetation and the slopes had a rugged and inhospitable look.

Gwar explained, "The sphinx lives at the pass through the mountains between the Enchanted Forest and the Southlands. This is the only passable route through the southern mountains, and he and his ancestors have long guarded it. Anyone using the crossing must answer a riddle of the sphinx. If they answer correctly they may pass. If they fail they will die.

"One other thing you should know. If you answer the sphinx's riddle correctly, you are free to go. However, he will consider it poor manners if you leave without a proper riddle of farewell. Ask him, 'What first must I do, before I may return?' Can you remember that?"

"What first must I do, before I may return?" Shane repeated.

"Yes. That is the polite way to say farewell. Now, we are an hour's flight from the crossing. I will bring you there after we eat."

Shane and Gwar ate in silence. When they were strengthened by the food, they took off again. Now that they were close to the southern mountains, Shane could see from the air that these would indeed be difficult to traverse by foot, for they were full of loose and jagged boulders, with cracks and crevasses deeper then the eye could see.

The sphinx's crossing was not hard to find. He had positioned himself at the top of the only natural pass through the mountains, a steep and narrow canyon cutting between two massive peaks. A smooth-worn path wound up through the canyon and down the other side, joining the forest to the southern wild lands. Steep walls rose up on either side, disappearing into the frosty air of the glistening summits.

Toward the top of the path, just a few minutes' walk from the cave of the sphinx but out of sight from it by a sharp bend in the trail, Gwar landed. "This is where I leave you," he told Shane. "I will wait here for your return."

Shane dismounted, shook out his arms and legs which were very stiff after two days on the dragon's back, and secured his sword. He started up the slope along the path and rounded the corner. He could no longer see Gwar but could still hear his breathing. There directly in front of him, blocking the path, stood a hideous monster. It was large, about the size of a horse, with the powerful body of a huge lion and the head and arms and chest of a man. Its face was that of a man but it had the teeth of a lion as deadly as daggers.

"Who comes to cross my mountain?" roared the sphinx.

"It is I, Shane-Torh, King of Medarya. I have not come to cross your mountain, but to ask you a riddle."

The beast laughed. "A boy king? Come to ask a riddle of me? This is extraordinary. As a rule I am the one who asks the riddle. But I will be a sport. What question could a child ask that I cannot answer? Once I answer it, I will ask you a question that you must answer, or forfeit your life. Ask!"

Shane stood straight and in his most commanding

voice said, "I ask you *by what the death at future looms*?"

"Hmm," said the sphinx, more serious now and pacing back and forth. "An ancient question for one so young. Do you seek the answer yourself? Or do you already know it, thinking I do not and intending to take my head?" The sphinx whipped around and glared directly into Shane's face. "I know the answer, young fool. Ages ago a hideous creature – a man, but rotten and eaten almost beyond recognition – told us this riddle, and we have kept it in our traditions ever since. The answer to your riddle, however, is not an answer to your question; it is another riddle:

> The pests from seraphim's gardens rid –
> An object in their lair is hid,
> To which they worship, their prayer is bid.

That is my answer," said the sphinx, "and my riddle to you: What is this object?"

Shane was stunned. He understood even more clearly now the diabolical design of the mage. This was not an answer, it was a trap! He hesitated, and a tense silence ensued as his mind worked through the problem.

"You cannot answer my riddle!" snarled the sphinx triumphantly.

"Yes!" said Shane boldly. "I believe I *can* answer your riddle!" It had dawned on him that the answer to the sphinx's riddle was also the answer to his own. And he suspected he already knew what that was. "It is a golden sphere – a biological bomb of sorts."

The sphinx's eyes widened in surprise and rage. "Your answer is correct! You have outwitted me and have denied me my feast. Ask me another riddle," he challenged.

"I do have one more riddle," said Shane: "What first must I do, before I may return?"

The sphinx's expression changed. He was still fierce and unfriendly, but now there was something like respect in his look. "You must depart," he answered.

"I will go now," said Shane, "but I will be back. It has been many ages since you and your fathers had a king, but now you know that I, Shane-Torh, have returned to restore the throne."

The monster made a haughty bow as Shane turned and slowly walked down the hill. When he reached Gwar, the told him what had happened. "So, you see," he said, "we're no further ahead than we were before, because the sphinx's answer was just what we already knew – the mage's golden sphere is supposed to cause my death."

"On the contrary, your majesty," contradicted Gwar, "I think we know a great deal more. There was one very important clue hidden in the sphinx's riddle: the sphere is hidden in the lair of the seraphim's garden pests. So now it simply remains to find out what the seraphim consider to be a garden pest. We shall find them in their lair worshipping the bomb like a god – if it is still there after all these years."

"You're right," Shane agreed. "But then we have to find a way of destroying their idol without upsetting them."

chapter thirty-six

Shane arrived back at the dwarf caves just a few days before the seraphim were to come and take him to the banquet that their commander-in-chief had declared in Shane's honor. Much preparation was being made. Lyric, who was now much better though still limping on three legs, fussed over Mia's clothes and behavior.

"I don't know how to act queenly," pleaded Mia.

"Just don't say much and smile a lot," coached Lyric.

In response Mia flashed a mischievous grin that would have worried any adult.

"And, no, you can't wear your antennae."

"Why not? They're a part of my queenly garb. They go with my wings! Besides, Moogkey would be disappointed."

Uncle Garrit was running about excitedly, clapping his hands with delight. He had selected some kingly robes from the dwarf armory for Shane to wear.

Damien by now had recovered completely from the

lotus and was not at all keen on going to some stuffy social event. He stubbornly refused until Uncle Garrit pointed out that the four-faced beasts were well skilled in weaponry and strategy, and this would be an excellent opportunity to learn what they had to teach. This sounded more interesting to Damien – it definitely beat all the silly eating etiquette Lyric had been spending hours trying to teach them.

"I don't see any purpose in this *eddy-kit*," whined an inattentive Mia for the hundredth time.

"The purpose," Lyric repeated for the hundredth time, "is for you to learn how to act like a queen at this banquet."

"It is a very serious event," Cyril interjected, also for the hundredth time. "Shane has to establish himself as king of these lands, and you, Mia, as queen. The four-faced beasts have kept the forest for many years, and if they are to keep the forest for the king, they must be established as his devoted allies."

"Shane's not a king – he's just a *brother*," said Mia disparagingly.

At that moment Shane came up, and suddenly Mia was the picture of diffidence. "M' liege," she declared with an exaggerated bow, "your humble servant awaits your command." Shane regarded her quizzically.

"The four-faced beasts are great warriors," warned Cyril. "You children must take them seriously. They would make a fearsome enemy."

"Yes, the dwarves left Medarya in ships because they could not maintain a war against the four-faced beasts and the goblins," said Shane. "Gwar told me about it."

Mia's eyes got big. "The four-faced beasts were on the side of the goblins?" she asked.

"Of course not," said Uncle Garrit.

"But Shane just said," she insisted.

"It was a three-way war, Mia," Shane explained. "The goblins against the dwarves against the four-faced beasts. When the dwarves left, the four-faced beasts could not defeat the goblins alone, and their numbers grew. One of our first missions will be for Damien and Gwar to organize an attack and drive back the goblins so that the forest is safe again. Before we can do that, we will have to gain the friendship of the four-faced beasts."

"And I will have to act like a lady. Oh, very well, m' liege!" With another bow she ran off.

When Damien found Mia she was in the shuttle, trying to teach Moogkey to stay in her pocket quietly.

"I think you should take our summit a little more seriously," said Damien.

"What's our summit?" she asked, trying to act as if Moogkey wasn't trying to get out of her pocket.

"It's our meeting with the leaders of the four-faced beasts. They're very serious and I think we should be too," said Damien. "I want to drive out the goblins so the forest is safe again."

Now Mia was fiddling with her feathers.

"Think of it like we have a secret club and we're making allies with the seraphim club to get the goblin kids out of our territory," said Damien.

"Hmm. Well, that makes more sense," said Mia

thoughtfully. "What we need is a secret weapon."

"We do need a secret weapon," agreed Damien. "Any ideas?"

"We can find out what they think smells bad," suggested Mia.

"Okay, as commander of the army, I commission you to find out reconnaissance information on the subject. You must not give yourself away, though. You need to know how to properly converse and fit in like a queen so no one will suspect."

Mia let out a big sigh. "Okay. I won't fail you, commander."

After that Mia was a more attentive student.

chapter thirty-seven

The morning of their audience with the commander-in-chief of the four-faced beasts arrived as did their escort to the banquet.

"They will be here in about twenty minutes," said Damien who had been keeping watch with Gwar. Gwar himself was not to attend the banquet this time. It was too much of a complication to include him at the introduction. Shane thought it best to establish himself and Mia first, and to introduce Gwar later.

"I'll bring you back some dessert," Mia promised in Gwar's ear.

Everybody was clean and dressed – Shane and Mia in royal garb; Damien and Cyril in battle garb (Cyril proudly sporting his battle claws). Lyric was simply Lyric and Uncle Garrit had on long bright robes like a wizard with an tall, elaborately decorated hat.

Mia was fidgeting with a bulge in her pocket as the escort marched up to the gate. It was indeed a royal procession. The escort was practically a legion of four-faced beasts, marching to the rhythm of their pipes. The rhythmic crunch of their hooves set the cadence to the erratically sweet and eerie sounds of the many instruments. In the front and the rear, the beasts held torches that were burning aromatic herbs. The smell seemed to fill the whole outdoors. When you saw the procession you had no doubt who ran the forest, for it opened up before them to lay out a smooth path.

"What a wonderful smell," piped Mia. "What is it?"

"It gets rid of itty-bitty bugs, little bugs that make you sick," answered Uncle Garrit.

"A bactericide?" asked Lyric, astonished.

"Bactericide, virocide, itty-bitty bugicide," Uncle Garrit said.

Mia looked alarmed and felt her pocket. "Does it hurt bigger things?" she asked urgently.

"It doesn't harm big bugs – or sucker anemone," said Uncle Garrit with a wink.

Mia look relieved and took a deep breath of the aroma. She was being ushered and scooted into line. The beasts were walking six abreast so that Mia and Shane marched side-by-side, flanked by two beasts on either side. Then came another row of beasts and then Lyric and Cyril and another six beasts, and after that Uncle Garrit and Damien. They were followed up and led by four rows of beasts in front and rear.

Mia found herself face-to-face with an ox. Thinking she was backward she spun around, only to find herself looking straight into the eyes of a lion, "How confusing," mumbled Mia as she turned herself frontward again. Just then the ox started moving away. It appeared to be walking backwards.

"You need to march towards me," it said.

"Eep!" said Mia. "You can talk."

"Of course," said the ox. "Can't oxen talk where you are from?"

"Well… no," answered Mia.

"How sad," said the ox. "That must be very frustrating for them."

Mia wondered if oxen on Earth knew they couldn't talk.

"I understand you speak Medaryan," said the well-dressed ox in front of Shane, trying to make polite conversation. Soon Shane and the ox, whose name was Tsar, were discussing how the phonology and syntax of the Medaryan language had changed through time. Soon their conversation turned to the forest language.

"Mia, you've got to listen to this. We've been pronouncing it all wrong."

"It's so like you to make a lesson out of this," grumbled Mia, rolling her eyes.

"It is so like Tsar," concurred the ox in front of her, startling her all over again.

The beasts stopped at the edge where the forest got denser. They paused, then their song launched into an unusual rhythm. The trees like a heavy curtain parted before them. Mia gasped and Shane looked amazed. The oxen looked pleased.

Uncle Garrit had broken rank and the beasts were

fussing at him. "Remember what I told you? Like those Earth plants that fold their leaves when you touch them..." but he got no further before he was escorted back into place.

Tsar explained, "Different plants respond in different ways when touched by our rhythms. How we mix our music controls the result. For example," he said, taking a small pipe from a pocket inside his cloak, "if I stand in front of the marsh grasses and blow in this opening they bend north. If I blow in this one, they immediately bend to the right of their last motion. It is similar with the trees. We can direct how they move. Every keeper of the forest is a musician."

Shane thought about his own chanter with its rune-marked holes. He was very interested in how the plants responded to the musical vibrations, and his conversation with Tsar continued along these lines.

The march was long but passed pleasantly. Shane found Tsar to be a most interesting ox. They quickly became quite good friends.

"You know," Shane confided glumly at one point, "I am supposed to be the king, but the truth is I really don't know how to be a king. I'm just a child."

"I think you're doing fine," encouraged Tsar.

"Maybe so – I don't know. I mean, I need to make an alliance with your chief, but I don't know if I can actually succeed. I mean, what if he won't?"

"Don't worry. He will," said Tsar confidently.

"How can you be sure?"

"Let me put it this way – would you be able to make

an alliance with me?"

"Well, yes."

"Then you've already succeeded. I am the chief."

Shane looked confused.

"I introduced myself as Tsar. That is short for Tsargahn. I am the commander-in-chief of the keepers of the forest. Our lore has told of the return of King Shane-Torh, although, to be honest, few of us really took it seriously before now. I thought on such an important occasion I should come personally to escort the new king to our banquet in his honor. That is why I was positioned in front of you."

Shane was relieved, and smiled. Tsargahn nodded pleasantly. He probably would have smiled, too, but an ox's face is not made for that.

"I thought you'd be much more severe," said Shane.

"And I thought you'd be much less serious," said Tsar. "As far as we knew, all Earthlings were like your Uncle Garrt. I have to say, I'm quite relieved to find it isn't so. I think we shall become the best of friends."

The camp of the four-faced beasts loomed ahead. It was a tent city. Mia was relieved when they were allowed to break ranks and Uncle Garrit and Damien rushed up to them. Shane introduced Damien to Tsargahn.

"Let us all go out to see the war exercises," suggested Tsar. "I have someone I want you to meet, Damien." He led them out to a large field.

The war games were impressive. Wave after wave of soldiers attacked and fell back, making way for the next wave. When they were over, the onlookers were approached by a large beast who came up to them with his lion's face forward. Tsargahn introduced him to Damien.

"Shikhar, I would like you to meet Damien, the new Medaryan army commander. Damien, this is Shikhar. Shikhar is my general. We will be giving Damien some training in war tactics. Supper is at high sun. Will you join us, General?"

"Certainly," was Shikhar's answer. "Is it all right if I take Damien with me for now? We might try some sparring."

"I want to go, too!" Mia spoke up.

"Mia," ordered Lyric in a whisper, "hush!"

"It may be all right," said Uncle Garrit, "but we need to get their permission first. Hold on a minute." Speaking to Shikhar he asked the lion's face if he minded. Of course he didn't. Then Uncle Garrit moved around to his ox head. "Do you mind if Mia comes along?" he asked most politely. Then he asked the eagle and then the man. "It's unanimous," said Uncle Garrit. "They don't mind if Mia goes along, too."

Thus it was decided. Shikhar, Damien, and Mia headed off to the field. Shane had a little time to be given some musical instruction on the chanter that Tsargahn had given him. The rest of the party returned to the tents where the preparation for the feast was taking place. The whole camp was alive like a beehive. They watched as the tables were lavishly laid out with crimson cloths and golden platters. Around the tables were small square stools.

"I wonder how they sit," thought Shane. He was soon to find out, as the guests had begun to arrive. Their party was ushered up to the head table. Then Shane saw that the four-faced beasts simply straddled the stools, human face forward and eagle face back.

"Please don't expect me to make a speech," whispered Shane to Tsargahn.

"No speech," promised Tsar.

Shikhar, Damien and Mia rushed in at the last minute. Moogkey was perched on Mia's head and her clothes were rumpled and sweaty, but there was nothing Lyric could do at this point. Damien, Mia and Shikhar all had broad smiles on their faces as they were seated at the head table. "Excellent potential," said Shikhar to Tsargahn.

When everyone was seated, Tsargahn stood up. "I have called you all here in honor of King Shane-Torh of Medarya, who against all hope has returned to restore his kingdom. We have agreed to renew our friendship of old, and to be allies forever." Tsargahn spoke in English out of respect for his guests, but not all of the keepers of the forest had learned the "language of Garrt" as they called it. There was a brief pause as the interpreter translated the announcement into their own language; then a cheer arose and the feast began.

Tsargahn was sitting between Mia and Shane. He was eating with his ox face, speaking to Shane with his human face and to Mia with his eagle face. Moogkey seemed quite alarmed at being so close to such a big beak.

Many delicious-looking plates were brought around. Shane noticed Tsargahn wave away a couple of platters that appeared to contain roasted antennae. Fortunately Mia and Moogkey were too distracted by other sights and smells to notice.

"The first thing we need to do," said Shane, "is clear the forest of goblins. If we can drive them south of the mountains the sphinx will guard our southern border and not let them pass back into the forest."

Tsargahn looked sad and all four faces sighed. "Try as we might, we have not been able to drive them back."

"We just need a secret weapon," said Mia boldly before Lyric could hush her.

"A secret weapon?" asked Tsargahn.

"Well… yes," said Shane, a little embarrassed. "We were trying to think of one."

"They have a secret weapon to use with the enchanted forest-smells and music and stuff," Mia went on, "and on Earth some people use sound frequencies to drive away termites and mosquitoes – maybe there would be a sound or smell that would drive away goblins."

"Now that's an interesting thought," said Uncle Garrit. "I like the idea of a secret weapon, Mia. If we could find a frequency that the goblins don't like, then I could make radio transmitters. I could make radio transmitters, couldn't I? *Could* I?" He muttered with himself for quite a while before he answered, "Yes, I do believe I could."

"If we could find a way to drive back the goblins through this or other means, can your men hold territory gained?" Shane asked.

"That we can do," said Tsargahn. "I believe we have our first treaty."

The conversation proceeded from one subject to another. Eventually Shane asked as nonchalantly as he could, "What is your worst garden pest?" Tsargahn looked a little surprised, so he added quickly, "It's an ancient riddle I got from the sphinx."

"From the sphinx!" exclaimed Tsargahn. "You talked to him? And got a riddle from him? I am very impressed. Well…," he said thoughtfully, "A long time ago, when the forest was safe and peaceful we did have quite some trouble with pixies. Pixies were always eating the flowers from our gardens."

Nobody noticed that Damien was blushing.

"It's kind of an old folk joke now, because we see few pixies nowadays. Not many are willing to hatch. You see, they emerge only when it is safe to do so. During bad times a lot of them choose to spend their entire lives inside their egg. But that is just as well. We have little trouble with them now."

"What exactly are pixies?" asked Shane.

"In a word, pixies are a nuisance. They are actually a type of winged mushroom, though bigger and more bothersome than the stationary varieties. The goblins, in fact, like to chop them up and sauté them to serve them on their salads – if they can catch them. Pixies are a bundle of energy, wild and untrainable. They can make noises, but they don't talk. They live for eighteen years, and when they die they just disintegrate in a cloud of spores which produce more pixie eggs. That is how they reproduce."

"Do you know where they keep their eggs?" asked Shane.

"Nobody knows. Pixies are nocturnal creatures, and flighty, and impossible to track. Nobody has ever succeeded in following them."

Tsargahn was poking at his meat, looking dolefully at it with big ox eyes. "Excuse me," he said and spun around on his stool until the lion was facing his plate. The lion ate the meat ravenously while the human face winked at Mia. Mia giggled.

"We'll have Damien and Shikhar devise a battle plan against the goblins," said Shane. "Damien is better than I am at aggressive strategy. Meanwhile, I'll have Uncle Garrit work on Mia's secret weapon."

At the end of the banquet, Tsargahn presented Shane with a wind bag which the four-faced beasts had made to go with his chanter. It was made of new leather, decoratively fringed and equipped with three finely crafted drone pipes and two additional holes for the chanter and the mouthpiece. Tsargahn showed him how it was to be assembled.

When the banquet had finished, the party began the very long trek home. Shane was carrying his gift. Mia held a basket laden with desserts for Gwar. Several beasts were helping Uncle Garrit carry some of his laboratory equipment back to the cave. It was quite an exit processional as they marched out to the rhythm of the seraphim's pipes.

chapter thirty-eight

That night Damien and Shane had retired to their cavern and were lying on their beds, unable to sleep. "So the biological weapon was hidden in the pixie lair and now they worship it as a god," said Shane. "So we need to find their lair. But how?"

"Um… Shane, you know when I was missing…" began Damien slowly. "Well, I saw a pixie. It was a pixie that led Gwar and me to the lotuses."

"Really? You know where to find a pixie? Maybe we could follow it to its lair."

"Well, I know where we could *look* for pixies," said Damien, "but I don't know if we could follow them. They camouflage themselves and it's like they disappear. They can even camouflage against mist."

Suddenly Uncle Garrit peeked around the door. "I hear you're planning on going pixie hunting," he remarked with a chuckle. The children hadn't realized how well their voices carried in the rock enclosure. "Why don't you put a bug on a pixie?"

"What's that you're saying, Uncle Garrit?" asked Shane.

"A radio-transmitter bug," said Uncle Garret. "The kind that scientists use to track birds." He was fiddling with his ring. He took it off and peered at Damien through it. "Cubic zirconium," he said. "Sparkles just like a diamond, but costs a lot less."

Shane and Damien both stared at him, puzzled. They were not following his train of thought.

"Pretty," said Uncle Garrit. "Shiny. Pretty shiny."

Damien suddenly understood. "I'll bet pixies like pretty, shiny things."

"I'll bring you your little shiny bug tomorrow night," Uncle Garrit said as he waltzed out the door.

4. The Chanter

chapter thirty-nine

The next day Damien went off looking for Gwar, and Shane dug out some of the old manuscripts their mother had sent with them so many months ago. He settled down with the ivory chanter that Tsargahn had given him. Shane worked on matching up the symbols of the manuscripts with the markings on the chanter. Then he tried to make the sounds. It wasn't working very well and he soon became frustrated. He made up his mind to ask the four-faced beasts for lessons.

"Whatcha doin'?" asked Mia. "Is it true you're going pixie hunting?"

"I'm working on the riddle," said Shane, ignoring her second question. "Once we find the biological weapon, we still have to destroy it."

"With the chanter?"

"Yes. I mean – no. Not exactly. Or at least – maybe," he ended lamely.

"Huh?"

"Well, I haven't figured it all out yet, but I've been thinking, and I'm sure the chanter is the key to destroying the bomb."

"How do you know?"

"I don't *know*. I just think so because it fits with what I do know."

Mia made an impatient little noise. "Shane, you're confusing me."

"Okay, look, I've been trying to put myself in the mage's shoes and figure out how he was thinking. It is as if this whole complicated puzzle was like a big joke to him, pitting his knowledge and cunning against ours. The riddle in the throne room warns of his plans to destroy the new king with a plague, but it was written in Sumerian, an Earth language that no one left on Medarya would be able to read. The riddle he left with Gwar mentions the guardian of Pharaoh's tombs, a detail of Earth's legends that no Medaryan would be likely to know. The riddle he gave to the sphinxes contains the clue about the garden pests that only the four-faced beasts have the answer to. But even they don't know where the pixies' lair is.

"So he was very thorough. He left a twisting trail of steps, and at each step he left a genuine clue that has a genuine solution if you know the answer. Therefore, since the clues so far have led us to find this deadly object, it stands to reason that the remaining clues will lead us to be able to destroy it. Does that make sense?"

"I guess so," Mia said a bit dubiously.

"That means the solution should be contained in the

last half of the Sumerian riddle. Do you remember how it goes?"

"Shane," said Mia, exasperated, "you *always* ask me that! You're the one who is good at remembering riddles. I just remember it had big words about neophytes and rancors and banes and cankers, and firegrasses, or something like that."

Shane quoted patiently:

> ...for fools can't hold
> The molten rock to burn the gold –
> Though song from yonder ledge be told.
> Lead, firegrasses! Path behold!

"It mentions burning the gold with molten rock. I think that is probably the way to destroy it. It also mentions a song from a ledge. That must be connected with the musical runes below the riddle, and the instrument the mage made. And it mentions firegrasses and a path. My guess is that this has something to do with the way the plants respond to music, but I'm not sure exactly what. So I've been practicing the chanter to find out."

He blew a few more notes on the instrument.

"Are you going pixie hunting?" Mia returned to her unanswered question.

"No," replied Shane evenly, "I'm practicing my chanter. But if you want to be of help, you could go search the library for anything about firegrasses."

"That's okay," said Mia lightly, and skipped off as

Shane returned to his instrument. At the door she bumped into Damien.

"What's that spooky music?" asked Damien. Shane set down the pipes. "Gwar is here," Damien said. "He's got some important news for us. He is waiting outside. He would like it if you came out and talked to him."

When they came out to the main gate, they saw Uncle Garrit pointing a speaker box at Gwar who held a goblin clutched in his claw. There was a soft humming noise coming from the box. The goblin was struggling desperately to wriggle free, and not just out of fear of the dragon. It had its gnarled hands clamped over its ears, its repulsive face screwed into a most horrific grimace. As soon as Gwar dropped it, it scurried off into the forest. Uncle Garrit switched off the humming.

"That might do it," Gwar growled.

"It's my anti-goblin machine!" exclaimed Uncle Garrit happily. "We can try it out for real when we go pixie hunting."

"Aha! So you *are* going pixie hunting!" cried Mia.

Uncle Garrit winked.

"Pixie hunting!" bellowed Gwar in alarm. "I'm not taking anybody pixie hunting! You will all end up with addled brains."

"We discovered yesterday from the keepers of the forest that pixies are their garden pest," Shane explained. "So the golden sphere is in the pixies' lair."

"Hmph," grumbled Gwar. "This is bad news. But it is other news that I have come to report to you. I heard something interesting yesterday from the colony speech that incessantly echoes through my caves. Two humans named Rockwell are here. If I am not mistaken, these are your Earth parents. Two days after they arrived, someone they call "Dumsford" and the "Secretary of Defense" also landed on Meta. He has placed them under house arrest. They may not leave their confines while it is being decided whether they are guilty of some great crime back on Earth. Secretary Dumsford is claiming evidence from Earth, and says they are subject to the death penalty."

That evening Shane, Mia, Damien, Cyril, Lyric, Uncle Garrit and Gwar sat around a small fire just outside the Queen's Gate entrance for hours, scheming. But nobody came up with a realistic rescue plan – not even Damien.

"I'm supposed to be a king and I can't even free my parents from prison or death," said Shane dismally. "There's just too much going on. We're supposed to stop a biological bomb set five thousand years ago. But before we can do that, we have to solve an impossible riddle. And now Mother and Father need rescuing. I just can't deal with it!" He threw up his hands and stomped off into the cave.

"Poor lad," said Cyril sympathetically. "There is a great weight on his shoulders and he feels it all too keenly. And that puzzle about the firegrasses has been getting him down. He is like a bulldog – he can't let go of something until he has defeated it."

"What puzzles him about the firegrasses?" asked Gwar.

Cyril briefly explained the riddle to Gwar.

"He should have asked me about that," said Gwar, frowning. "I could have told him. Among the many things the mage experimented with were the firegrasses. He found that when certain notes were played on a chanter they would burst into flames…"

"Oh!" Mia interrupted, her eyes wide.

Everyone looked at her questioningly.

"Back in Daddy's lab," explained Mia, "the firegrasses exploded once when Shane was playing his wooden flute. It was so unexpected, we didn't connect the two."

"That would do it," agreed Gwar. "The mage learned how to manipulate the grasses, for there are different varieties and each behaves a little differently. He would plant green and yellow and orange and red and purple grasses, and write music that would make the colorful flames unfurl in magnificent patterns. He planted grasses on the terraces below the Cliff City, then let animals loose on them to wander and graze. Far up on the ledge of the throne room he would play his music and trap the prey with the flames. In his madness he considered it artistic sport."

"I'll go tell Shane what you said," said Cyril and padded off after him. Shane was nowhere to be found in the dwarf caves. On a hunch, Cyril went up to the Cliff City throne room. There he found Shane sitting on the platform where the king's throne used to be, his head in his hands. Cyril quietly told him what Gwar had said about the firegrasses.

Shane looked up at the throne room's grand arched entrance which overlooked the terraces and the plain below. "Then I suppose that is *yonder ledge* where I am supposed to play the mage's song."

"I don't doubt it," Cyril replied.

"I've been thinking about how to free my parents. If I just showed up at the colony's gate and told them I was king and demanded they free Mother and Father, what do you suppose would happen?"

"I suppose they'd arrest you and lock you up, too."

"Yeah," said Shane, "but how about if I came with Mia showing off her wings, and I wore a cape so it doesn't show that I don't have wings. And we came with a large entourage of four-faced beasts and Damien and Gwar as an army escort. And we act as if we only spoke Medaryan so they would need to get my mother to interpret. Do you think we could really convince them that I am the king?"

"Hmm," said Cyril. "It might work, at that."

Neither of them had heard Mia creeping up on them so they both jumped when she spoke. "We should drink glow pop, too," she announced. "That will *really* make us look alien."

chapter forty

Damien had arranged with Gwar to go in search of Veque-xi the following night and try to get her to take the ring in which Uncle Garrit had hidden a tracking chip. Uncle Garrit insisted on coming too, to see his handiwork in action.

"This is a historic event, you know, finding a pixie's lair. Never been done before!"

As they were getting ready to go, Shane came up to wish them well. On a whim, Damien suggested, "Why don't you come too, Shane? You've been so serious lately. Getting out and seeing a pixie would be just what the doctor ordered."

"No, I'd better not. I have too much to do tomorrow, working out how to free my parents and learning to play a new instrument and all. I need a good night's sleep."

"But you probably won't get much sleep anyhow. You'll be awake half the night worrying about all your responsibilities. This would be the perfect way to get your mind off your worries for a little while. And then when you get back to them you will be able to tackle them fresh. Besides," he added, seeing Shane still looking doubtful, "as king you need to get to know your whole realm. That includes the pixies."

"Well... you might have a point there. Okay, I guess you're right – I'll go."

"Excellent!" cried Uncle Garrit.

The three of them dressed warmly and took off into the moonlit night on the back of Gwar, flying low over the trees so as to avoid being spotted. When they neared the pool of water where they had last found the pixie washing her hair, they heard a faint singing.

Gwar touched down in the same place that he had hidden the last time. "Now remember," Damien instructed Shane in a whisper, "she'll be a bit flighty. If you see her shake her wings you, jump back fast as you can or you'll get dusted." Shane nodded and the two boys crept down off the dragon and quietly approached the pool.

Veque-xi was again sitting on her moss-covered rock, ringing water out of her light green and brilliant blue hair, glowing warmly. Shane was entranced by the unusual sight.

The boys were so quiet that Veque-xi didn't hear them until they were almost upon her. Then she jumped up with alarm and chirped out, "*Veque-xi!*" Both boys immediately knelt down on the ground, and while Shane stared in amazement Damien put a finger over his lips as if to say *shhh*. Veque-xi glanced from Damien to Shane and back to Damien, and then did an unexpected thing. She copied them. Kneeling with a wide-eyed expression on her face, she put a finger over her mouth and giggled. Damien tipped his head to the right and Veque-xi tipped her head the same way. Damien squeezed his eyes shut and opened them again, and so did Veque-xi.

"And they say you're not trainable," he remarked.

"*Traimble*," echoed Veque-xi. By now she had caught sight of the sparkling ring on his finger and was staring at it intently.

Damien held his hand out to show it to her. She backed away in fear. Then with a sudden flick of her wings she let loose a cloud of pixie dust at the two boys. Damien was ready for this and leapt clear of it, but Shane was taken entirely by surprise and got a thorough dusting. They heard Uncle Garrit's chuckle from the bushes behind them. (At least, Damien heard it – Shane seemed beyond hearing anything at the moment.) Veque-xi heard it, too, for she looked in that direction with alarm. Her eyes darted back and forth as she tried to watch the shrubbery and the ring at the same time.

Damien slowly took the ring off his finger and held it out to her temptingly. She hesitated for one moment longer and then snatched it away, doing a furious little dance as she clutched it in her fists. She flew up into the air and down again, making tight circles and figure-eights above the water. Then she disappeared.

Damien made his way back to Gwar with an absent Shane in tow, who followed amiably along, gazing about with a vacant smile on his face and humming softly to himself. "It happened too quickly for him. He must have let down his guard," Damien explained apologetically. Gwar looked anything but pleased.

Damien noticed the dragon was alone.

"Where's Uncle Garrit?" he asked. Following the direction of Gwar's gaze, he saw. Uncle Garrit had made his way to a clearing some twenty-five yards distant, where he stood holding a black box in his hands. Soon Damien noticed shadows, scores of them, stirring in the bushes all around. Goblins! Uncle Garrit, seemingly unaware, let them edge closer and closer, closing the circle. Right when they were about to pounce, he flipped on the switch. All Damien heard was a pleasant hum, but the goblins shrieked in fear and ran in all directions with their hands over their pig-like ears, bumping into trees and into each other in their mad haste to get away.

Presently Uncle Garrit switched the gadget off again and came back to the others, looking pleased. "Well, that worked as well in the field as it did in the lab," he said happily. "As effective as a dragon for scaring off goblins. So now let's see where our little pixie has flown off to." He pulled out a battery-operated radio receiver and direction finding unit, unfolded the antennas, and turned it on. He made a few adjustments to the frequency setting and moved the unit this way and that until he found the homing signal. His face flickered oddly as it reflected the lights on the display.

"Right, here we are. From the direction and strength of the signal, it looks like she's flown all the way to the other side of the lotus lagoon."

They climbed onto Gwar's back and took to flight across the big, dark lake. Damien held tight to Shane, who seemed inclined to dismount in mid air every time he noticed something interesting below – and in his state of mind, that happened every few seconds. They finally landed at the opposite edge of the lagoon. Shane immediately saw the lotuses and went to investigate. It was a good thing Gwar was paying attention or Shane would have been in even worse trouble.

The first thing Damien noticed was that the gnarled tree walls had shifted – changed shape or moved, or both. Also, some new ones seemed to have recently migrated into the area. The next thing Damien noticed was the spiders.

"Yech!" he said. "There are enough spiders here to catch a dragon."

"Shh," rasped Gwar, "I can hear her." Listening intently, they could all hear Veque-xi's entrancing tune. Shane in particular seemed eager to follow it. They crept toward a thickly overgrown knoll where the sound was coming from. The glowing light of the pixie slowly grew stronger. When they saw her, she was in a thicket teeming with spiders. Her fist was full of glow bugs which she was feeding one by one to her favorite spiders. One of the them lay on its back so she could tickle its belly, and she giggled as it wiggled its legs. Then she jumped onto the back of a larger one and held on as it zipped up a web which Damien hadn't noticed before running about ten yards above their heads.

At this point Veque-xi spied them. She gave a shrill

little scream and disappeared behind the thicket of webs.

The spiders had noticed the intruders, too, and began to close in threateningly.

"Quick, guys, let's get out of here!" Damien cried urgently, scrambling onto Gwar's back and helping Uncle Garrit on behind him. Gwar grabbed Shane who was busy peering behind a curtain of moss, looking for something – probably Veque-xi. They were airborne in an instant.

"We'll have to come back in the daytime," said Uncle Garrit. "These spiders are nocturnal like the pixies, so it will be safer then."

Ugh! thought Damien. These spiders are creepy! Not at all like Matilda. She was... well, not exactly cute, but at least she wasn't so scary. He didn't relish the thought of going back, even in the daytime.

When Gwar landed at the Queen's Gate, Uncle Garrit was the first through the net root veil, looking pleased as punch. Damien was slightly delayed because he had to retrieve Shane who had started wandering aimlessly back towards the woods.

Inside the caves Lyric met them and politely inquired as to whether they had found the mage's sphere.

"No page's smear, only phixies," replied Shane confidently.

"Excuse me?" said Lyric.

"No, accuse me. No phage's spear, only mixies," he tried to clarify.

Lyric turned to Damien and Uncle Garrit. "What's

wrong with him?" she asked them sharply. Uncle Garrit seemed surprised at her question and looked at Shane inquiringly, as if he hadn't noticed that there *was* anything wrong with him.

Damien spoke up. "We did find a pixie and got her to take the ring with the tracking device. We now know where the lair is. Unfortunately, Shane kind of got pixie dusted in the process and he's not quite himself at the moment."

"How did that happen?" There was a distinct note of accusation in her voice.

Damien looked sheepish. "It just, well… happened. I did warn him ahead of time to be on his guard, but when it actually happened I guess he just didn't see it coming."

"Did *you* see it coming?" she asked sternly.

"Yes, but not in time to save Shane. I'm sorry, Lyric. I would have been more careful if I had known what would happen."

"Child, none of us can know what *will* happen. We have to plan for what *might* happen, and be guided by what *has* happened in the past. Is he going to be out of it for days now, the way you were?" Now the note in her voice was one of worry.

Damien frowned. "I really don't know. In my case, I think it was actually the lotus that did me in for so long. So hopefully with Shane— hold on—"

He broke off suddenly and ran after Shane who was wandering toward the stairway that led down to the dwarf city, smiling and humming to himself. Damien laid a guiding hand on his shoulder and steered him back.

"Are we going to see more Veque-xis?" asked Shane hopefully.

"Not right now, Shane... you need to get a good day's sleep before you can see the pixies again."

"Oh, okay, in that case, let's get some sleep." Stretching and yawning, Shane let himself be led to his room.

chapter forty-one

"Hey, guy," said Damien, flopping himself down beside Shane who was sitting at the table in the main cave reading an old book on music magic. "You look like you've recovered from last night's little mishap."

"I am doing better this afternoon, since I slept away most of the day. But I'm still finding it hard to focus my mind on what I'm reading. Why did you set me up to get pixie dusted?"

"Honestly, Shane, I didn't set you up. Though I must say," he added with a twinkle in his eye, "it couldn't have worked better if I *had* planned it."

"Hmph," replied Shane.

"But I do owe you an apology. I convinced you to go against your better judgment, and then I didn't take enough precautions to keep you from getting pixie dusted."

"No, it was my decision to go, and I don't see how you could have prevented the pixie from dusting me."

"Well, something Lyric said to me last night got me to thinking. My own experiences with that pixie could have made me more cautious, and would have if I had not been so overconfident. I should have been forewarned by the past. A good general needs to listen to the lessons of history."

"Yeah, I know. So does a good king," said Shane glumly.

"What's eatin' you, pal?"

"It's just that I'm losing time while the bomb keeps ticking away and my parents remain under arrest."

"I understand. Any ideas how to free them?"

"One," said Shane, "the most harebrained of them all – just march in there and convince them that almost fourteen-year-old me is really the king of this place. Fat chance of that!"

"Oh, who knows? It's so far out they might actually fall for it."

"Cyril thinks so, too."

"And don't forget, we are making progress in the other areas, too. We know for sure that the anti-goblin frequencies work. And we have found out where the pixies' lair is, so we are closer to destroying that bomb."

"Which reminds me – when are you planning on returning to the pixie lair to get the sphere? The sooner the better."

"The only thing holding us back is those giant spiders it's infested with. I don't know how we can get past without getting caught in their webs."

"We have some anti-stick acid among the shuttle

supplies," Shane pointed out. "You can use that."

"*I* can use that? So I take it you're not planning on coming."

"Oh, no. This king is going to learn from history. I can't risk another pixie dusting."

"Well, I don't look forward to going back there, either, with those huge, ugly eight-legged creatures running about."

"Oh, I don't remember their being so hideous," said Shane. "And if I can contact the research colony and claim to be king, I think you can face a few spiders. Or do you want to switch jobs?"

"No, no," said Damien quickly. "I'd just as soon try to make friends with the spiders."

Gwar poked his nose through the door at that moment.

"Hello, Gwar," said Shane.

"Greetings, your majesty." The dragon's piercing yellow eyes inspected the young king intently. He said nothing more, but Shane suspected that Gwar had come by mainly to see if he was all right.

"I'm glad you are here, Gwar. I have been meaning to ask you something. Do you remember or know of any underground lava streams or volcanoes, or anything about volcanic activity in the area?" asked Shane.

A troubled look spread across Gwar's face, and he heaved a great dragon sigh. "Come outside, your majesty, and I will tell you what I remember.

"This is not something suitable for Lyric's ears," he explained once they were outside. "I was just a very small dragon, small enough for the mage to carry me on his back. In this way we explored the caves together. There is a place under the ground where the lava flows, but I never knew where the entrance was. The sorcerer found those caves by himself and built his laboratory there. He always blindfolded me before taking me there. It was there that he experimented on the cats when he was developing the death. Then he would have me drag the dead ones down to that place where the lava flowed, and push them in. The air was too hot for him and the bodies too heavy. I remember the path from his laboratory to the lava flows all too well." Gwar clawed at the ground as if in anguish and torched a nearby sapling. "It took me hundreds of years to grow higher than his shoulder. By then he was dead. In all that time, I never knew where his lair was, nor could I find it after."

chapter forty-two

The next day Damien and Shane went on Gwar to visit Tsargahn and Shikhar. An angry stir ran throughout the seraphim camp when they saw the dragon, and many appeared as if out of nowhere fully armed and at the ready. Gwar glowered menacingly but fortunately kept his mouth shut and Shane spoke up. "Gwartár son of Wirtár serves with Damien, the commander of my army," he announced firmly. "He is not an enemy. All reasonable creatures must live in harmony in this realm if we are to succeed in reestablishing it. We bring important news."

Tsargahn bowed graciously, although his face was grave. "Let us sit at drink and discuss the news you have brought. My apologies for our rudeness." He and Shikhar led them to the camp's central marquee which was even big enough to accommodate Gwar once half of the tables and stools were cleared out. This was done within a few minutes and Tsar directed his other guests to sit at a nearby table. They were brought aromatic mugs of mead.

"We believe we have found a way to drive back the goblins. We plan to force them over the southern mountains, if only your men can hold land gained," said Shane.

"Mia's secret weapon?" asked Tsargahn with a rare smile.

"Yes, Mia's secret weapon," said Shane. "Uncle Garrit helped develop it from a method used on Earth to drive away insects. There are particular frequencies of sound, higher than what we can hear, which they find unbearable and flee from. Uncle Garrit has found the frequency that drives away goblins. If we can build a chain of these transmitters, we can sweep it across the forest and corral the goblins over the southern pass. The sphinx will not let them back into the Enchanted Forest."

"Excellent," said Shikhar.

"I thought we could leave it to you and Damien to decide how to proceed. Maybe Uncle Garrit can get your help in making the machines?"

"I will talk to my men," said Shikhar. "Come, Damien, Gwar, we will plan the advance."

When the others left, Shane took out a neatly written manuscript and held it out to Tsargahn. "Have you ever seen anything like this? If I am not mistaken, it contains music to be played on the pipes you gave me."

Tsargahn studied it for a several minutes. "Yes, and no. This is definitely music, though it is a writing system we use very little these days. Our writing, like our language, has changed over time. Do you understand any of it?"

"I have been able to decipher some of the symbols, because they are also written on the chanter itself. But there are other markings that I cannot figure out. I was hoping you might be able to help."

"I can tell you what many of the symbols mean – they indicate the tempos, rhythms, and the lengths of the notes – but the notes themselves are tied to your specific instrument, so I cannot say exactly what they will sound like. Your instrument is similar in some ways to our own pipes, but it is different, too. We never dared to play it. I would caution you to be careful with the mage's instrument, and with his music. Our legends portray him as a dragon-lord with the power to control fire – a sorcerer who did terrible things. The power of this mage was deadly."

"I will be careful," Shane promised solemnly. "But will you show me as much as you can about this musical notation, and how the pipes are played? I believe my survival depends on it."

"Very well," agreed Tsargahn. The next two hours were spent teaching Shane how to read the musical writing and how to play the bagpipes. By the end Shane was quite confident that this new knowledge, combined with what he already knew of the symbols written on the chanter – plus a good deal of practice – would enable him to play the mage's song.

When the lesson was over, Tsargahn fixed a discerning look on Shane and said, "Something else troubles you, friend. Tell me what it is."

"There are many things troubling me," Shane

admitted. "First of all, are you familiar with the Medaryan prophecy about my return?"

"It is part of our lore, too," answered Tsargahn.

"Well, it was also known to the Earth man who brought Gwar here. He was the one responsible for killing all of the winged people with the plague five thousand years ago. I have discovered that he has prepared and hidden another outbreak of that disease to be released in these days. That is one of the things that are bothering me. The other is that my parents – I mean, the mother and father who gave me life and raised me on Earth – have now arrived here, but they are at the research colony, being held under arrest. I want to free them, but I feel powerless. I am just a child," Shane ended in exasperation.

"Let's take a walk," said Tsargahn, leading Shane towards a far clump of tents that were set in a square with a central courtyard. "These are our schools," he said as they entered the courtyard.

Shane gasped. There were rows and rows of plants with thick stalks and blossoms at the top shaped like lions' heads and oxen's heads and eagles' and men's. Their arms grew out like branches and their wings like big fronds. There was row after row of fledgling four-faced beasts, organized according to their stage of development. Tsar took Shane up and down the aisles toward the plants that were further along in their growth. At a certain point the young creatures were clearly aware of their surroundings and interacting with them. The older ones could talk, and waved a greeting to Tsargahn and Shane.

"These are our offspring," said Tsar. "They cannot move independently until they reach near-adulthood. We have always considered it strange that the young of animals – and people – can run about freely from the time they first sprout. It must be very difficult to keep them out of trouble."

"It is," agreed Shane.

"So, you see, we have a natural kinship with the Enchanted Forest. That is why we have always kept it – or tried."

"You are a little like the pixies then, aren't you?"

"In a way, I suppose, but the pixies will always be wild. And when there are many of them, we have to watch our flowering sprouts very closely. I think they mean no harm but are simply incapable of understanding what our flowers mean to us."

"Why are you showing me this?" Shane wondered.

"For two reasons. First, so you may know a little bit more about us, for we must seem very strange to you. But also, to let you see that, though a child, you are in a much better position to do what you must do than those of comparable age among our young would be. Your efforts to rid the forest of the goblins are very much appreciated."

On the way back to the main tent, Tsargahn told Shane more. "In the ancient days, the rulers of the winged people kept the peace in all of Medarya among the diverse peoples who lived here. After they were wiped out, those of us who were left were unable to live together in harmony, and everything fell apart. The dwarves eventually fled when their numbers became too small to sustain their safety. Goblins overran the forest, and we, the keepers of the forest, were driven back to our present holdout, only a small portion of our former domain."

"I have read much of this in the history books, although the accounts never tell what happened after the dwarves left."

"The state of things you see now was the outcome. Much has happened but little has changed in thousands of years. The instinctive reaction of my people when your dragon showed up, I fear, is part of the reason we were never able to maintain peace with the others. And without peace, progress has proven impossible."

"So now it falls to me to bring peace, too? I'm afraid this just adds to my burden."

Tsargahn sighed. "Then, my young royal friend, let me remind you of what you have already accomplished, since you seem not to recognize it." Tsar's voice was firm. "Without an army or any force of numbers, you have already gained the confidence of an ancient and bitter dragon, of a wild sphinx who would as soon kill and eat you as talk to you, and of the keepers of the forest who prefer to keep to ourselves. Any one of those alone would be an accomplishment; together they are nothing short of remarkable. And how have you done this? By approaching all in friendship and honesty, showing unfeigned respect, and insisting on building alliances instead of hostilities.

"Such a thing has not been done since the days of the first King Shane-Torh and his fathers – and probably his son, too, though he never lived long enough to prove himself. You have already shown by your actions that you are a cutting from the same root. Do not let your doubts convince you that you are helpless. Do what you have to do – do not give up even if things go badly at first – and you will succeed in the end."

Shane was still serious, but he seemed encouraged by Tsar's words.

Tsargahn then asked gently, "Is there any way I can help you free your parents?"

"Perhaps there is. I have to establish my position as king – to the Earth colony, I mean," said Shane. "Can your men escort me when I approach their gate?"

"Do you think it is time to let the colony know of us?" asked Tsargahn. "We have kept ourselves out of sight for so long."

Shane weighed the question carefully. When he answered, his mind seemed made up. "I think it is time to let them know that the forest belongs to you, and that the fields and mountains belong to me – that they are welcome, as guests, to farm the lower lands. As I revive the Cliff City with winged people, we will farm the upper terraces."

"If that is what your wisdom tells you, then we will support you with a show of strength," said Tsargahn.

"Thank you," said Shane, "...for everything. The shadows are starting to lengthen, so it is time for us to go now."

chapter forty-three

At the dwarf caves Damien and Uncle Garrit were preparing for their incursion into the pixie lair. As they were discussing their plans, Uncle Garrit donned a belt with an arsenal of tools – files and chisels, screwdrivers, wire cutters, pliers, a small level, a T-square, measuring tape, a hammer, a battery-operated drill, and bag of assorted nails and screws. "You never know," he said. "*Always be prepared* is my motto."

"I want to go, too," complained Mia in a huff.

"There are spiders guarding the lair. Spiders that are as big as you are," said Uncle Garrit in his spookiest voice.

"Yeah, their eyes are kind of buggy but they're really affectionate," Mia returned. "I'm sure they are just like Matilda."

"Matilda was big and hairy, too, but she wasn't creepy like these spiders," Damien assured her.

"I'm not afraid of big hairy spiders," insisted Mia.

"You're not afraid of big spiders?" asked Uncle Garrit. "Then maybe we *will* bring you. We need something to feed the spiders to keep them busy while we are searching."

"You'll do no such thing!" snapped Lyric, glaring at Uncle Garrit.

"Spider bait! Spider bait! I get to be spider bait!" sang Mia, dancing about as if she were wielding a sword against some invisible giant spider. "I want to see the giant pixie flowers that open at night," she insisted.

"We'll be home snug in our beds by night," said Uncle Garrit.

"Does that mean I can go?" asked Mia.

"Mia might be useful," intervened Damien before Lyric could say no. "She has a way with creatures. They all like her. She might be able to get near Veque-xi more easily than the rest of us."

"Hmm," said Uncle Garrit, "good thinking."

Soon the hunting party was assembled. Lyric was furious but said nothing. Shane paced about. He was unsure about sending Mia as well, but he had also learned not to underestimate his sister. She could be amazingly bold at crucial moments. "Make sure you save enough anti-stick acid for your retreat," he fussed.

The three adventurers – Damien, Uncle Garrit, and Mia – mounted on Gwar's back and took to flight. The sun hadn't reached its peak yet and there was still the glistening magic of morning in the air as Gwar dropped down toward the far end of the lotus lagoon. Its tree-like walls once again were rearranged. It was like a Alice-in-

Wonderland landscape with the huge flowers and exotic plants and creepers that shifted towards them.

Mia looked warily at the large drooping yellow pixie flower, remembering the time at age seven when she had gotten trapped in one back at the estate. "There is somebody in it," she whispered to Uncle Garrit as they tiptoed by. Then she added in a louder voice, "I guess we don't have to be so quiet. They can't get out even if they wake up." She knew this from her own experience three years earlier.

As they approached the hillock that contained the lair, they saw that there was a small, deeply worn path that went straight into the worst of the spider webs.

"Thankfully the spiders are nocturnal like the pixies," whispered Uncle Garrit.

Behind them a furious clatter and chatter suddenly broke out between two orange lilies. They were energetically snapping at each other. Mia giggled.

"Well... if nobody was woken up by that..." mumbled Damien. "I will keep my sword ready and Uncle Garrit and Mia, you can start spraying anti-stick on the webs. Try to use as little as possible" – which turned out to be impossible. There were just too many webs. But slowly, layer by layer, Damien helped them to peel back the curtains of web until they could see the entrance of a cave glowing from a soft light within. It was arduous work but they were finally able to let the veils of web fall behind them.

The threesome quietly crept through the worn crevice into a large room. Glowing from the walls were sacks of all colors and sizes: mint green, lemon yellow, peach and raspberry, from the size of a pin head to almost as large as Mia.

"Pixie eggs!" said Mia in a hush.

"A lot of them are full-grown pixies," whispered Damien. "Tsar told Shane that in bad times a lot of them choose not to hatch at all."

Deep within the cave they could hear the sound of weeping which sounded strangely hollow. This, they found out, was because it was reverberating off of an underground lake – the rhythm of dripping water echoed like the heartbeat of an ancient god. Quietly they followed the time-worn path toward the heart of the cave, over cracks and under boulders, downward into damper air toward the forlorn song of cries. When the cavern opened up again, they were at the edge of the underground lake. Suspended from the rocks above the water hung a golden sphere etched with runes. Veque-xi, in her glowing green flower-petal dress, was kneeling with her back to them, head bowed as if she were praying to it. The pixie was clutching and holding out the diamond ring as if it were an offering to a god.

It was Mia who reacted first. Before anyone could stop her she crept up beside the pixie and knelt, sobbing with her. Veque-xi leaned against Mia's shoulder and wept even harder. Mia's gold bracelet gleamed warmly in the soft light that fell from Veque-xi. The pixie saw it, and once caught by its glint, she couldn't take her eyes off it. She tugged at Mia's bracelet trying to take it from her. But Mia wouldn't let her have it. So Veque-xi bit her with her pointed little teeth.

"Ow!" cried Mia, leaping up. The pixie leapt after her. Mia got an idea. "You want this, you little brat, don't you?" she said, holding out the bracelet. The pixie sprang madly at it. Quick as a cat, Mia dashed out the entrance of the cave with the pixie flying after her. It was pure luck that at just that moment a raspberry-colored pixie flower yawned. Mia tossed the bracelet into it and the pixie dove in after. The mouth of the flower snapped shut on the sound of Veque-xi's angry chatter, but no matter how much she complained and struggled, she was trapped until nightfall.

Mia dusted herself off smartly and grinned at Damien and Uncle Garrit.

"You were brilliant!" said Damien. Now they could steal the pixie god unimpeded.

The sphere was hard to reach. Uncle Garrit helped them gather wood from outside to build a makeshift scaffold from which they could lie on their back and file at the millennia-old metal chain. Damien tried it first.

"Be careful not to bump the sphere," warned Uncle Garrit. "The wood inside is probably very fragile by now."

The chain was exceptionally strong, and it took a long time for the file to make even a mark on it. "The guy who made this sure knew what he was doing," grumbled Damien. After half an hour he had still only made a shallow groove in the metal. "My arms are hurting," he announced finally, "and I'm getting blisters."

"Let me work at it for a while," said Uncle Garrit, and

the two swapped places. For the next few hours he and Damien spelled each other off, the one taking over when the other got too tired to continue. It was Uncle Garrit who was lying on his back and filing at the chain when a distant humming drifted into the cave. At first it sounded like a low rhythmic hum but as it grew louder and closer it could definitely be recognized as a chant.

"It's coming this way," hissed Damien.

Mia looked down and shuffled her feet. "I didn't tell you guys before, but when I trapped Veque-xi in the flower I heard her crying something that sounded like *xzerklan*. She sounded more scared then angry. Pixies can't talk, so I didn't think it meant anything. But now I'm not so sure. Maybe it's a name. Maybe Xzerklan is coming."

"Well, whatever it is, it is coming here!" said Damien.

"Hey, I got it!" exclaimed Uncle Garrit. "Damien, here, can you help me with this? It is very heavy. Gentle now. Don't know if the wood inside is going to crumble. Quick! Hide in there." Uncle Garrit pointed to a shadowy hollow that neither Mia nor Damien had noticed before. The children entered first, followed by Uncle Garrit who pulled the scaffolding in after them.

They just got into the shadows when the blue and purple glow of a boy pixie appeared. The light emanating from him was dim and dull, and his skin had a dry leathery look to it as if it had been exposed to the elements for too long. His movements were slow and labored.

The pixie looked briefly in their direction, bright blue

eyes flashing as if he could sense the intruders, but he continued his chant without a pause, solemnly marching as if in a trance to the rhythm of his voice. In fact, his steps appeared to take such effort that it seemed to be only the chant, more than his own will, that moved him onward, head down, towards the lake. In his hand he held a pixie thorn honed into a long dagger. This he raised above his bowed head towards the missing sphere.

Damien whispered, "Remember what Tsargahn told us about the pixies, how they only live until they are eighteen and then they spore? This pixie looks old and worn out. Maybe it was this death ceremony that Veque-xi was crying about."

"He's not going to kill himself?" Mia exclaimed, more loudly than she intended.

The pixie's head jerked up at the cry and he looked directly at the empty rock where the sphere had hung. He let out a clear screech of rage and turned towards the intruders, dagger raised to strike. Damien leapt forward, sword out, and the dying pixie met him with unexpected strength. Damien parried his blow. The pixie prepared for another inhumanly strong strike, blade raised above his head – but Damien's sword met open air. The pixie had vanished in a puff of spores; his dagger fell to the floor and slipped into the water. All that was left was a gentle wind which carried the colorful dust on its current back through the tunnel.

Silently Mia, Damien, and Uncle Garrit followed the sparkles drifting though the tunnel and watched in a hush as most of the spores settled and attached themselves to the jagged walls of the cave, as an unborn baby clings to the wall of the womb. Mia felt a warm sensation at her side and saw the faint sparkle of pixie spores attaching to the inner lining of her coat. Quickly she zipped up her jacket and clung to her treasure, realizing that they may have been the only humans ever to witness the sporing of a pixie.

The colorful mist that didn't find a place on the cave walls wafted outside, riding the last breath of Xzerklan. The party followed the sparkles out of the cave where Gwar was impatiently waiting. Dusk had fallen. Soon the lair would stir with life and the pixies would realize their loss. In fact, the pixie flowers were already beginning to yawn open, one by one, letting out their cargo In a flash Veque-xi was free, and she started performing a violent little dance, which the others around her began to copy. The sound of her warning chatter reached inside the lair, and unhatched pixies began to stir, too. All over, sleepy pixies were struggling out of their flowers to see the war dance of their brethren.

Suddenly a large spider dropped down from above, snapping its mandibles ferociously.

"I think we're in for some trouble," warned Damien as they ran towards the dragon.

"Pixies are always trouble!" barked Gwar. "Get on, everyone, *now*!"

Damien leapt onto Gwar, pulling Uncle Garrit behind him who nimbly plucked Mia up, too, and Gwar instantly launched into flight. By now, the angry voices of the pixies had grown into a violent buzz, and they were swarming after the dragon. New pixies were hatching from their sacks and joining the mad pursuit, more and more of them, until the swarm had swollen into the hundreds. Gwar took a zigzag path with the pursuers close behind, while Uncle Garrit and the children held on for dear life. Uncle Garrit still clutched the chain with its golden sphere, trying to keep it from joggling too much. It wasn't until the dragon burst above the clouds that they realized they had succeeded in losing the pixies.

chapter forty-four

When Damien brought him the golden sphere, Shane was practicing the mage's instrument which the four-faced beasts had given him. It was the most unusual instrument he had ever come across, and equally difficult to play. It was a kind of bagpipe – you blew air into a leather bag which was then channeled out through several other pipes to produced the tones. Three drone pipes produced an unchanging chord while you fingered the tune on a multiple-piped chanter which could play several notes at once. The sounds it made were also strange. Some were clear tones, but others sounded more like wind howling through a crack, and there were clicks and rustling sounds like leaves in a breeze. The result was both eerie and stirring. Shane, who was quite gifted in music, was only learning to master this challenging instrument with great effort.

He gave the sphere a troubled look. "I don't like that thing being here. We need to find some place to put it until we can destroy it. Is Gwar here?"

"Yeah, he's just outside," Damien replied.

Shane went out to see him.

"Gwar," he said, "I am eager to be rid of this plague-bomb as soon as possible. I feel we are so close, I want to make sure we are on the right track." He repeated the mage's riddle to him. "This riddle was carved on a stone and placed in the throne room. Do you think *yonder ledge* in the riddle is the ledge that looks out over the terraces from the throne room?"

"Everything I know of the mage would lead me to believe so, for he himself played from that very ledge. He was both a magician and a musician. He had an entire terrace planted in firegrasses, and he would sit up there in front of the king's throne and play his songs to make the firegrasses dance for him."

"But how is that going to destroy the golden sphere?" asked Damien.

"Oh, that would not destroy the sphere," said Gwar, "but it might show us the path to the underground volcanoes where we can destroy it."

"That's exactly what I was thinking," said Shane. "So it just remains for me to learn how to play this instrument, before it's too late."

"But why would somebody go to such lengths to destroy the returning king, and then turn around and leave clues on how to save him?" Damien wondered.

"He was insane," said Gwar. "He considered it a grand joke because he did not think the riddle was actually solvable. He delighted in the thought of the desperate young king frantically trying to solve the riddle, but to no avail. It was for the power to cause anxiety and torment that he loved it – to create a sense of tantalizing hope that would only be frustrated. And the thought of creating such anguish for thousands of years in the future, he found invigorating – it represented a kind of immortality."

"That's horrible," said Mia. They all spun around with surprise. Mia was standing there, protectively cradling her side.

"When did you come out?"

Mia shrugged. "Did Damien tell you about the pixie swarm?"

"Yes," said Shane. "I wish we had known to bring something to replace their idol."

Mia's face darkened. "They shouldn't have it anyway. Maybe this is an opportunity for their society to progress. You know... to evolve... into something more based on reality."

"Pixies are untrainable," said Lyric, who had padded out with Cyril to see what the conference was about. "We will have no pixie nonsense, Mia."

Mia got a stubborn look on her face and hugged herself. Moogkey also got a stubborn look about him. Fortunately for Mia, Cyril changed the subject. "Shane, I have been thinking that part of your problem with the instrument is trying to concentrate on everything all at once. Would it help if one of the others of us blew in the wind bag so that all you had to think about was fingering the chanter?"

"It's worth a try," said Shane

As it turned out, Gwar was excellent for the job. With his help it almost started to sound like music, and Shane quickly caught on.

chapter forty-five

Mia was sitting inside the shuttle all alone, studying the lining of her jacket, counting the little dots. They were hardly bigger than the point of a pin, but were definitely there. One... two... three... four... Yes, she counted thirteen little eggs, and she could see that they were already bigger than the night before. There were two blue ones and three minty green ones, a yellow and two peaches, two raspberry, two purple, and one silver.

Mia wondered how big pixie babies were and what they ate. She skipped out of the shuttle determined to act as if nothing were up.

chapter forty-six

The next day Shane, Cyril and Damien took a trip to the four-faced beasts' camp to discuss tactics. Damien and Shikhar had agreed upon a route by which to drive the goblins south.

"I still need to speak with the sphinx to request that he allow the goblins south through the pass but not to allow them to return," said Shane.

"Are you sure you want to risk meeting the sphinx again?" asked Tsargahn.

"Yes," said Shane. "I cannot be afraid to talk to the subjects of my realm. I will leave to go see him tomorrow morning. If this kingdom is to thrive we cannot remain in hiding. I would like to make contact with the research colony as soon as possible after that. When I return – perhaps in a week – I shall come to see you, and we may march on the colony then. I'm hoping a show of force will be enough to bend the Secretary of Defense to my will, for he is set to convict my parents for bringing Lyric and

Cyril to life. Gwar has informed me that the trial is to be concluded in ten days. I would like to confront them before it is finished," said Shane.

"We will be prepared to escort you," said Tsargahn. "How many of our troops do you need?"

"A thousand would be enough," said Shane. "If they do not agree, I would like to surround the colony on four sides with a full force of tens of thousands. I have no desire to really attack them, but they must realize we have the ability. And if it comes down to it, as a last resort I may call on the use of your tranquilizer darts. But it would be better that the colony willingly recognize our sovereignty and we gain my parents' release without hostility."

"That would be best for all of us," said Tsargahn solemnly. "We will be prepared."

chapter forty~seven

This time it was Cyril who flew Shane southward toward the border lands. He could not fly as far as Gwar could with Shane's weight on his back, so it took longer before the jagged mountains loomed close. Cyril flew much closer to the ground, affording Shane the opportunity to survey the terrain. There was indeed a bad goblin infestation, although the land was beautiful.

The vegetation was rich and varied, and had a different look from the lush greenery of the north. Shane decided that he wanted to study the botany of the region – not only the characteristics of the different plants but also how they reacted to the seraphim's music. No wonder people thought the Earth scientist was a magician – the mage having control of the forest and fire. Shane filed that bit of understanding away for future use.

They arrived at the sphinx's crossing on the afternoon of the third day. Shane had Cyril stop just before the last bend in the mountain pass as it approached the sphinx's lair. He left the cat and approached the sphinx alone.

"Who dares come here?" roared the sphinx from the mouth of his cave. "Is it the child king again?"

"If the child king is your king," said Shane. "But if he is not, I have no further business with you."

"What kind of business would a child have with a monster like me?" asked the sphinx, coming out to meet him.

"Is that your riddle?" asked Shane.

"That is my riddle," said the sphinx.

"Then the answer is easy. The child has made an alliance with the keepers of the forest to drive the hordes of goblins south beyond our border. He wishes to ask you, as the guardian of the southern border, to prevent the goblins from returning through your pass."

"And what would the monster gain from such an arrangement?" asked the sphinx.

"You already asked your riddle and had it answered," Shane pointed out. "It is my turn. A tyrant desires the dread of his enemies; the wise king desires a greater power."

"Not difficult," replied the sphinx after a dramatic pause. "A wise king desires the respect of his friends, for there is greater power in respect than fear. But no matter how wise, one may still have enemies. So – what is the best way to eliminate your enemy?"

"Not by eating him," replied Shane decisively. "No, the *best* way to eliminate an enemy is… well, I think it would have to be to turn him into a friend."

The sphinx's toothy mouth widened into what must

have been intended as a grin. "So it is," he said. "I believe we understand each other, then."

"Yes, I believe we do," said Shane. "Now I have one more riddle for you:

> How may I know the path to read
> Where chanter's song and firegrasses lead
> To earth's deep hearth, the place to purge
> With molten rock the mage's scourge?"

There was silence as the sphinx mulled this over. "That's a hard one," he said finally. "A chanter's song and firegrasses will lead you to fiery depths under the ground where molten rock will cleanse the mage's deadly scourge. That is clear enough. But how you will know this path to follow – I don't know."

"I see you cannot answer my riddle," said Shane. "The last riddle you gave me led me to the lair of the pixies, for they are the garden pests of the seraphim. There they worshipped the mage's golden sphere, in which he left his deadly plague. The answer to this riddle would tell me how I might destroy that sphere. Since you cannot answer it, now you are indebted to me."

"I am now in your debt," said the sphinx inclining his head in a kind of bow. "I will guard your southern borders."

No sooner had the sphinx said this than they heard a hideous screech and terrified braying followed by the crunching of metal hooves on rock. From the southern wild lands a horse-like animal came crashing along the

— 313 —

path with a snarling goblin on its bare back. It was a dappled grey unicorn with a bright silver horn and hooves. Red blood trickled down its neck where the goblin had dug in his claws. Fear showed in the unicorn's sapphire eyes but it stopped short before Shane's drawn sword, stumbling to the ground and dashing the goblin against the stone wall. Before the goblin could recover, Shane had him cornered with his sword. The unicorn had scrambled to its feet again and was backing against the cliff wall at the elbow of the pass, where the sphinx had it cornered.

"Let me take the unicorn," shouted Shane. "You take the goblin."

"Agreed!" the sphinx returned. He backed up, allowing Shane passage to the unicorn and then turned his fury on the goblin that had tried to cross his pass. Shane climbed a cleft in the rock wall and swung onto the unicorn's back. The animal reared up on its hind legs and then shot down the path past Cyril in a frenzied charge north.

The unicorn ran the rest of the waning day and into the night, lathered and foaming, while Shane hung on the best he could and Cyril followed from the air. Its pace eventually slowed, but it wasn't until morning that the animal finally stopped in exhaustion near a brook to drink. Shane didn't dare dismount for fear the unicorn would bolt, but fell asleep on its back as it waded into the water and fell asleep on its feet. Cyril kept out of sight, guarding his sleeping charges.

When they awoke in the afternoon the unicorn, which

Shane named Sapphire for the color of its eyes, seemed to have grown more accustomed to Shane on its back, and he urged it onward to the north at a more reasonable speed. Cyril hovered overhead, occasionally having to herd the animal in the right direction, and they managed to continue towards home. The exhausted unicorn began to lose its fear and to understand Shane's gentle guiding so that they succeeded in making it back home in seven days. Shane made immediate arrangements to meet with the four-faced beasts the next morning so they could march on the research colony.

chapter forty-eight

Secretary of Defense Dominic Dumsford arrived at the research colony with all the pomp and ceremony that a government official of his rank could demand. The sparse army – and it was sparse, only about twenty men and one senior officer, Col. Clarence Mustard, of which none (except the Colonel) were combat troops – were lined up outside the shuttle when the Secretary and his distinguished company stepped out onto the tarmac. They were duly saluted and rushed inside, being shown every hospitality and honor available in this distant outpost.

The Secretary of Defense, however, was not a man often given to being pleased, and he was certainly not in such a frame of mind today. He had wanted to impress the international delegation of important guests that he was hosting on this trip to Meta. In his estimation there had been too few troops there to greet them on the tarmac and their salute had been sloppy – just what one would expect of a colony gone to weed. There was some house-cleaning to do. (The Secretary had been ruminating on the Boston Tea Party during his whole flight and was rather more inclined toward sympathy for the British than any American politician had a right to be.)

Then there was the matter of that capital crime that had been committed eighteen years ago, but the prisoner had escaped before he could be executed (with the help of the Colonel, the rumor was). Now, to make things worse, the escaped convict's twin brother and his sister-in-law were seeking refuge here at the colony, having fled from a Government investigation back home for the same capital crime. Well – fool me once, shame on you; fool me twice, shame on me! This time *they* were not going to get away before *their* execution. He, Dominic Donnelly Dumsford, would personally see to that. (The Secretary had always liked his name. Dom D. Dumsford. It had a martial sound to it, like a drum-beat.)

And then there was this silly legend of flying people – *bah!* A few fanciful statues and rock carvings and people let their minds go into absurdity. The Secretary of Defense was determined that his opinions would remain his own until he had a good look around. But the first order of business was to have that criminal couple put under house arrest. Then he would take a few days to rest up as the Colonel had urged. After that well-earned rest, he would arrange for a military tribunal – pitiful as it was – to convict the fugitives. A trial of ten days ought to do it. Once that whole messy business was over, he could turn his attention to Col. Mustard, who had let things fall into such anarchy.

Colonel Mustard – what a ridiculous name for a military man. Next thing you know, he'd be introduced to Professor Plum!

5. The King

chapter forty-nine

As tired as he was once he got back to the dwarf caves, Shane could sleep for only a few hours. He awoke a couple of hours before dawn, his mind racing. He lay awake, listening to the stillness of the night and going over and over exactly what he planned to say to the leaders of the colony. He imagined the sun rising on that sleepy outpost unaware of the surprise that lay ahead for them. He thought about the unsuspected preparations of the seraphim in their battle regalia. No doubt the troops were already on the march. Finally Shane got up in the darkness of the cave and took a cold bath. Just before his odd little family began to stir, he grimly put on the clothes that Uncle Gerrit and Cyril had chosen for him. Instead of a coat they had selected a cape that hid the fact that he had no wings. Mia was to be beside him, her wings in full view, to add to the illusion.

He was surprised at the door by Mia who nearly ran into him. "Oh!" she exclaimed. "Sorry." She was holding two bottles of light blue glow pop. "I think we should drink these before Lyric sees."

"If we drink them, Lyric will see soon enough."

"I know, but it'll be too late to stop us then." Mia's lower lip was protruding, and she was staring down at the ground and kicking a toe into a crack. She looked so forlorn that Shane accepted her offer to drink the pop. Mia's gloominess disappeared as if by magic, and soon they were both glowing an eerie cyan.

Shane put his arm on his sister's shoulder. "Let's go out and meet Tsargahn. I hear their music and their march. No doubt the colony hears it as well." For with so many troops and pipers, the sound could be heard for miles. Shane and Mia went out of the gate just as Tsargahn emerged from the woods with ranks of troops behind him.

"You've been eating glow bugs?" he asked with surprise. "I didn't know humans ate them."

Mia giggled and Shane felt a little foolish.

Soon Gwar arrived by air and Damien stumbled out of the cave followed by Cyril and Lyric. Lyric scowled when she saw the bright-blue glowing Shane and Mia. Mia just smiled at her sweetly.

Damien spoke for a while with Shikhar and then came over to Shane, taking a bottle of glow pop from Mia in stride. "Here is our plan. We are going to advance on the colony from all four sides. Shikhar has his men almost in place." The forest was indeed teaming with four-faced beasts, so many that they looked like a living sea among the trees. Each regiment held their standard high with the incense burning beneath it which wafted through the air, cleansing as it went. The music of the pipers rippled through the forest.

It was decided that Mia would ride behind Shane, both sitting on Sapphire who was proving to be an intelligent and devoted steed. When they had approached the colony on unicorn back, Mia would then make a show of flying off Sapphire and alighting on the ground in front of the Secretary of Defense. Shane was to stay on Sapphire and to speak to them from his mount. Shane and Mia were to be escorted by Lyric and Cyril, followed directly behind by Damien on Gwar's back. The dragon and boy were to be flanked on either side by six four-faced beasts and followed by hundreds more. Uncle Garrit would also be in the company, hidden under an overly large helmet.

Once all were ready, the orders were given to march, and they set off in an orderly fashion.

When Shane and Mia emerged out of the forest with Damian and Gwar following a wingspan behind, they could see the small colony surrounded on four sides in the regular square formation of the four-faced beasts.

"Brilliant!" cried Uncle Garrit from underneath his helmet. "We've got them sur-squared on all four sides!"

The marching of the troops shook the ground in time with the droning of the war pipes, so that if anyone at the colony had been asleep, they were no longer. Several of the more curious colonists climbed up onto their roofs to get a look at what was going on. The troops stopped advancing about ten yards from the closed wooden gate and palisades of the colony. The glowing Shane and Mia on their mount, flanked by Cyril, Lyric, and six seraphim, approached until they were directly in front of the gate. Damien stayed behind. The four-faced beasts stood ready with their broadswords and crossbows just several strides from the wooden enclosure.

The gate slowly opened and a pale Secretary of Defense along with an anxious Colonel Mustard stepped out, followed by a measly twenty soldiers trying to make a brave show.

With great flair, Mia stretched and flapped her wings and then flew down in front of the troops. Shane guided his steed up to the Secretary of Defense and addressed him in Medaryan, a language that the colonists had never heard before. Shane spoke several sentences to them and then was silent, looking expectantly at the Secretary.

"Umm... greetings, my young man" said the Secretary. "I don't speak your language, but welcome to our colony. We are here in peace."

Shane let out another torrent of what sounded like gibberish. He was frowning and looking impatient. Some of the four-faced beasts moved restlessly.

"WE – COME – IN – PEACE," the Secretary repeated loudly, as if raising his voice would somehow make English understandable to this foreigner. His exaggerated hand gestures may have also been intended to be helpful, but their precise meaning was lost on everyone but him.

"Excuse me, sir," said the Colonel aside to the Secretary of Defense, "but there may be someone here who could translate; only, she is currently under house arrest. It is Serena Whitman Rockwell. She has studied the languages of this land and is an expert on them."

"Get her quickly," ordered the Secretary, and the Colonel immediately sent a sentinel after Serena. The Colonel looked awkwardly at Shane and then smiled kindly – he looked like a nice boy, this lad who had come at the head of this terrifying horde that now surrounding them. By now the marching and the pipes had stopped and it was so quiet you could hear a pin drop.

Serena came running out to the gate barefoot and hair unbrushed. What she saw absolutely stunned her. Thankfully she was a quick study and managed to hide her joy at being greeted by her son, and the confusion on her face was in no way out of place. Colonel Mustard led her up to Shane and asked her if she thought she could translate his speech.

"*Prék uᵇ, apò ðiyk théʔi mil nignuᵇtíy um,*" Shane said to her in very fine Medaryan – "Please act as if you don't know me. Please tell them I am Shane-Torh, King of Medarya. That we welcome them to our kingdom."

Serena repeated the message in English, and the Secretary of Defense shifted uncomfortably from one foot to another. He believed in democracy, not monarchy.

Shane spoke again.

Serena interpreted. "He says: You are welcome to reside on this land and farm his lower fields, as long as you live in peace. The Enchanted Forest, however, is kept by the four-faced beasts and is their domain. He asks if it is agreeable to you to dwell on his lands in peace?"

"Of course," said the Secretary. "Tell him so."

"May I address him as 'your majesty', sir, from you, since he is the king of these lands?" asked Serena.

"No, you may *not* address him as 'your majesty' for me, but do tell him we intend to live in peace."

Serena translated this into Medaryan, and Shane spoke again.

"He says," said Serena, "We are going to drive the goblins back beyond our southern borders and you will see us doing this. Please stay out of the way for the safety of the colony. One reason we have chosen this time to contact you is because our activities will make our presence visible and we wanted to give you an explanation. No harm will come to your people as long as you adhere to my words."

The Secretary looked briefly confused. "Ask him why they are going to take action against... goblins, did he say? Who are they? Are the goblins intelligent beings, worthy of a democratic voice?"

Serena translated the question to Shane and he gave his response, pausing every sentence or two so Serena could translate. "Sir, he asks: Have we not noticed that nobody who has entered the Enchanted Forest from this colony has returned again? They were eaten by goblins. The goblins are not intelligent. They are wild and a threat that must be removed. It is my duty as king to see that my realm is safe. And because you are guests in my land, I must be concerned for your safety, too. For this reason the Enchanted Forest is to remain off-limits to your people, for there are carnivorous plants and other dangers that will always grow and live there. The Enchanted Forest is your western boundary. The terraces of the Cliff City are your northern boundary. We will reopen the Cliff City for recolonization of the winged people. Again, you may have use of the meadows around your colony, up to the forest edge. Is there anybody else among you who speaks our language?"

"Your father is here, under arrest," Serena told him in Medaryan before she translated the question.

"Tell him there is nobody else," said the Secretary.

"I have already told him there is. Jerrod speaks it," said Serena.

Shane spoke again.

"The king would like to speak to Jerrod," Serena reported.

"Tell him that's impossible," said the Secretary. "Does he have any other questions?"

Another exchange. "Yes, he has one more question: Why is that impossible?" Serena relayed.

"Tell him that the man committed a heinous crime and is imprisoned for it," said the Secretary curtly. He was beginning to grow testy.

"He asks what the nature of his crime is, and what punishment awaits the man," translated Serena.

"Tell him it is an internal matter that does not concern him and ask him what else we can do for him," snapped the Secretary, his face starting to grow red.

Serena and Shane exchanged a few sentences, then Serena turned back to the Secretary. "The king asked if the death penalty awaits Jerrod," she said quietly. "I told him the truth. He is greatly concerned. He says that by the laws of Medarya, judgment of a capital crime resides with the king alone. This is a matter of grave importance, for he feels this execution would be an affront to his sovereignty. The king requests that the prisoner be transferred into his custody."

At this the Secretary of Defense lost his temper. What happened next wasn't planned, except perhaps by Gwar. With a mighty roar, the dragon the size of an airplane launched into flight, spitting fire into the air as high as the colony was wide. With the precision of a surgeon, Gwar torched the colony's northern and western walls which almost immediately crumbled into coals.

Sitting on top of the buildings so they could see what was going on, the whole scientific colony along with the visiting foreign guests watched in dread as the large purple dragon and small cyan-colored boy retreated and the four-faced beasts closed in. To Damien's immense surprise and delight, there sitting atop one of the nearest roofs was his father. Their shocked eyes met just before Gwar retreated into the shadows of the forest.

The Secretary of Defense was speechless. The colonists were terrified. The four-faced beasts resumed their battle-stirring piping and began to march in place. Then they stopped again, and all was silent.

Shane had been as surprised as everyone else, but quickly recovered his composure. Seeing the color rising again on the Secretary's face, Shane realized that there was nothing to be gained by pushing the matter any further today. Addressing him again – and Serena translating – he said, "We will give you a night to consider my request. Tomorrow morning we will come for the prisoner. Good evening."

The glowering Secretary did not respond.

"The king also wishes to know if I may go with him," said Serena.

"No. You are a prisoner as well," said the Secretary.

With that Shane gave the sign to retreat, and the convocation withdrew, leaving the Secretary of Defense alone in his shock and anger.

chapter fifty

The night was falling when the entourage stood out at the entrance of the dwarf cave. "What do you intend to do?" asked Tsargahn.

"I don't know," Shane answered truthfully. "I can't actually attack them, but I can't let them execute my parents either. The Secretary does not look as if he is going to back down. I really don't know what to do."

"Then let us wait and see what the morning brings. Whatever it comes to, we will be by your side," Tsargahn assured him.

"Thank you," said Shane. "Now the troops should take a rest. Gwar, Damien, go get the sphere and my pipes. I'll meet you at the throne room. Damien, have you seen Mia?"

"I think she's already gone to bed," answered Damien.

"That's strange," said Shane. "She's been going to bed early every night. Yet she still seems tired in the morning. I hope she's not getting sick."

chapter fifty-one

Mia wasn't getting sick. She was just very busy at night – anybody would be, with more than a dozen babies to take care of. Mia's pixie eggs had hatched. Being nocturnal creatures, they peacefully slept during the day, curled up in Mia's hair or ears. But at night they were awake. And now Mia's pixies, which were about the size of her little fingernail, were just waking up.

Mia was learning a great deal about pixies. Pixies look the same all their life. Even the little ones are fully formed in their pixie, babyish sort of way – just in miniature. When they first hatch (in good times, that is), they are hardly bigger than a pinhead. Mia's pixies obviously thought these were good times because all of them had hatched. At this age they ate their weight in flowers so Mia was constantly making them floral salads. Mia had even sent Gwar after some of the lotuses, because Uncle Garrit had whispered to her that they needed to eat the lotuses if their pixie dust was to be effective. Mia thought

it would be useful to have pixies with healthy dust.

Tonight Mia decided that her pixies needed a bath. So she set down a teacup saucer on her nightstand and gingerly sat the pixies all around the edge. Then from a pitcher she poured water into the center of the saucer. It made a nice, deep little puddle. One by one she began pushing her pixies into the puddle from the rim where they had been perched. They chattered angrily at her like tiny little squirrels and flung themselves into a tantrum of a dance. Mia smiled encouragingly at them and continued pushing the others in. Smiles the pixies understood; and when they saw their tantrums were getting them nowhere with Mia, they accepted their fate – after all, she was much bigger than they were. But they were very sulky as they sat in the water, their flower-petal clothes dripping wet.

It was interesting to Mia that the pixies understood her smile. They also seemed to pick up on motions like nodding and shaking her head – but not on words. They could make sounds like words and even imitate her speech, but when she spoke they did not respond as if her words had any meaning.

Mia watched the pixies splashing around in their little puddle. One of the raspberry ones began tugging on the antennae of one of the green ones. Mia observed, fascinated, as another green pixie noticed this and immediately launched into a furious dance while her color-kin (the other green) watched attentively. Suddenly the little green dancing pixie shot her fist from her ear out toward the raspberry antenna-puller. The other green nodded enthusiastically and the two of them flew to rescue their friend.

Mia made a mental note of the motion. Was that how they talked? Their little tantrums and dances were not just unbridled emotion. They meant something. Mia plucked them out of the water and handed them bits of fuzz to dry off with. Then she gave them their first lotus. Shortly before morning she would give them more, but this time the lotus was to be spiked with No Doze. Mia wanted them awake for the next day.

chapter Fifty-two

Cyril flew Shane up to the throne room where he paced around for some time, still glowing from the pop that Mia had given him. The night was very dark – no moon had risen in the sky yet, and a high cloud cover obscured the stars. Shane was clearly visible from the colony far below, and he looked like an apparition. Nevertheless people knew it was he. They couldn't hide from the ghostly sight because Gwar had burned down their northern and western walls. It was like a theater and Shane was the show. *Just as well*, he thought. *Maybe the specter before them will bend their hearts*. But he knew the only problem was with the Secretary of Defense who seemed bent on executing his parents.

Gwar and Damien arrived in the solemn silence, carefully carrying the golden rune-engraved sphere and the pipes.

"I am going to play the song that the mage left, from this ledge overlooking the terraces. They are overgrown with firegrasses. I'm not sure what is going to happen," said Shane, "but we are looking for something that will indicate a path or be a path to follow. We are looking for the way to the underground volcanoes. If you see anything that might show a path, then Damien, you take the sphere, and Gwar, you and Damien fly after it, wherever it takes you. With luck this will lead to the destruction of the sphere. If you have to leave, I will finish the song by myself."

Shane first fixed the mouthpiece to the chanter and blew a few experimental notes to get the feel of the instrument again. Once he was confident, he assembled the whole instrument, attaching the drones and chanter and mouthpiece to the air bag. He slung the bag under his arm,

took a deep breath, and began to blow.

The drones started up first, and then the melody as Shane began to finger the chanter, following the music he had by now committed to memory. The music was loud, amplified by the rock walls of the room behind him, and carried well across the terraces and plain below. Anyone who had not been watching from the colony now rushed out to see the specter and listen to the eerie, spine-chilling sound. Even from the distance they could see that the instrument was like one of the war pipes of the four-faced beasts, but the music was unlike anything they had ever heard. Then the firegrasses on the terraces between them and the king began to stir.

At first thin needles of orange flame rose straight up and danced around each other in a spiral. Soon short red flames began to blossom and mix with the orange in a large ring that spread outwards. A thick smoky cloud began to form in the center of the ring, smoldering with blue; then shimmering flames appeared in it, and its smoky form stretched out and hung like a menace over the dancing orange and red flames. As the music of the chanter became more complex, a series of small explosions occurred and yellow firegrasses began to ignite, one after another. Yellow fire snaked out, emerging from the cloud like fractal patterns giving birth. Flames leapt up and died down, then leapt wildly again into the air. Pushed and pulled by bursts of yellow flame, the blue-colored smoke turned a glowing teal and writhed this way and that as if in agony.

Watching this fireworks display spread across the

plateaus above him and listening to the whining, crackling laughter of the flames as bits of grey ash wafted down around him, the Secretary of Defense stood with an unaccustomed feeling growing inside of him. He had never believed in magic. He had always regarded superstition as the folly of weak and ignorant men who were not in control of their own lives. But now a small voice nagged at the back of his mind: *Maybe this alien king is a sorcerer. Maybe you should try appeasing him.*

—*Ridiculous!* his rational self retorted. *I don't even believe in such nonsense.*

—*You don't believe in dragons, either*, replied the doubting voice, *but you can't deny what you saw today.*

—*Bah!* countered the voice of reason. *I will not be cowed by intimidation, especially from a mere child.*

—*But how can you know he is a child? Maybe this is what they look like when they're full-grown.*

And so two wills fought within the Secretary, one will wavering in doubt, the other hunkering down in stubbornness.

As Shane neared the end of his song, the licking flames of orange, red, and yellow began to melt away, and the bluish fire in the center began to abate, too, and the smoky shape began to dissipate as if it had finally died. Damien and Gwar looked on, their hearts sinking. Nothing had appeared that looked remotely like a path. Had Shane played the song wrong? Or was this another of the mage's diabolical jokes?

On Shane's last sustained note, a clear and piercing tone, a small green flame flickered in the center of the dying conflagration. As everything around it settled, the lone flame skipped and spiraled upward like a charmed snake, a single dancing needle of green. The note ended in a fancy flourish, and the green firegrasses suddenly ignited. A straight line of bright green flames shot off like an arrow into the night.

"After it!" cried Shane, but Gwar and Damien were already gone in a purple streak. Shane collapsed beside Cyril and below them the firegrasses smoldered to embers.

chapter fifty-three

Gwar followed the bright green flame that hugged the earth. It went to the edge of the plateau around the eastern face of the cliff and continued northward for some distance before turning up a narrow gap in the mountains. The floor of the gully was covered in firegrasses, and the whole thing lit up for a brief minute in the dazzling multicolored flames. Then the blaze died out, until all that was left was a small brush fire that had caught on some shrubs and old net roots at the very end of the gorge.

Gwar and Damien landed beside the kindling and stood silently watching the flames cast ghostly shadows on the cliff face. It appeared to be a dead end, and the sinking feeling of defeat crept over them.

"Where are we, anyway?" asked Damien.

"It's a place I normally stay away from, this northern frontier of Medarya. It has always given me a bad feeling," said Gwar. "You can't see the rest of the realm from here."

Indeed, Damien realized, he never even thought about this corner of the land before. The shuttle had landed near the Enchanted Forest and the Cliff City, and his attention had been toward the west and the south. He had not paid attention to what lay across the plain or north around the mountain.

"I don't know what we were expecting," Damien said moodily as he watched the fire lick deeper into the ground. He noticed it was not going out by itself and realized with a little alarm that it could spread up the mountainside if they didn't put it out. He handed the golden sphere to Gwar and began stomping and kicking at the fire on the ground. Unexpectedly his foot broke through and Damien went tumbling, along with the crumbling earth and the ash of the burnt vines, down into a hole. In a panic, he scrambled back out as fast as he could and brushed the embers off his clothes.

"It doesn't seem you were expecting this," remarked Gwar dryly. "Stand back!"

With a blast of fire he disintegrated the old growth of net roots to reveal a gaping hole at the base of the rock face. It must have had a wooden door at one time, but that had long since disintegrated and the net roots had taken over. The opening yawned wide for them to enter as if it had been asleep for a million years. A few steps led down into a cavernous black space – but it was impossible to see how big the space was in the uneven glow of the still-smoldering net roots.

Gwar handed Damien the sphere and poked his head

into the opening, but stopped short – that was all that would fit. A puff of his fiery breath lit up the inside enough to reveal that it was a large cavern which led further into the mountain. A few small rocks fell around his shoulders as he pulled his head back out. Looking closely, Gwar saw that the rock around the opening was soft and crumbly from long exposure to the elements.

"Stand back!" he ordered again. Damien stepped back a few paces. "No – far back," Gwar said. Damien obeyed.

Wham! Gwar's massive tail dealt the cave entrance a powerful blow and the rock shook. A few more pieces fell. *Wham! Wham!* Cracks began to open up in the stone with each blow and more chunks fell to the ground. The fire was completely gone now, stamped out by his blows. Impatiently Gwar scraped the loose rubble out of the way and tried to push his bulk through the hole which was somewhat larger now. He strained and the rock groaned but did not give way.

Wham! Wham! Wham! Larger rocks broke off as Gwar hammered more with his tail. Again Gwar cleared the pile of rubble and pushed his body into the entrance. With a mighty heave and a crash, the stone gave way, and Gwar was inside.

Damien followed carefully when the dust settled and found himself inside a pitch-black cavern. The darkness was so thick and warm he almost thought he could grasp it and move it aside like a curtain. The blackness of the night outside shone cold and pale gray in comparison through the ruined entrance behind him. Suddenly the room lit up – Gwar was blowing a small blue flame from his mouth, providing enough light to illuminate their surroundings. What it revealed took Damien's breath away.

The walls of the cave were a deep, shiny black, intricately carved in reliefs that depicted all sorts of frightful and bizarre creatures, along with mysterious symbols and unintelligible writings. The domed roof overhead was also ornamented in carvings of evil-looking plants and gargoyle-like heads with jewel-studded eyes that leered down on the viewers below.

The light went out abruptly, and Gwar spoke. "I know these caves," he said in a gravelly whisper, and his voice echoed hollowly off the walls. "This is where the mage kept his laboratory, where he would do his experiments. His lair was over there, through that arch." Damien could not see where he was pointing, but he remembered catching a glimpse of an arched opening in the right-hand wall which led to more dark unknown chambers. "We can look in there on our way back from the volcano, if you wish."

"Do you remember the way to the volcano?" asked Damien.

"Of course. I never forget a thing," snapped Gwar. "Besides, I was the one who would have to pack the carcasses down to the rim. It is too hot for any human. I will have to take the sphere there, too. You won't be able."

"I will go with you as far as I can," said Damien.

Gwar took a breath and began to blow the torch-flame from his mouth again. He could keep up the small stream of fire for over two minutes at a time before he had to stop and take another breath. They walked straight on, past the arched doorway that led to the mage's laboratory and into the darkness that loomed ahead.

A wide passageway led out of the opposite side of the cave into a large tunnel that immediately began to curve down and to the right. The tunnel ended in another huge cavern, twice as big as the grand entrance hall. Here Gwar stopped and they were enveloped in blackness again.

"Stop walking," he warned. "The floor disappears in an abyss a few yards ahead."

When Gwar lit his torch again, Damien saw what he was talking about. About twenty paces in front of them the cave floor simply ended, plunging into nothingness beyond. They were standing on a ledge about fifteen yards wide which followed the cave wall around to the right. About fifty yards away, half of the ledge dropped away in a broad stone stairway leading down, and some distance later the rest of the ledge descended in a second stairway. One above the other, the two stairs snaked in a continuous spiral down the wall of the chasm, deep into the belly of the mountain.

Strange stone pillars lined the two staircases, pillars which had serpents coiling up around them, ending in flat heads like a cobra's. In the glow of Gwar's flame they seemed to slither and squirm – though it must have been an optical illusion, for in reality all was still and dead.

Carved between the twisting snakes were runes of a forgotten tongue, bearing unknown messages of nameless spells. Niches carved into the walls must have once held torches to light the way, but now they were no more than holes of shallow blackness.

Gwar took the sphere from Damien's hands, and holding it in his mouth by the chain, he started down the first stairway. Damien followed. Gwar's girth almost filled the breadth of the stair, but he found there was room to spare if he stretched out to his full length. The stone steps were smooth and well worn, especially in the middle. Evidently they had seen much use in timeless ages past.

Now that Gwar was no longer providing a light, Damien realized that the blackness here was not absolute. A very faint red glow could just be seen emanating from the depths below. He began to smell the acrid reek of brimstone and feel the rock walls growing warm. The air became heavier, and Damien's mind thickened, as they descended deeper and deeper towards the heart of the volcano.

Damien lost all track of time as he stumbled ever downward, following the hulking form of the dragon. He felt numb. Finally, as if in a dream, he had an indistinct impression of the stairs ending and the corridor opening up, and far below the sight of a red river of flowing lava teeming with large fiery lizards; and then the heat and noxious fumes overcame him and he passed out.

chapter fifty-four

Morning came and Shane knew he had to face the research colony again – this time without his friends Damien and Gwar, for they had not returned from the previous night's quest for the underground volcano. Pacing about in his solitude, Shane reflected on the state of affairs. If Secretary Dumsford refused to release his parents, what *would* he do? Would he be forced to attack – to make war to save his parents' lives?

Mia solemnly brought Shane his glow pop. Today he was to be a royal purple. She had drunk hers already and was glowing lime-green. Mia was hiding something, Shane could tell – he could see it in her eyes that too quickly shifted away.

Just then Lyric entered the room angrily. "Mia-Ryall Rockwell! What were you doing with that No Doze? I found it on your night stand. Have you been taking No Doze?"

"I only used a speck," said Mia truthfully. "Together

with the tiniest piece of lotus. It's a new potion I've been inventing."

"I do not want you taking any more of that potion, young lady!" ordered Lyric. "You know it is dangerous to mix chemicals from the medicine chest. They can react with each other in unexpected and dangerous ways!"

"Yes, Lyric," said Mia meekly. "I promise I won't take any."

The children quickly dressed and were ushered outside to where the pipes of the four-faced beasts were already droning. Once they arrived, the march began. When the army had again surrounded the little research facility, now missing two of its protective walls, the Secretary of Defense was already out and waiting for them at the gate. He wore a stubborn look on his face.

Shane approached on the back of Sapphire with Mia and Cyril and Lyric, Tsargahn and six of his men. They waited for the droning of the pipes to stop. When it did, silence thickened the air.

"Mr. Secretary of Defense," Shane spoke through his mother's translation, "We greet you. Have you considered our request?"

"Mr. King," said the Secretary, bowing, "I have given your request all the consideration it merits. I thank you for your hospitality, and I recognize that you are a great magician. But you must realize that I represent a great and sovereign nation. We have power, and the will to assert our power. We intend to stand our ground in the name of liberty and the lawful rule of democracy by which we live."

Shane replied, "We respect the greatness of the nation you represent, and you do us honor to accept our hospitality. As you are no doubt aware, we of Medarya, too, live by freedom and the rule of law – laws, indeed, that go back thousands of years. As guests in this land you are free to live under the laws that govern this land. This freedom is granted to every man. Even a criminal worthy of death is entitled to a royal hearing, under the jurisdiction of these laws."

"Then our disagreement is easily solved," said the Secretary in his most smugly reasonable voice. "As I indicated yesterday, this is an internal matter that does not concern you. We will take our prisoners back to our world with us, and they will no longer be under your jurisdiction."

Shane's eyes flashed and he sat up straighter. He was getting nowhere. Then an idea struck him – he wondered why he hadn't thought of it before. A look of understanding spread over his face.

"Ah, Mr. Secretary, I see the source of our misunderstanding. You must be referring to the act of awakening the ancient cats from death. That may be a crime under your laws – our laws do not address this offense. But, you see, the first wrong was committed against *us*. For those cats slept in the tombs of the Cliff City. The royal catacombs of Medarya were pillaged and our dead were desecrated when their bodies were stolen. This crime was committed before the other, and therefore the Royal Court of Medarya has first jurisdiction in this matter. If you hold the perpetrators of this heinous crime in your custody, then we are confident of your willingness to turn them over to us."

Secretary Dumsford was aghast. He had been outmaneuvered. Now the entire research colony was in danger of being incriminated in the desecration of the royal Cliff City. Maybe it *would* be best to turn over his two prisoners to Shane-Torh after all. They could be the scapegoats, and the rest of his men would be spared. The more he thought about it, the more appealing this option seemed. That wretched kid king! How did he know so much?

I told you he was a sorcerer. He divined it! said the nagging little doubt in the back of his mind.

This was the last straw. Something snapped in the Secretary's mind. He had had enough of this nonsense. No more Mr. Wishy-Washy. *I know where that royal brat learned it!* he practically shouted at himself. *He has spies! Serena Rockwell blabbed it all right under my very nose, while she was pretending to interpret for me! No doubt Colonel Mustard is in on it too! Well, the lot of them are in a whole pile of trouble now. No more Mr. Nice Guy – I am through playing these games!*

The Secretary's eyes began to bulge and his face to turn crimson. He was just about to erupt in a tirade of threats, to cow this young royal upstart and put him in his place, when something very peculiar happened. Mia started acting very strangely – doing an odd little dance. Then she drew her clenched fist to her ear and punched it forward toward the Secretary of Defense while he gawked in puzzlement at her strange antics. A bunch of what looked like brightly colored mosquitoes flew out of

Mia's hair and attacked the Secretary. They swarmed around him, shaking their wings furiously as they danced and zipped about his head. He swatted at them, but they were too quick for him and gave him a good dusting before returning to hide in Mia's hair.

Everyone stood staring in shocked silence.

The Secretary of Defense dazedly shook his head. Then he calmly brushed off his shirt. He smiled up at the wise young king. Then he looked at the charred grass where the colony walls used to stand, and out at the legions of fearsome four-faced beasts.

"Well… Your majesty, this has been such a nice chat. Major Mayonnaise, – er, Colonel Ketchup, – I mean, Colonel Mustard, please go get the prisoner that this fine young king has requested, along with the rest of his household. (That includes the ones they call Nanny and Matilda, if I am not misinformed.) They will go with you, King Shane-Torh, and you judge them as you see fit. Now, is there anything else I can do for you before I leave on the next shuttle?"

"Yes, there is," said Shane. "Our throne was removed from the Cliff City. Will you return it to the throne room where it belongs?"

"Yes, yes, certainly," said the Secretary, "and with our apologies."

"And if you ever need us, you may come look us up at the Cliff City," said Shane, turning Sapphire around to leave. He didn't dare stay to greet his father when he was released, lest the joy and relief show in his eyes.

Mia lagged behind for an instant. She took a parcel

which had been tucked into her tunic and ceremoniously handed it to the Secretary of Defense. Speaking through her mother's interpretation, Mia said, "This is a gift for your return trip. Please do not open it until you are on your ship returning home. It is something to eat – a Medaryan treat." Then Mia turned and joined the retreat, the prisoners following solemnly behind.

chapter fifty-five

They marched back in silence, save for the *tramp, tramp, tramp* of the four-faced beasts' hooves on the forest floor, and occasional strains of humming from the direction of Uncle Garrit – "Dum-de-dum-de Dom D. Dum, Dom D. Dum de-dum-dum-dom." Nobody broke rank until they reached the dwarf caves, except that Mia was holding hands with Daddy. Shane turned around with tears streaming down his face and gave his parents a hug. Uncle Garrit, who had removed his helmet, was bustling about importantly congratulating everyone. Then he started into his ceremony of shaking all the hands of the four-faced beasts, a task that would occupy him for a while.

Shane introduced his parents to Tsargahn and Shikhar and explained their role in the rescue. Suddenly a shadow darkened the sky. A moment later Gwar swooped low with a limp Damien clutched in his claws. The seraphim parted to allow the dragon to land and then began their return march home.

Damien looked up weakly. "I'll be all right," he said. "My mind needs to clear of the volcanic fumes. But we succeeded – we destroyed the sphere! And," he added with a weary smile, "I saw my dad at the colony! What is he doing *here*?"

Jerrod spoke up. "I believe I can answer that. Back at home I was unable to learn anything about your father's whereabouts, but here on Meta it was common knowledge. As a high-ranking negotiator for the State Department, he had been chosen to help lay the groundwork for this trip. As you can imagine, it takes a lot of money to maintain a continual presence here on Meta, and our Government seems to think this planet also has strategic importance. For the past several months your father has been traveling around the world, holding top-secret negotiations and conferring with heads of state and other dignitaries in order to promote greater interest in Meta and build international cooperation to fund its continued exploration – and also to prevent rogue nations from getting a foothold here. He was unable to breathe a word about it to anyone. And his assignment culminated in actually accompanying this international delegation of high-profile guests to see the planet in person. So that is why he is here."

Mia understood very little of her father's explanation, but one thing was clear to her. "Well, he's *got* to believe in Meta now."

"Good! Fine! Excellent! Great!" cried Uncle Garrit, clapping his hands. "Let's make a feast to celebrate!"

Just before Uncle Garrit and Nanny set off to prepare the meal, Jerrod asked his brother, "What finally changed the mind of the Secretary of Defense?"

Uncle Garrit's eyes twinkled. "We'll never know for sure if it was fear of our armies, or Shane's wisdom – or Mia's pixies."

"What do you mean, Mia's pixies?" asked Mother.

Lyric sat silent. She was just glad she no longer needed to feel so responsible for her lively charge.

Mia plucked a groggy pixie out of her hair and held it up for her mother to see.

"And what was that package you gave the Secretary of Defense?" asked Mother.

"Just a bit of lotus," answer Mia, "– with the roots."

epilogue

In the months that followed Mia was very busy taming the pixie population and bringing them under the crown. Having destroyed the toxic sphere, Damien and Gwar spent their time driving back the goblins with the help of the four-faced beasts and Uncle Garrit's invention. Serena was living in heaven with all of the literature of the dwarf library at her fingertips, while she awaited the birth of twins. Garrit and Jerrod set their minds to learning the technology of the Medaryan civilization and repairing the infrastructure of the Cliff City and the Dwarf City. Lyric and Cyril had kittens – eight of them. (No wonder Lyric had been cranky.) And Shane spent his days in the throne room of the Cliff City. Occasionally someone from the colony or seraphim camp would come to seek him out, but most of his time he spent sitting on his throne reading books.

Appendix

CONTENTS

The Dragon-Slaying Myth of Vedic India.......359

The *Annunaki* of Sumer 361

The Flood Story 363

The Magi of Persia.............................365

The Sphinxes of Greece, Egypt and India.......367

The Lotus Eaters of Homer's *Odyssey* 369

The Language of Medarya...................370

The Dragon-Slaying Myth of Vedic India

The hymn to Indra is found in the first book of the *Rig-Veda*, a collection of over 1,000 sacred hymns, or chants, of ancient India. The hymns were probably composed before 1500 B.C. but were not actually written down until 1,000 years later when writing first came to India. Every word and every syllable of these hymns was considered holy and always had to be pronounced perfectly, so they remained unchanged for hundreds of years as they were passed down orally through the generations. In this way the *Rig-Veda* has preserved the oldest variety we have of Sanskrit, the language spoken by the Indo-Europeans who migrated to India.

There are many hymns in the Vedas dedicated to the god Indra. One theme that keeps recurring is the famous story about mighty Indra slaying the fearsome dragon Vritra. We don't know all the particulars of what actually happened, because the hymns never relate the whole story – the ancient Indian audience already knew the tale well and didn't need to be told again. We today are not so fortunate, however, so we are left trying to piece together the legend from the many small allusions scattered throughout the Vedas.

As we present him, Indra was a human warrior who was later deified for his daring defeat of the dragon Vritra. The word we translate as "dragon" comes from the Sanskrit word *ahi*, which literally just means 'snake'. But 19th-century scholars identified him as "the dragon of the sky" and this idea became firmly entrenched. Our Medaryan creature Gwar is a dragon, the offspring of Vritra, the last survivor of a species that was driven to extinction by man in olden times, but still survives in the memory of legend and myth. His physiology resembles the European concept of a dragon that has been popular since the Middle Ages.

The Annunaki of Sumer

Sumer was a civilization of the Ancient Near East occupying part of Mesopotamia, the land between the Tigris and Euphrates rivers, in the area of modern-day Iraq. The Sumerian civilization was one of the earliest on Earth and the very first to invent writing, which they fashioned by pressing wedge-shaped (or "cuneiform") marks in clay. When talking about the written record of ancient Sumer, it is important to keep in mind that the oldest symbols were pictographic in nature, so it is often hard to decipher exactly what they meant. Later writings are better understood, but even these contain many doubtful details of grammar and meaning. For this reason the literature of Sumer, surely the most ancient of human written records, is open to a lot of interpretation and disagreement as to what is history and what is myth.

In the Sumerian writings is mentioned a race called *Annunaki,* whose name may mean 'those who came from Heaven to Earth.' They are often referred to as gods and are depicted in Sumerian art and artifacts as winged men. From these and other clues, a handful of scholars have thought that the Annunaki were a human-like race who came from another planet and ruled over men in ancient times, and in some cases even intermixed with people to produce children.

Needless to say, the majority of Sumerologists think this theory is pure fantasy – so, of course, it is not out of place in a fantasy novel. The historical myth of the Annunaki forms the inspiration for our legend of a noble winged race from Medarya with an ancient Sumerian connection.

Œhe Floob Story

Most people in our culture are familiar with the story of Noah and the Flood as told in the Bible, but not as many are aware that legends of a great flood exist in almost every major culture of Earth. Besides the biblical Hebrew account we know best, other ancient versions can be found in Sumerian, Assyrian, Babylonian, Vedic, Persian, Greek, Celtic, Chinese, Polynesian, Eskimo, Aztec, Incan, and Mayan literature and lore – to name just a few!

The Sumerian version of the flood is recorded in an epic poem about Gilgamesh, a historical king who ruled in the ancient city of Uruk around 2700 B.C. In the poem Gilgamesh seeks out Utnapishtim, the man who survived the flood, and hears the story from him: The gods had become angry and decided to destroy all mankind; but forewarned and instructed by Ea, the god of wisdom, Utnapishtim built a great ship and he, his family, and the "seed of all living creatures" were able to escape.

For our story, this catastrophic flood serves as the crucial event that causes the Medaryans (our Annunaki) to flee Earth and return home. Human civilization survives and is rebuilt, but the Medaryans are gone, and only rare traces survive to tell that they were once here.

The Magi of Persia

Our English word *mage* can be traced, step by step, back to ancient Persia and the Near East, and beyond. The English word was borrowed in the 14th century from Old French, which had inherited the word from Latin *magus*, which had borrowed it from Greek *mágos*, which in turn had adopted the word from Old Persian *maguš*. Ancient historians describe the magi as a priestly caste in Persia and Media, and throughout the Near East. The Chaldean magi (the wise men of Babylon) were often considered soothsayers and astrologers and diviners. Our modern concept of magic ultimately stems from the sciences and arts of these magi – and, in fact, the same root lies at the base of the words *magic* and *magician*. If we look farther back into the dim recesses of time, we find a Proto-Indo-European root **magʰ-* meaning 'be able, have power'. And like the word, the concept of a class of powerful "wise men" who practiced the divine arts and were regarded as "mighty ones" is far older than ancient Persia and Babylonia. It doubtlessly dates back as far as Sumer.

The mage in *The King and the Fire Chanter* is a priest, magician, and scientist – for in those days no sharp distinctions were made between science, divination, astronomy, and astrology. He served in the White Temple of Uruk, in Sumer, around 3000 B.C., only a few centuries before Gilgamesh and during the lifetime of Utnapishtim (though they probably did not know each other). The remains of the White Temple can still be seen in Uruk, which is now in southern Iraq.

The Sphinxes of Egypt, Greece, and India

The sphinxes of ancient Egypt were guardians of the pharaohs' tombs. They had the body of a lion with the head of a ram, a hawk, or a man. There are many statues and images of sphinxes, but the best-known is the Great Sphinx of Giza. The Greeks apparently borrowed the idea of the sphinx from the Egyptians. But in Greek mythology there was just one Sphinx, the daughter or Chimaera, who was part lion, part woman, and part bird. She terrorized the travelers of Thebes in the mountain pass where she would stop them and ask a riddle. Those who could not answer correctly, she would kill. Eventually Oedipus bested her by answering her riddle correctly, and in despair she took her own life. India also has a sphinx, the *purushamriga* ('human-beast' in Sanskrit), not a fearsome monster but a guardian that wards off evil.

Our sphinx combines these traditions. Designated "the guardian of pharaoh's tomb" in a riddle left by the mage, the Medaryan sphinx guards the pass over the southern mountains, asking riddles of all who try to cross, and preventing goblins from entering Medarya.

The Lotus Eaters of Homer's Odyssey

We don't know exactly when the ancient Greek poet Homer composed his great epic poems, the *Iliad* and the *Odyssey*, but a good guess would be about 750 B.C. In the second of these adventures, Odysseus (or Ulysses), king of Ithaca, attempts to find his way home after the Trojan war and encounters many perils along the way. When his ships are blown off course in a fierce storm, he and his men find themselves in the country of the lotus-eaters. The natives are friendly enough and hospitably offer their own food, the lotus plant, to some of Odysseus' men to eat. At once the men are overtaken by forgetfulness and happy indolence, and lose all thoughts of returning home. All they desire is to stay where they are and eat more lotus. Odysseus is forced to drag them struggling and weeping back to the ships and to tie them under the benches while he makes good their escape.

Medaryan lotus is a mainstay of the pixies' diet. It doesn't seem to affect them the way it does humans, but it is the ingredient that makes their pixie dust so potent.

The Language of Medarya

Medaryan was a contemporary of Sumerian about 5000 years ago. The Medaryans who came to Earth spoke a dialect of this language, and some segments of the human population they ruled over adopted the dialect as their own tongue – but slightly altered by the ingrained speech habits of their native language. (To the Medaryans they always spoke with an "accent.") After the upheaval caused by the catastrophic flood and the disappearance of the Medaryans, these speakers (that is, those who survived) became known to history as the Indo-Europeans, and their descendants migrated far and wide. Ironically, this language which did not even originate on Earth has become the ancestor of the most widespread family of languages on Earth. Its modern descendants extend all the way from India in the East, through Europe (including English), and over the Atlantic to the Americas in the West, encompassing most of the languages in between.

The Medaryan language is made up, of course, but the Indo-European language family is not. Proto-Indo-

European itself was never written down, but linguists have been able to reconstruct quite a lot of its vocabulary and grammatical structure, working backwards from a careful comparison of its descendants – one of which is the language you are reading. The grammar of Medaryan is realistic, and some of the words will actually be recognizable because they are based on the ancestor of our own language.

The following notes are provided for those who want to know how to pronounce Medaryan. Spelling is consistent – every symbol stands for one sound – so anyone who knows how the letters are pronounced can read Medaryan even if they do not understand what it means.

The majority of Medaryan consonants will pose no serious difficulties for speakers of English. Those that do not exist in English may seem strange at first until you are used to them. Note the following details:

th	always the voiceless *th* of *thin*; never a voiced *th* sound, for which *ðh* is used instead
dh	like the *th* of *then*; the voiced counterpart of *th*
kh	a spirant *k*-sound like the *ch* of German *nach* or Scottish *loch*; it is not strongly pronounced
gh	a spirant *g*-sound, the voiced counterpart of *kh*
qhu	like *kh* + *w*
ghw	like *gh* + *w*
zh	like the *s* in *measure*
l	always the 'light' *l* of *light*; never the 'dark' sound in *call*, for which *ll* is used instead
ll	like *ll* in *call*

r	a light tap of the tongue, like the *r* of Spanish or Italian
ʔ	a glottal stop, which is the break in sound between the two syllables of *uh-oh*; this is every bit as much a consonant in Medaryan as are *p*, *t*, *k*, etc.
ʰ	a sound pronounced far in the back of the throat; similar to the uvular *r* of French or German

The rest of the consonants are pronounced as in English.

Medaryan has a rich vowel system, including some that do not exist in English. These, like the consonants, may take some getting used to.

á	like the *a* of *father*
ä́	like the *a* of *bad*; may also be pronounced like the *e* of *bed* without any difference in meaning.
ǻ	like the *o* of *for*
é	like the *é* of *attaché* or the *a* of *bake*
ë́	set your mouth as if to say *ee* but say *oh* instead (without moving your lips!); the vowel *ó* may be substituted if this proves too difficult
í	like the *i* of *machine*
ó	like the *o* of *bone*
ő	set your mouth as if to say *oh* but say *eh* instead; like the *ö* of German or the *eu* of French; the *oo* in *foot* may be substituted
ú	like the *oo* of *boot*
ű	set your mouth as if to say *oo* but say *ee* instead; like the *ü* of German or the *u* of French

Stress is always indicated in writing. The two accents

in Medaryan specify the pitch or tone of the vowel. The primary accent (´) is somewhat higher in pitch than the surrounding syllables, while the secondary accent (`) is somewhat lower. This gives Medaryan a kind of lilting rhythm.

Unstressed vowels are shorter and less distinctly pronounced than stressed vowels, and have no special tones. There are three of them:

a   like the *a* of *about*
i   like the *i* of *pit*
u   like the *u* of *put*

A *w* or *y* following a vowel does not change its basic pronunciation. The combination is pronounced as a strict sequence of the two sounds. Thus *ów* is always *ó* + *w*, like the *ow* in *low*, never as in *cow*; that sound is spelled *áw* (*á* + *w*). Similary *áy* is always *á* + *y*, like the *ay* in *aye*, never as in *day*. And so on.